A Different Kind of Magic

A Fantasy Romance
By Chesney Infalt

BookDragon
PUBLISHING

Dedication

To my wonderful friend Lydia who encouraged me and helped me with this project from the beginning. Nate might not have made as much of an appearance had it not been for how much you love him. Here's to being writing buddies!

Books by Chesney Infalt

Warrior's Song Series
~Haeven Short Stories Collection

~The Three

Warrior of Laurele Series
~Warrior's Heart

Standalone Books
~Worth Fighting For

Chapter One

Isabela

Sanctuary

I ran, thanking my lucky stars I'd found trousers to change into before trying to flee. Branches tore at my clothes, hair, skin—anything they could snag. I kept one hand on the top of my hat, hoping to keep it on my head.

Barking. Yelling.

I dared not look behind me in fear of losing my footing, but my mind was coming up with all sorts of heart-pounding imagery of my pursuers being right on my heels. In the dark, I'd hoped that I could slip away before they had caught on to my disappearance, but the hounds had not been as susceptible to the sleeping powder as I'd anticipated, and I had had no time to remedy it before their masters had realised what was happening.

A shot rang through the air, followed by a fiery pain in my upper arm. Hissing through my teeth, I stumbled, letting go of my hat to grip my injury. I scrambled back into a sprint, feeling my shirt sleeve and hand becoming wet. *Just focus,* I told myself. But on what? Surviving? My plan to climb the gate to freedom was now out of the question... but I was not going back with them, no matter what.

I followed the wall enclosing the city and tried my best to ignore my burning lungs and shaking legs. Stopping was not an option. Letting them catch me was not an option.

But was fighting?

I peeked over my shoulder quickly. Based on the bobbing lights, there had to be at least three of them, not to mention their hounds—to call upon that much magic to fight them would be akin to signing over my sanity. For a split second, a dark thought crossed my mind: if I were insane, would I care if they took me back, if they won?

No. I would not risk it unless it was the very last option available. Although the likelihood of that was increasing more and more by the second.

As if to answer an unspoken prayer that was forming on my lips, I noticed a chapel not too far away. With what I had left in me, I rushed to it and pounded on the door. "SANCTUARY!"

The sounds of the pursuers got louder.

"SANCTUARY!"

The door opened, and a priest answered. "Come in."

I did not need to be told twice.

And he did not need to be told to shut the door behind me and lock it.

"Priest! Let us in! Let us have the girl!" shouted one of the men above the snarling of the dogs.

The priest looked at me with a slight amount of surprise to his face. Trembling, I took off my hat, letting my hair tumble out of its containment.

"Please," I pleaded, my accent apparent in my state of panic, "help me, *padre*—father. I have no other options."

The priest stared at me long enough that my hope deflated and I considered seeking out a back door to flee once more. Just when I was about to turn away from him, the priest opened the slat in the door and said, "It is past visiting hours, gentlemen. I suggest you go home and return at a more reasonable time."

"Give her to us!"

"She is not mine to give," the priest replied calmly. "She has claimed sanctuary, and so she has it until she leaves these premises."

"Surely you would not give sanctuary to a spell-caster?"

I held my breath.

"I give it to whomever needs it," the priest stated matter-of-factly. "Good night, gentlemen." He closed the slat and turned to face me, ignoring the curses on the other side of the door. His face was younger than I had expected of one of his station, and there was a kindness to his eyes that made me want to let my guard down.

"You are wounded," he said, his eyes going to my arm. "Did they do this to you?"

My blood had stained the white shirt, making it rather obvious. I blinked, having thought that he would have started with questions about why a woman was fleeing a group of men in the middle of the night... in men's clothing, no less. Or that he would have asked if I was what they claimed me to be.

I flinched when he stepped toward me, and the priest lifted his hands in surrender.

"You may call me Abel," he said gently. "Your arm needs tending to. If you will allow me, I would like to call one of the priestesses to inspect your wound."

"You..." I started, not entirely sure which question I wanted to ask first, or at all. I swallowed and tried again. "You want to help me?"

Abel looked at me as if the answer should have been obvious. "Any proper clergyman would tend to someone in need."

My eyes stung with tears creeping up on me; my throat tightened. Something in my face must have made him understand because Abel offered a faint smile and told me to sit and wait there until he returned with help. I sank to the ground and leant against the back of one of the pews, not wanting to go any further. Especially in my current state, I did not want to see the judgment in the stained-glass faces. I closed my eyes and took a few deep breaths before I processed my current predicament.

For the moment, I had sanctuary. However long it would last, it was not guaranteed to be more than the night, so I had to make some sort of plan. Granted, that was about all I could come up with, given the biting pain in my arm and the way the room felt like it was spinning.

It was not long before Abel returned with a priestess, just as he had said. Her brown dress matched the priest's robes so well that they almost looked to be the same, shapeless and simple.

"Miss, why are you on the floor?" the priestess asked. When I couldn't come up with a good enough answer, she said, "Never mind that. We need to see that arm. Come with us."

Abel helped me to my feet, and we followed the priestess to a side room with various medical supplies. She bade me sit on a cot while she tore at my sleeve to get a better look at my wound.

"You did not tell me that she was *shot*," the priestess said in shock. "We will need Doctor Cornelius's assistance for this."

"Doctor Cornelius will be home, asleep, like everyone else. Just do what you can for her, Priestess Margaret."

The priestess seemed to not hear what Abel was saying. "She will also need a dress. You must be in grave trouble to have had to wear a man's clothing!"

I pressed my lips together to keep from making a face. It seemed that Abel had not told her what the men had said about me. If he would have, there was a good chance she would have thrown me back outside so that my pursuers could do what they pleased. Although to be fair, Abel had not done so, so there was a chance that she was not rotten like some others I'd met.

She wrapped my arm in a bandage and tied it carefully. "I will have the girls do another wash in the morning so that she has proper, fresh, clean clothes."

"I am fine in this," I said without thinking.

Priestess Margaret took my chin in her hand and said, "But we will make you even better. Worry not."

The chapel bell tolled twice.

"Do try to sleep," Priestess Margaret suggested before scurrying off.

"She means well," Abel told me as he handed me a blanket he had gotten from a cabinet. "I will fetch some tea to help you sleep and numb the pain a little."

I found myself not wanting him to leave but said nothing until he returned with a steaming cup.

"Thank you," I said quietly, suddenly feeling very drained.

"Of course. As I said, it is what any good clergyman would do."

I shook my head. "It's not. At least, not the ones I have met."

His grey eyes followed me as I took a sip of the tea. My injured arm was not responding well, and I didn't want to move it much, so I balanced the saucer on my lap and used one hand on the teacup.

"Are you going to ask me?"

His eyes refocused like I had drawn him out of his thoughts. "I beg your pardon? Is there something you want me to ask you, miss?"

There were plenty of things he *could* have asked me. No matter how badly I wanted to blend in, things like my accent tended to draw the wrong sorts of attention, and that was even before any of them dug any deeper.

I'm not sure whether it was delirium from being hurt and fatigued, or if it was the fact that I felt strange accepting his help when most people would not deign to even answer one of my questions when they knew what I was, but I almost felt like I *wanted* him to ask me, like I owed him the answer for some reason. There was a chance that he could get into trouble for helping me.

"You have had a very long night," Abel said in a gentle tone. "I suggest you rest. Doctor Cornelius will be here in the morning to dress your wound properly."

Properly. I wanted to roll my eyes. That seemed to be one of their favourite words.

"Sleep well, miss." Abel dipped his head and left the room.

I drained the remainder of the tea. It warmed me and eased some of the aches in my body but did not settle my mind.

Temporary safety... I had to make the most of it. Waiting for the doctor to patch up my arm required me to stay at least until he left. After that, I'd slip out of here and flee before *los cazarrecompensas* could stop me.

Before I could begin to formulate a plan, sleep overtook me.

Chapter Two

Thomas

Surprises

"Good morning, Master Grahm."

The sudden sunlight made me squeeze my eyes shut even more tightly. "Archibald, is this necessary?"

"I am afraid so, sir. Your father requires you and your brother to dress and eat quickly. There is something to tend to at the chapel that requires your presence post-haste."

My groggy mind took its time to process what he said as I made myself get out of bed. "What could have possibly happened that requires our attention? Did the Chantry call for us?"

"I have no more knowledge of the situation than you, Master Grahm. I just do as I am told." Archibald got out my outfit for the day and then bowed before taking his leave. He chose my rune-writer attire, a black and white suit with loose cuffs to make it easy to push them back or roll them up.

Post-haste. I doubted there was any reason for my brother and me to join our father in whatever the Chantry needed. Chances were that our father had caught on to the fact that we were out late last night and wanted to punish us in his subtle way. Although, given the recent string of strange attacks and burnings, perhaps the police had decided to bring rune-writers into the situation in hopes of better luck solving the case.

When I was presentable, I made my way through the manor and sat down at the dining table for breakfast.

"Good morning, Thomas."

"Good morning, Father."

He did not bother to lower his newspaper as he asked, "How did you sleep?"

He definitely knew.

I focused on eating. "Well enough." I hoped it did not sound like a grumble.

Father refrained from saying anything else. He did, however, fold the paper and place it on the table when Nate entered the room. "Nathaniel! Good of you to join us for breakfast."

Nate slipped into his chair and kept his gaze downcast.

"Well? What is the story this time?" Father took turns looking at the two of us. "Surely there must be a wonderful story to go along with that glorious bruise colouring your cheekbone, Nathaniel." His gaze seemed to be more accusing whenever he looked at me than when he looked at Nate. I cut the sausage on my plate with more force than necessary, causing a scraping noise that earned me a glare from Father.

"Nothing special, sir," Nate mumbled.

"It must be," Father pressed, leaning forward, "for two grown men to be acting like foolhardy boys."

I inhaled slowly through my nose, but that did little to temper my rising irritation.

"I strictly forbade you from going to taverns anymore," Father said sternly. He turned his attention to me. "How could you take your younger brother there?"

"I did not," I replied. "He makes his own choices. I was trying to protect him."

Father raised an eyebrow. "You did an outstanding job."

Mother entered the room, keeping me from one of the things I was about to say and immediately regret. We all stood.

"Good morning, my darlings," she said with a smile that vanished the instant she looked at Nate. "Nathaniel! My dear, sweet boy, what happened?"

"We were just discussing it," Father informed her. "Take a seat, love. He's not a child to be mollycoddled anymore."

Hesitantly, Mother did as she was told, sinking into her chair.

"If you continue to sulk, you will get frown lines," Father said and patted her hand. "You are far too pretty for those."

Mother offered him a small smile that held very little warmth, if any at all.

"Now, tell us what happened. I cannot protect you if I am not aware of the facts." He eyed both of us boys. "All of the facts."

Nate peeked at me, but I wanted to throw my hands up and stomp out of the room. A good portion of me wanted to let him fight his own battles.

"There is not much to say," I said, giving into my younger brother. "You know how people can be when they drink: given to all sorts of wild behaviours."

"Why did they hit him? Who hit him?"

I exhaled through my nose. *Feel free to speak up anytime now, Nate.* "No one important."

"What leads you to believe that?"

"You are the one who taught us to ascertain someone's status by their clothing and the way they speak and carry themselves."

"What was this man wearing?"

To my credit, I kept a straight face as I answered, "Trousers and a cotton shirt. Farmer's hat and worn boots."

For what felt like an eternity, Father said nothing. "You will not do anything of the sort again." He waved his hand. "You two get into the carriage. I will join you in a moment."

Trying not to look too eager, we left the room. As soon as we went outside and got into the carriage, Nate said, "I cannot believe Father did not press for more details. We are lucky."

I frowned at him. "*We* are lucky? You rarely get more than a tongue lashing from Father over your recklessness."

Nate snorted and crossed his arms. "You get to inherit everything. The least you owe me is a little fun." A smirk crossed his lips. "You have to admit it was fun last night."

"Fun? It was *fun* to get punched by a woman in men's clothing because you made a pass at her?"

"A little. It was better than spending another dreadfully boring night here."

"I'll give you that."

We exchanged smiles.

"Hey… my thanks again."

"No need to mention it again," I told him just before Father reached the carriage.

"You must stop worrying your mother," was the only thing Father said the entire ride to the chapel. We knew better than to ask him questions about where we were going and why. It was much better to suffer in silence.

When we finally arrived, I tried not to show that I was surprised to see not policemen but bounty hunters standing just outside of the chapel doors. By the weariness of their stance and their agitation, I assumed they had been waiting for an hour or so at the least. Did the Chantry call for them? I could not imagine the clergymen leaving them outside if they had...

"Lord Grahm!" One of the men—their leader by the newness of his hat and coat in comparison to the others—stepped forward and bowed his head. "Thank goodness you've arrived, sir. There is—"

"I am well aware of what is happening," Father snapped as he walked up the steps. The bounty hunters stepped aside, leaving a pathway for us to pass through them. He started to reach out to the doors when he paused. I glanced over his shoulder to see blood splotches on it.

"Spell-caster blood, Lord Grahm."

Well, that answered why the bounty hunters were standing outside of the chapel like vultures waiting to swoop in on dying prey. But then why were we called?

Not bothering to respond, Father knocked on the door. "Lord Grahm and his sons to see Priest Abel."

I felt some relief that Abel was the one we were going to interact with. Of all of the priests and priestesses, he was the most amicable.

Abel let us in not too long after that, once again shutting the door to keep the bounty hunters outside. "Good to see you all," he said to us. "Follow me, if you please."

It was strange to see the chapel so empty. Granted, we were not here often other than Sundays and the occasional celebration. I noted a few spots on the floor behind one of the pews. Before I could investigate, Abel brought us to one of the medical rooms. Doctor Cornelius was already there, tending to someone's arm. Someone who, when she looked up, made me much more interested in the situation: she wore the same clothes from the tavern last night, albeit torn and dishevelled. After all of Nate's boasts of previous conquests, it'd given me no small amount of amusement to see her reject his advances with a punch to the face.

I sneaked a peek at my brother, who had reddened slightly. Her eyes widened at the sight of us. Without her hat on, her light brown hair was free and so long that it almost reached her hips. If she really was a spell-caster, then Nate did choose the wrong person to mess with last night.

"Doctor Cornelius," Father greeted. "Thank you for your help and discretion."

Doctor Cornelius finished tying the bandage before he faced Father and answered, "Of course, Lord Grahm." He looked between Father and Priest Abel. "She needs to have this applied to the wound and to have it redressed twice a day for the next week. I would like to check on her again soon. Let me know when and where I might find her."

"Of course."

The doctor set a bottle of medicine and some neatly rolled bandages on the counter and then took his leave, shutting the door behind him.

Chapter Three

Isabela

Interrogation

Out of all of the people who could have walked into this chapel, I was not expecting the handsy idiot and his companion from the tavern last night. His brother, I assumed by the similar facial structure. Following that assumption, I guessed that the older man with them was their father. Lord Grahm. Of course—those two idiots had to be a part of the most prestigious family of rune-writers… unless that happened to be a commonplace surname, which I found unlikely. Even if it was, the way their father carried himself with a pretentious air, I had to believe that he was the notorious rune-writer.

I hoped they could not tell that my pulse was raging and my palms were sweaty. Who had called for them? As part of the Chantry, it was possible that the priests and priestesses were required to call upon rune-writers when dealing with a spell-caster like me. Or *los cazarrecompensas* outside called for help.

The doctor had been kind enough, doing his job without saying much other than to ask a few questions about my injury. Now I felt like I was on display. At least Abel had stayed. Whether or not he would speak up for me remained to be seen, but I was glad for a friendly face regardless.

"You have met my sons," Lord Grahm guessed as he caught the looks between us, studied my clothes. "You were the one at the tavern last night?"

What is it with these people and not asking things like others do? I supposed that was not a true complaint. However, by the way that the handsy idiot blushed and looked down at the ground, it was rather obvious that something had happened. I would have judged the man for *not* asking about it.

"I would not say 'met,'" I replied.

His brows raised slightly. "Your accent. You are not from here, are you?"

I stopped myself from making a sarcastic comment. If he thought me to be a spell-caster, I would obviously be from the country of Isouldia, not Glennad. "No."

"Priest Abel," Lord Grahm said, "is there anything for her to wear that is proper and suitable for her gender?"

"Priestess Margaret will be bringing her a dress shortly," Abel explained.

I fought not to roll my eyes, although it was strange to be sitting there in dirty and torn clothes while the others were in nice attire. Doctor Cornelius had cut up my sleeve to deal with my arm, leaving it bare except for the bandage.

"Very well." The man turned his attention back to me. "My name is Lord Gerold Grahm, and I am a very powerful man in this country, in case you were not aware. I would be very honest if I were you."

Have I lied yet? I just stared back at him, hoping that my face remained calm in spite of my heart hammering in my chest. He had just confirmed that here, before me, was the Grahm patriarch, one of the most powerful of the rune-writer families. I had not lied yet, but I was certain that I would have to soon unless I was ridiculously lucky.

"What is your name?"

"Isabela Fuerte."

"Are you a spell-caster?"

There was no use lying to him when those *cazarrecompensas* outside had seen me use magic—when Gerold Grahm's own sons might have seen me. "Yes."

By the way the younger men's brows went up, I figured that they had not seen me use magic. Or were not expecting me to admit to it so easily.

Lord Grahm reached into his pocket, taking out a pocketknife, and sliced the back of his wrist. He dipped his index finger into the welling blood and made a motion in the air, and the room thrummed with magic. "As I am sure you are aware, I have created a protective barrier against anything you could do, so do not think to use your magic against us."

I wanted to huff in annoyance. His blood hung in the air in the particular pattern he had drawn. I had heard that rune-writers were prominent in this area, that most of them had risen to positions of authority. This would make things more difficult. Of course I had run into the worst of all of them.

"I do not believe she has any evil intent," Abel said. "She has yet to raise a finger against any of us."

Lord Grahm threw the priest an annoyed look but said to me, "Prove it."

I fought the urge to cross my arms. Of course he would want proof, but did I have to give it? What would happen if I refused?

As if he read my thoughts, the Grahm patriarch warned, "I could hand you over to the bounty hunters and see how you fare with them."

We locked gazes with such intensity it reminded me of wolves circling, snarling to provoke the other to attack first.

This lone wolf knew how to survive.

I closed my eyes and inhaled slowly, deeply. Magic pressed against the barrier in my mind and seeped in the moment I cracked it open. It rushed through my veins, and I guided it toward my hands, cupped like I was holding something fragile and precious. I opened my eyes, and the magic danced in my palms as swirling iridescent colours. It swayed and warped as my will fought to control it. Fatigue washed over me again, reminding me how little true rest I'd had in the past week. The magic surged up; I regathered my strength and overpowered it before it could lash out at the rune hovering in the air. It finally settled, melting into a puddle of water in my hands.

The men watched intently, eyes unblinking as if they were afraid to miss a single moment.

My hands trembled. Breathing again, I willed the magic back into myself, funnelling it into my mind and out of the barrier before sealing it shut.

Silence reigned. I stared at Lord Grahm, awaiting his response. All I noted was the set of his jaw, the slight widening of his eyes. Fear kept me from looking at the others, especially Priest Abel. What would he think of me now that I'd given proof of what I was?

Lord Grahm demanded, "What is your business here?"

"Freedom."

My answer seemed to throw all of them off-kilter.

"Explain yourself."

I sighed. "I would rather not live the life I was living, so I was trying to leave and find somewhere I can start over. As you could probably guess, very few people trust a spell-caster enough to let me do much of anything."

Not fully turning away from me, Lord Grahm looked over his shoulder at his sons. "You saw her at the tavern last night?"

"Yes," the bruised one said. I could not help but smirk with pride at the shine of colour on his cheek.

"She spoke to someone about getting passage on the next boat out of here," the other said. My smirk disappeared, realising that he had been paying closer attention to me than I had originally thought… which could tilt the situation in my favour.

Lord Grahm stared me down. "I cannot just let you leave. You have stirred up a lot of attention."

You could, I thought. *You just refuse to so you can keep an air of control.*

"Lord Grahm, if I may," Abel suggested, "you could take her on as your personal spell-caster. That would give her a new life than the one she had, and you would gain even more prestige having someone so powerful at your command."

I jumped up from the cot, making all of them flinch. "You want to keep me as a *pet?*"

"A personal spell-caster," Abel corrected not unkindly. "You would protect his family—more with just being present than anything else. It was a common practice a few generations ago."

Before my people fled to create new lives for themselves.

"Good idea, Priest," Lord Grahm said with a smile that made my stomach churn. "Your choices are simple, Miss Fuerte: agree to become my personal spell-caster or take your chances with the bounty hunters."

How courteous of you. Instead of saying that, I pondered my options, knowing fully well that there was only one choice to be made. I raised my chin. "I will agree to become your spell-caster, Lord Grahm."

"Splendid." He undid his protection rune, the blood dissipating along with the magic. Squeezing a fresh bit of blood, Lord Grahm grabbed my wrist and wrote out a much more complicated rune. It tingled against my skin, and the moment it was completed, it felt like a manacle.

Priestess Margaret arrived with a clean dress the same dull colour as hers and just as shapeless. Even the fabric looked to be low quality.

"Get dressed," ordered Lord Grahm. "We have a lot to do today."

What have I done? I wondered as fear clamped around my chest. Priest Abel offered me a reassuring smile that made me think that at least I could be grateful to not be handed over to *los cazarrecompensas*. And, if I made myself useful, I would have protection— Lord Grahm seemed like the kind of man to protect his possessions. I tried to focus on the first part, the part that did not dehumanise me.

Chapter Four

Thomas

The Spell-Caster

Isabela. Something about her accent captivated my attention, made me mentally repeat her words.

And that display of power… I could feel it in the air, but it hummed differently than ours, like it was part of a separate song, a foreign one with notes I couldn't understand. To make water appear out of practically nothing… our runes could do no such thing. What was the limit to her power? Was I imagining that dark circles had formed under her eyes after she cut off the spell?

Father dismissed the bounty hunters, who were obviously less than pleased to learn that Isabela was out of reach. She stood behind us in her simple dress and kept her face from showing much emotion. But her dark brown eyes—they were filled to the brim with a mixture of things that I could not read.

I offered my hand when it was her turn to enter the carriage. For a moment, she glanced at it but got in by herself. Fine. Let her be that way… I was not the one enslaving her. Still, I was her new master's son, so I was probably the enemy in her eyes. She was the first spell-caster I had seen up close and unchained. On the carriage ride back to our manor, I ruminated on all of the things I had been told by Father and others about spell-casters. The last one I had seen was an older man who was quickly transported to the Queen for judgment. Nate and I had been children then, and all Father would tell us was that the man was a danger to society. Where that babbling, distant-eyed man seemed to be near death, this spell-caster was quiet and very much alive and alert, even with her injury. Keeping her gaze low, every so often her eyes shifted under her long, dark lashes, reminding me of a guard checking the perimeter. Even though there was plenty of room between her and Father, Isabela kept her right side against the wall of the carriage.

"So, Miss Fuerte," Father said in his business voice, "as our family spell-caster, you will have duties to attend."

Isabela looked at him out of the corner of her eye. "Duties? You *want* me to use my magic?"

I could understand her confusion: rune-writers were respected and trusted to use their magic for the good of the country, but spell-caster magic was dangerous, to be leashed and only used when absolutely necessary. Or to show off prestige, as Father seemed to be after.

"In certain circumstances and with permission, yes. Look at me," Father ordered.

Lips in a thin line, Isabela obeyed, lifting her chin slightly.

"Your duties will mostly be accompanying me to various functions and meetings, which will require you to be dressed properly and to act appropriately."

The muscle in her jaw flexed.

Father said nothing of it as he continued, "As I am sure I need not tell you, everything you do will be under the utmost scrutiny, reflecting upon the Grahm family." He did not look away from her as he added,

"Something my sons are still in the process of learning."

Nate fingered the curtain, letting a little light in. He left it alone when Father cleared his throat.

As she tugged at her sleeve, Isabela asked, "Am I supposed to wear this every day?"

"We will provide you with clothing," Father answered, his upper lip curling slightly. "You wear that simply to keep you decent until better wear is available. I'll not have anyone in my employ dressed so poorly."

Isabela knotted her hands together in her lap and stared down at them. A lock of hair just behind her ear had fallen out of her quickly put together bun, trailing all the way down to her ribcage. She must have missed it in her hurry.

"I will have your utmost obedience," Father stated. "Do you understand and agree to all of these terms, Miss Fuerte?"

Isabela lifted her face and met his gaze. "I understand, *Señ*— Lord Grahm."

I was certain that Father was going to say more, but thankfully, I was wrong. We arrived back at the manor, and Mother met us in the foyer.

"I am glad to see you home so early," Mother said, her smile waning when she caught sight of Isabela. "Who is our guest?"

"This is Isabela Fuerte," Father filled in, tossing his cloak in the direction of the nearest servant, "our new spell-caster. Perhaps, since you are not busy with anything important, you can help her find more suitable, dignified attire befitting one of our estate."

Mother put on a smile. "Of course. Miss Fuerte, would you follow me? Some of the servant girls should be able to help us find something."

Isabela hesitated. Out of everyone in the manor, Mother was the most harmless one; however, I guessed that, if I were in her shoes, I would have been wary of everyone, not just because of being a spell-caster, but also the fact that meeting Father alone was enough to put anyone on their guard.

No sooner had they gone halfway up the staircase than Father said to the two of us boys, "You will not disgrace our family again, understood?"

Or what? I wanted to say, but I really did not want to know what the "or what" would be, and I did not plan on finding out.

"Understood, Father," Nate and I said simultaneously.

"Luckily for me," Father said, "your blunder resulted in finding us a spell-caster. This will certainly tip the scales in my favour for when the League votes for a new leader."

Of course he would spin things his way yet again. Granted, it saved us from his wrath, so I could not complain.

"After Miss Fuerte returns, you two will apologise for your behaviour last night."

That was already the plan, but I nodded anyway. Nate mumbled his agreement.

"Good. Now, I have a meeting, so be sure to help your mother show our spell-caster the grounds."

Father left, and Nate and I went to our rooms to change out of our rune-writer attire and into something more casual. Then we waited downstairs for Mother and Isabela.

"That went pretty well, all things considering," Nate said as he crossed his arms and leant against the wall.

I shook my head. "Who knew your mess-up would gain father a valuable asset?"

"Is that what I am, Master Grahm?"

We whirled around to see Isabela. The new dress fit her much better, the top portion hugging her torso, and the skirt flowed out, almost touching the floor. She looked the part of a lady, not a monster spell-casters were said to be.

"That is not what I meant," I said quickly.

"But that is what you said." Her dark eyes narrowed.

"I was merely summing up what our father had said." I looked to Nate for help, but his attention was zoned in on Isabela.

"So, that gives you permission to repeat it without consequence?"

I tried to swallow but found my mouth dry. "I apologise."

"For saying it or for getting caught saying it?"

"Both," I said. "And for what happened last night."

Her expression softened slightly. "If I remember correctly, your brother is the one who made the offensive proposition."

Nate cleared his throat, replacing his smirk with a smile. "I apologise, miss. I was too bladdered to be my normal, charming self."

Pinning the blame on too much alcohol discredited the apology in my opinion, but it was not my place to judge.

Isabela watched him for a few moments longer. "Your mother is freshening up and will join us soon. She said something about a tour of the manor."

The urge to blush hit me. How did we forget to ask about our mother? Part of me wanted to blame Isabela's accent... among other things.

Now who is pinning the blame elsewhere?

It was a relief when Mother finally showed up. "Thank you for your patience, my darlings," she said, parasol in hand. "Oh, Priscilla, please fetch a parasol for Miss Fuerte."

"Please, call me Isabela," she insisted. "And I have no need for a parasol."

The servant glanced back and forth between the women.

"Nonsense!" Mother waved as if to bat away the notion like it was something in the air. "It is important to keep one's skin looking healthy. What if you should burn?"

Priscilla hurried to do as her mistress asked of her. Isabela's eyes narrowed, but instead of arguing like I feared she would, she seemed to think better of it. She put on a smile that was almost convincing as she said, "Of course, Lady Grahm. You are quite right."

That placated Mother, who accepted Nate's arm... leaving me to escort Isabela. Nate threw a quick smirk in my direction; I ignored him and offered my arm to the spell-caster. Isabela hesitated before taking it. Even though her touch was light, my heart thudded almost painfully the moment she wrapped her arm around mine, and the rune on my chest warmed.

Keep it together, I reminded myself.

Chapter Five

Isabela

The first day at the manor, Lady Grahm and her sons showed me around their estate, something I did not expect, considering I felt like I was supposed to be a glorified prisoner. I took note of the different exits for future reference and nodded along as Lady Grahm told me all sorts of facts about their family history.

The second day, a seamstress and a cobbler arrived to measure me for proper gowns, shoes, gloves, hats, and everything else a dignified young woman would need or want when it came to clothing. It turned out that my definition of "need or want" did not quite line up with theirs, so I kept my mouth shut and offered up the pretty smiles I knew they expected from me. I had to admit, I looked like a proper lady in them, and I was sure that Camila would have approved.

Camila… My heart ached at the thought of my friend. I had to find a way to send her a letter as soon as I could, to let her know that I was still alive but had not managed to make it to the ship before the departure date. With the amount of time I spent with at least one of the Grahms, that was going to make it difficult.

The third day, Lady Grahm and an elderly woman taught me how to behave properly, which included lessons on dancing, eating, speaking, and even smiling.

Lord Grahm was not to be disturbed in all this time, either in his office speaking with clients in need of rune-writer help or leaving for meetings in the city.

When he left on the third day, I sought out Thomas and Nathaniel, finding them finishing up their fencing lessons. Taking off their masks, Nathaniel said something that Thomas laughed at. Thomas handed his rapier to one of the servants and turned toward me, sweat making his loose curls stick to his forehead. His smile faltered when he caught sight of me.

"Miss Fuerte," he greeted, offering a dip of his head. "Can I help you?"

Nathaniel perked up but stayed where he was, watching from a distance. Clearing my throat, I walked toward Thomas. "Yes, actually. First, you can start calling me 'Isabela' instead of 'Miss Fuerte.'"

He blinked. "Very well, Isabela. What else can I do for you?"

There was something about his accent that made me want to keep asking him questions. All of the people in this region had a similar one, but for some reason, I liked the way he said things.

Focus. "I would appreciate it if you would accompany me to the chapel."

Another blink. "You want to go to the chapel? The service is on Sunday."

"No," I clarified, shaking my head, "I wish to speak with Priest Abel."

"Priest Abel?"

I pursed my lips, wondering if he would continue to waste my time by repeating everything I said in the form of questions.

"I do not believe Father would be pleased if you left the manor."

"Your father has been in meetings for days, and he is gone right now. If you are there to escort me, then surely there would be nothing to fret over."

"She has a point," Nathaniel chimed in, warranting a look from his older brother.

"I apologise, Miss F—Isabela. I doubt I could, in good conscience, take you off the property without permission."

My eyes flicked to the lingering servants; Nathaniel must have understood because he handed them his rapier and gloves, asking them to put them away.

"Master Grahm—"

"Thomas," he corrected with a small smile.

"And you can call me Nathan or Nate," the younger Grahm interjected.

"Thomas," I said, keeping my voice low, "let me make this clear for you: I am going with or without you, but I am giving you the chance to join me. Would that not, after all, ensure that I do not run away? Would your father prefer that you go with me or that you let me leave?"

Nathan snickered as he took steps closer to us. "We should've had you around much sooner. Where have you been all our lives?"

Thomas's warm brown eyes searched mine like he was trying to uncover what I might be hiding.

You will not figure it out, I silently promised.

"Come now, this'll be fun," Nathan interjected, clapping a hand on

Thomas's shoulder. "We could all use at least a few hours out of this stuffy house."

I opened my mouth to object but thought better of it: the brothers seemed to do most things together, so if it got me away from the manor, so be it. Plans could always be adjusted.

Thomas's lips pressed into a thin line before he relented. "Let us change, and then we will meet you in the courtyard."

True to their word, the Grahm men met me outside, having changed and freshened up rather quickly, Thomas's curls slicked back, no sign of the messiness the fencing mask had left behind. Where Thomas looked respectable, Nathan did not bother to do more than comb his hair and change his clothes. He looked much more relaxed than his brother, carrying an air of nonchalance and freedom.

The carriage showed up about the same time they did.

"I hope we haven't kept you waiting long," Thomas said, offering his hand.

I paused, fighting the urge to ignore his help out of sheer stubbornness. If I was being honest with myself, I would have had to admit that my frustration lay with Lord Grahm, not his sons—even Nathan was much more tolerable to be around since he stopped flirting. Granted, that might have more to do with the fact that the bruise on his face was a good reminder of what would happen if he tried that with me again.

"Not at all," I assured Thomas and then gave a small smile that I hope appeared less forced than it was.

"Let us be on our way then, shall we?" Thomas smiled back—just a subtle, small smile, but a true one nonetheless.

The brothers shared one side, giving me the appropriate amount of space. I appreciated having the room for my skirts so they would not end up rumpled or sat on. Lord Grahm pleasantly surprised me by having fine-quality gowns made for me—which, when I thought about it, made sense, considering everything associated with him was about his reputation. If these did not flatter me so well, I might have worn frumpy clothing instead to get under his skin.

"Father has a taste for the finest things he can afford," Nathan commented, eyeing the way I smoothed the fabric of my dress.

"And not afford," Thomas added.

"As of yet. But he's convinced he'll be one of the richest men in the country if he can get into the royal family's good graces."

"Is he not already a lord?" I asked.

"Father is not one to settle, so I doubt he will ever be satisfied with where he is in life, even if he were to be crowned king. I am glad the king had all sons, otherwise I am sure Father would have already arranged marriages for Thomas and me."

As Nathan spoke, Thomas stared out the window at the hillsides we passed. There was nothing but green hills and trees for miles, telling me that I was far from the ship I was going to use to escape just days prior. Going to the chapel would put me that much closer, but without a plan in place, I was not going to be able to slip away today. No, that would take time and a lack of attentiveness on the Grahms' part.

"Right, Tom?" He nudged his older brother.

"Right," Thomas said with a nod, permitting Nathan to draw him back into the conversation.

"It would have been wonderful to have the perks of being married to a princess, but what if they were ugly and boring, and we were stuck with them because we had no say in the matter?"

"What makes you think they would have been ugly and boring?"

Nathan shrugged at me. "Simple: the sons are. Why would the daughters be any different?"

I rolled my eyes.

"The princes are kind enough," Thomas commented.

"Being kind does not make someone not boring."

"You are exaggerating, nonetheless."

"You cannot tell me that attraction to someone is not important," Nathan pressed. "You can love someone's mind, but physical attraction is what draws you to them in the first place and keeps you there when they have nothing interesting left to say."

How long until we reach the chapel? I wondered but kept from asking. "So, you would have been fine with marrying a boring princess who was beautiful beyond your wildest dreams?"

To his credit, the younger Grahm took a few moments to think before responding, "Yes. I believe the perks of being married to a beautiful princess would outweigh the negatives, even if she were dreadfully boring."

"What are these perks you speak of?" I asked, and the corner of Thomas's mouth twitched upward. For reasons beyond me, I found that alone was worth spending the rest of the journey there listening to Nathan's colourful, ignorant ideas of life as royalty. At one point, he stepped so far past the line of ridiculousness that I could not help but laugh.

Nathan frowned. "What?"

I waved a hand, trying to compose myself. "Go on."

"Your laughter wounds me, Miss Fuerte," Nathan replied, putting a hand to his chest mockingly. "What do you know of how royalty live?"

I took a moment to weigh my words by pretending to control my laughter. In actuality, all mirth turned to heavy seriousness in my stomach. "I know some."

Opting for a sprinkling of the truth drew in their attention. "Come on," Nathan urged, "tell us. You must! You already have us baited."

I raised my chin. "Must I?"

"Yes!"

"Leave her be, Nate," chided Thomas.

The carriage pulled to a stop, and a footman opened the door. Thomas exited first and extended his hand to me again. In the daylight, the chapel looked more solemn and serious, its spires seeming to pierce the sky above. A last resort for the desperate.

Desperate, I had been. Still was.

"Are you well?" Thomas whispered, cutting through the shouts and barks plaguing my mind.

I released his hand; my cheeks warmed.

"How long will you be?" Nathan inquired, checking his pocket watch.

Thomas frowned. "Where are you going?"

The brothers stared down one another. With a sigh, Nathan relented, "I have a lady friend to visit. She lives near here."

"Be back here in an hour."

Nathan looked to me, but I was not much help: "An hour should be plenty of time."

"Two."

"This is not a negotiation," Thomas stated. "We'll return home with or without you in an hour."

I considered pressing for more time as well, but figured that Thomas was trying to help us return to the manor before their father did.

"As you wish," Nathan replied with a mocking bow. As he hurried off, Thomas called after him, "One hour!" but got no response.

"Will we actually leave him behind?" I could not help but ask.

"We probably should. No doubt he will expect me to go after him as always." Thomas offered his arm again. "Shall we?"

Together, we walked up the steps. I had to lift the hem of my gown out of the way. It had been much easier, running up these stairs in pants, but with Thomas's arm and the skirts I was used to, I felt much safer. Not to mention there were no dogs or angry *cazarrecompensas* after me.

The doors stretched more than twice the height of any person I'd ever known, and they were open, showing off the grandeur of the main sanctuary. Rows upon rows of pews filled both sides, with a wide walkway leading up to steps and the pulpit. People kneeled, scattered amongst various rows as though their prayers were not to be heard by anyone else.

Thomas pulled away from me and put his hands into a bowl of dirt on the pedestal, rubbing them together. "From the dirt we come, to the dirt we shall return," he murmured.

With practiced hands, I copied, mentally chastising myself for being so distracted that I had forgotten.

"Pardon me," Thomas said to one of the priestesses in a soft tone, "Miss Fuerte would like to speak with Priest Abel at his earliest convenience."

While we waited, I scanned the room, focusing on the stained-glass windows and the way the sunlight painted the colours on the stone floor. It did not matter what was depicted on them: the array of colours together held my attention.

"Master Grahm," greeted a familiar voice. "Miss Fuerte. Good afternoon. What can I do for you?"

While everything else seemed so different in the daylight, Abel remained the same. I let my shoulders relax and put on a smile. "I would appreciate a moment of your time…" My mind blanked as I tried to remember his title in their language. Graciously, he gestured for me to follow him into one of the smaller rooms off to the side. Unlike where he had me stay the first time, this one had just two chairs and a couple of dishes on the floor with water and what looked like mashed up food. Then I noticed a cat resting with its young amongst scraps of what looked like newspapers.

"This will give us privacy and keep others from gossip," Abel said so that only I could hear him as he shut the door. "These rooms are reserved for lightenings."

Of course he thought that I was here to unload whatever was troubling me and to receive encouragement. "Oh, pardon me, I did not mean—"

The priest waved a hand as he sat across from me. "Everyone has stones weighing down their souls. I am here to help you untie them." He smiled at the cat lying near my chair. "Even creatures do. She came to us about a month ago after that big storm. I call her Stormy because of it. That, and because she is grey."

Two of the kittens ventured toward me, inspecting the hem of my dress with their noses and paws.

"You may hold them if you wish."

I did not have to be persuaded. Gently, I brought the two into my lap, and they nipped at my fingers. The dirt from my hands was obvious on the white kitten. This was a strange lightening indeed—he had not even asked me a question yet. All the ones I had attended in my country were serious affairs.

"How are you feeling?"

His question took me by surprise. "I… My arm is healing slowly." After a moment, I added, "Thank you for all you did for me. Not many would have, knowing what I am." The dark kitten got restless, so I set it down but kept the white one with me. It looked up at me with its bright green eyes.

He paused, watching me scratch the kitten along its spine. "Are the accommodations at the Grahm residence to your liking?"

I had to ponder the meaning of "accommodations" for a few seconds. "I am being taken care of," I answered slowly. Even though there was no one near us to eavesdrop, I quieted my voice as I asked, "Why did you help me? You could have handed me over to the... *cazarrecompensas*." I huffed through my nose, frustrated that the translation eluded me.

"...Do you mean the bounty hunters? I have heard stories and find their methods... distasteful. Besides, you were someone in need, and the Maker has commissioned us to not turn away those in need."

The dark kitten mewled from the floor, so I gave in and picked it back up.

"But I am a heathen."

"Are you?"

I blinked, looking up at him. "Is that not what the Chantry teaches, that I am a heathen for being a spell-caster? A monster who can only fight my true nature for a short amount of time?"

After a beat, Abel replied, "My faith tells me to love people. Are you a person, Miss Fuerte?"

I snorted at the absurdity of the question; a few answers ran through my mind. "That depends on whom you ask."

"You *are* a person," he corrected kindly. "And, if you are ever in need again, you are most welcome to return here for sanctuary. I am certain these kittens would like your company again."

I swallowed. In a barely audible voice, I said, "Thank you."

Chapter Six

Thomas

Friends

As I waited for Isabela, I looked at where she had been staring, hoping to figure out what had her attention. The way she clung to my arm had me checking around the sanctuary as though I were going to find some sort of monster to protect her from. I saw nothing other than a normal, fairly vacant chapel, given that it was midweek.

Isabela returned not too long after she left, her brow furrowed and mouth in a tight line. She smoothed the front of her gown before she turned to bid farewell to Priest Abel. Little white and black hairs stuck to her gloves and skirt, barely noticeable.

"May the Maker's protection and favour follow both of you wherever you go," the priest said to us. Nothing in his expression betrayed what was said between the two of them, and I doubted either of them would be forthcoming if I asked.

"Thank you," I replied with a dip of my head. "And to you as well."

Before I could finish speaking, Isabela was already outside. I caught up to her on the stairs. "Miss Fuer—pardon me, I mean Isabela."

Her rich chocolate eyes met mine, within them a myriad of emotions railing against one another. "If you ask me again if I am well, Thomas, I will take the carriage home alone and let you walk with your brother."

We descended the rest of the stairs in silence, keeping space between us.

"We have plenty of time yet," I said after checking my pocket watch. "I can track down Nate so we can return home if it please you."

"No."

The abruptness of her response caused me to look at her curiously.

"I am going for a walk," Isabela stated. Then she added with a smirk and a gleam in her eye, "You may come if it please you."

I could not help a small smile as I matched her leisurely pace. "There is a park nearby." I was about to make a comment about how we had not thought to bring a parasol, but she had refused one before, so I let it go.

"That sounds lovely." She lost the edge to her voice.

Children played with a kite in the park, running through the grass as a dog nipped at their heels. Their giggles and shouts of glee carried far. In the shade of a tree sat two women on a bench, chattering away as they watched the children.

"I am sorry for snapping at you."

I glanced at Isabela. "Already forgiven and forgotten."

She frowned at me, making me wonder what on earth I possibly could say that would not offend her in some way. "How are you not bothered?" she asked, drawing closer to me so that we nearly rubbed shoulders. She looped her arm through mine and winced, so I stepped around and offered her the other one.

"Bothered by what?" I led us away from the children's wide running area.

"What I am," she said simply. "You, Nathan, and Priest Abel seem to be the only people in the world who haven't a care about it."

"Should I be bothered?" I asked, fully well knowing of what she was speaking.

"Rather unfair to answer a question with a question," she retorted, sweat beading at her brow.

I handed her my handkerchief and found us a spot to sit at that had trees to protect us from the sun. "I heard stories of spell-casters growing up," I admitted. "Nate and I both have. I would be surprised if anyone had not. But what good would it do for me to treat you poorly? You do not seem the dangerous monster stories make you out to be."

Isabela raised an eyebrow at me, the corner of her lip twitching.

"Well, perhaps dangerous," I amended teasingly. "There is a fire to you I would not want to be on the wrong side of—but I've never heard of a monster being so beautiful." The words came out of me before I thought them through, and I snapped my mouth shut as my mind reeled.

Her eyes widened drastically before she swatted at my shoulder with my handkerchief. "Here I thought your brother was the terrible flirt." She laughed, and I could not tell whether the red blooming on her cheeks was from the heat or for the same reason mine were.

I cleared my throat, stuffing the handkerchief back into my pocket. "I think we can agree that both of us are terrible in our own ways."

After a moment, she said, "*Sirenas.*"

"Pardon?"

"I… I am trying to remember the word in your language. They

would be considered a 'beautiful monster.'"

"Can you describe them?"

She pursed her lips, staring up at the sky. "I read about them in a book. They are women who live in water. Their looks and voices are so… enchanting—is that the word?—that men fall in love with them and jump into the oceans just to be with them, drowning themselves."

"That sounds rather morbid," I replied, almost laughing at the flash of a grin on her face. "Do you recall the name of the book?"

"It is in my language."

"We might have a copy in our language in the library."

"Library?"

"A room full of books. We have a library at the manor."

Her expression lit up; this time, I really did laugh, realising we had forgotten to show it to her on our tour.

"I'll show you when we return home," I promised.

"Now I actually have a reason to want to return," she commented. For a moment, I paused: what she said hit me strangely, leaving an aching feeling in my chest. But why would she have any desire to be in a place where she was a glorified servant?

I checked the time. "Nate has another quarter hour, but we can go looking for him if you'd rather."

"Does he always make you go looking for him?"

"Nearly," I said, standing up as two familiar figures came out of the trees. They giggled and stole kisses from one another, their clothes and hair rumpled. "You're actually about to be on time, Nate."

My brother pulled his face away from Caroline's. The sight of her pale complexion and bright blue eyes, so similar to her sister Abigail's, jarred me, leaving me irritated with Nate as he said, "Fancy seeing you here. I thought you wanted to go to the chapel?"

"We already did." In my peripherals, I could see Isabela positioning herself beside me, but I focused on Nate.

"Afternoon, Thomas," Caroline greeted, fanning at her flushed face.

"Miss Collins."

"I'll take her home and then meet you back at the carriage," Nate said. "Or—"

"That is fine," I cut him off.

"Or you could come," Caroline said. "I am sure Abigail would love to chat."

I grit my teeth so hard they ached. "Good day to you, Miss Collins. Nate, fix your shirt and do not dawdle." Then I took my leave, too quick to be considered walking but too slow for running. Out of all the people Nate could have been meeting, he had to be overly friendly with Caroline. At least it hadn't been Abigail herself—my brother would never cross that line.

Isabela hurried to catch up to my pace. "Thomas. Thomas. Thomas!"

I halted, making her run into me. I caught her before she could lose her balance; the children sprinted past us.

"What was that about? Who was she?"

"Caroline is the sister of the woman I used to court." I started walking again, and Isabela latched onto my arm, no doubt to keep me from going too quickly for her to keep pace. She fidgeted with my sleeve, so I answered the question before she could pluck up the courage to ask: "Abigail decided she wanted to court Prince August to have the chance to become a princess, so she ended things with me to pursue him. Things must have gone poorly, because she came back to me not a few months later saying that she wanted to try again. I refused her."

Isabela watched me. "You loved her."

"I thought I did."

"Why did you not take her back?"

"Could you be with someone, knowing that you were their second choice?"

There was nothing but the sound of our footsteps for the rest of the way to the carriage. By the time we arrived, I found that my muscles had relaxed, and I missed Isabela's touch as soon as she pulled away to get in. I gave the coachman directions and settled inside of the carriage.

"I thought the Collins' residence would be the last place you'd wish to go."

"Yes, but this way Nate has less excuses to dally." I locked eyes with her. "My apologies for not introducing you—that was impolite."

The corner of Isabela's mouth quirked up. "Already forgiven and forgotten." We shared a smile; she moved her skirts to pat the seat beside her. "You may sit with me if it please you, leave Nate to sit alone."

"That is a kind offer, but I'd rather look at you than my brother." I had no idea what it was about Isabela that made me say such things, but I found that this time I had no qualms about what I'd said.

"Nate does look a mess," Isabela said, "and this gown does flatter me well enough."

"Too true, *Sirena*." I inwardly cringed at how terribly I botched the pronunciation and hoped she took no offense.

Isabela shook her head with a chuckle. "You are a terrible flirt."

"The worst."

Chapter Seven

Isabela

 Gossip

The smile I had managed to get onto Thomas's face fled the moment Nathan entered the carriage. A few terse words were exchanged, and then the rest of the way back to the manor was shared in silence. At least Nathan had the decency to straighten up before we made it back...

...because their father was waiting at the front doors.

"You made your mother worried sick," Lord Grahm said before we had even made it out of the carriage. "You'll be the death of her yet."

I, of course, had to wonder why, if she was so distraught, she was nowhere to be seen.

"And you have the audacity to return home looking like ragamuffins." He gestured toward Nathan, who I'd thought did a decent job cleaning up, all things considered. No more twigs and leaves, no dirt smudges. I did not know exactly what "ragamuffin" meant, but I could guess, so before I could take offense, Thomas said, "We apologise for worrying you and Mother."

"Where did you go?"

"I asked them to go with me to the chapel," I clarified. "I wished to thank Priest Abel for his kindness in person."

Lord Grahm lifted his chin. "You expect me to believe that

nonsense when—"

"It is the truth," I countered, taking a step forward. "You are more than welcome to inquire of Priest Abel."

"Do not interrupt me, girl."

I pressed my lips together but refused to look away from his glare, refused to show how his eerie calm voice caused my pulse to quicken and hands to tremble.

"Get inside and change," Lord Grahm ordered. "We have guests joining us for dinner—I'll not have you embarrassing me."

Guests? I then noticed how his attire, notably his tailcoat with gold buttons, was fancier than what I'd seen him in previously.

"After they have all gone, we shall speak of consequences."

"You would punish us for going to the chapel?" I asked without thinking.

Lord Grahm's shoes made the only sound as he approached me.

"Father," Thomas interrupted, only to receive a crippling look.

Stopping in front of me, Lord Grahm straightened, making himself appear taller. "You would do well to learn your place, spell-caster. I took you in out of the goodness of my heart, but if your disobedience continues, be rest assured I will have no qualms handing you over to the bounty hunters."

There were so many things I wanted to say in response, but, even if I could, I had no idea where I would have begun, which point I would have argued first.

"Father, she—"

"Enough, Thomas." Lord Grahm demanded, "Do you understand?

Will you behave properly?"

"…yes…" I said, forcing the word from my mouth, nearly having to yank it out.

"Very good. Go inside and get ready for dinner."

Thomas and Nathan waited for me to move first. I made my way inside and up the grand staircase, and they caught up to me rather quickly then. After checking over my shoulder that Lord Grahm had not followed us, I said, "I am sorry: I did not mean—"

"No need," Thomas assured me.

"That was one of his more amicable moods," Nathan added. "Count it lucky we have guests coming. He must be pleasant, at least until after they leave. By then, he shouldn't be quite as mad." His half-hearted smirk did little to put me at ease. "Besides, you did not force us to leave the manor without permission."

"I did manipulate you a little," I admitted, gripping the banister as I brought myself to meet their gazes.

"We wanted to leave," Thomas said. "We're too often stuck here for our liking."

"Glad to hear you finally admitting it instead of pinning it on me." Nathan gave a playful shove, making him bump into me.

"Are you all right?" Thomas inquired, his hand on my forearm to steady me.

I chuckled, "I am fine. Remember what I said about you asking me that?"

"Well, we're already home, so I would not have to walk far." Thomas let go of me and smacked the back of Nathan's head. "You could have hurt Isabela."

"She said she's fine."

I ducked out of the way before the two of them could grapple each other. "I will see you at dinner."

If they responded, it was too muffled by their scrap.

I slipped into my room to find a few servants already there, waiting for me. The time it took them to ready me for the dinner party was enough to let myself run through the events of the day… and the lack of action on my part.

As they laced me into my corset and petticoats, I pondered Priest Abel and his words. Could I use him as a way to escape? I ran my fingertips over the rune on my wrist, tracing its lines. It thrummed with magic. Although I knew better, I had tried scrubbing it off, only to have the blood remain like it was seared into my skin. That, at the moment, was the one thing keeping me from escape. But each rune-writer's magic worked differently, and Lord Grahm had not told me what the consequences of my trying to leave would be.

Dare I try?

The corset forced me to have good posture. The servants brought over a dark blue gown, slipping it on over my head and then situating the rest of it.

No, I would not dare try that—yet. My meeting with the priest was not in vain: I had his sympathies, and so, if need be, I could perhaps call upon him to help break the bond. That was a bit of a longshot, since the priest would have to petition Lord Grahm's treatment of me to the Crown, and there was no telling how that would go over. I might get myself into a worse situation.

Thomas was another option. Perhaps he knew how to get rid of the rune, and, after today, I might have cracked open a door of trust between us.

Sirena, he had said—or, rather, tried to say.

"Are you excited for the dinner party?" asked one of the servant girls, a dark brunette named Gianna. "You're already all smiles, miss."

The vanity mirror confirmed what she said; I fought not to blush, and I pushed away those thoughts.

"It seems one should be excited given the guests coming," commented another, an older woman named Priscilla, as she twisted pieces of my hair to pin into place so that I had a beautiful updo that showed off the silver necklace and matching dangling earrings. I had seen her here and there since the manor tour on the first day, but this was the most I'd heard her speak. "Prestigious, the lot of them. Although I do hope Master Thomas doesn't feel put out by Miss Abigail's presence."

I looked at Priscilla through the mirror. "Abigail Collins will be attending this evening?"

Priscilla grimaced. "Pardon me, Miss Fuerte—I know I'm apt to the sin of gossip."

"I'm not bothered, Priscilla," I assured her. "Quite the opposite, actually. What can you tell me of her and her relationship with Thomas?"

Why do you care? I teased myself, but all I could think about was the way he stormed off, the sudden shift in demeanour. The way he answered my questions without me giving voice to them. The way he looked at me after I let go of his arm to get into the carriage, like I was his comfort.

But was it truly for any of those reasons? *No,* I told myself. Not if I wanted to escape and find a better life. I had to know all of my options, all of the people who could help me unwittingly or not.

"If you insist, miss," Priscilla said, her voice dropping into a conspiratorial whisper. "I heard Miss Abigail is the desire of most lads, given her beauty and voice."

"Then why did the prince break it off with her?"

Gianna situated herself in front of me and picked up a cosmetics brush. "Close your eyes, please."

"Word is that she was too much for the prince to handle," Priscilla answered.

"What does that mean?" I asked, trying not to sneeze as Gianna powdered my face.

"Knows what she wants, that one."

"What's wrong with that?"

"Nothing at all except when she throws a tantrum to get her way."

"A tantrum?"

"A fit, miss. Like when children wail over not getting dessert."

A laugh escaped me before I could stop myself. Gianna shook her head and wiped at my face with a cloth before starting again.

"I can't imagine an adult behaving in such a manner."

"You'd best believe it," Priscilla said seriously. "We were rather glad when she and Master Thomas were through—mind you, not glad of his broken heart, but glad to not see the likes of her around much anymore. Demanding, that one. Thomas catered to her every whim and fancy, letting her walk all over him."

I thought of his relationship with his brother and his father. I had seen little of how he interacted with his mother, but what Priscilla said seemed to add up. It was no wonder I so easily got him to take me away from the manor.

"Finished," Priscilla announced.

I stood and inspected myself in the full-length mirror, feeling like a princess in the elegant gown. Camila would have approved, although she would have wanted a version of it in her signature red instead of this deep blue. The corset gave me an hourglass shape, and the dress hugged the curves up top.

Priscilla said, "If this is not too far in saying so, miss, you look beautiful, and I hope Miss Collins finds you a threat. She deserves to be knocked down a peg or two."

Chapter Eight

Thomas

The moment my mother asked me to bring Isabela down for dinner, I excused myself from the sitting room and tried not to look like I was rushing my way up the stairs. I could feel Abigail's eyes on me—everyone's, really. Why Father had invited her family was beyond me, and questioning him would only result in a tongue-lashing.

I knocked, and Gianna opened the door not a few seconds later, stepping aside so that Isabela and I could see one another.

"Thomas," Isabela said, walking away from the mirror. "Am I late?" Somehow, the servants had managed to pin up her long hair, exposing her petite ears and slender neck, which were both graced with silver jewellery. The hem of the dark blue dress nearly scraped the floor as she approached me. Up close, I could tell how much cosmetics they had put on her: the tiny mole near the corner of her left eye was covered.

"Not yet," I replied, scrambling for my brain to put together words. "Mother sent me to fetch you so we could begin."

"Have the other guests arrived?"

I said, "Yes," refraining from talking about how long it felt they had been at the manor already.

She looped her arm through mine and slowly walked down the hall. "Then you've already seen her."

There was no mistaking whom she meant. "I have. And I've been avoiding her as best I can." Stopping just before the stairs, I lowered my voice even further, leaning in toward her. The smell of her perfume beckoned me even closer, but I resisted. It took me a moment to recall what I was about to say, especially when Isabela tilted her face my way. "She has been staring at me. Everyone is tense, like they are waiting for us to either confess our love or have it out right there in the middle of the sitting room."

Isabela grinned mischievously, and I realised that our noses were nearly touching.

"Might as well have fun with them then," she said. "Let them watch you walk in handsome as you are with a beautiful woman on your arm."

I blinked. Her words ran through my mind a few times.

"Let's not keep them waiting. I am certain they are dying to meet the monstrous spell-caster." She winked at me. "*La Sirena.*"

I still did not know what that meant, but I smiled. "They have no idea what they're in for." *And neither do I.* As much as I tried to look away from her, my eyes kept wandering back and forth between her eyes and lips. If I focused enough, I could tell where that mole was hidden, seeing just a hint of it.

The rune on my chest heated up. Between me trying to puzzle out what that meant and Isabela tugging on my arm, I was saved from staring like an idiot any longer. We descended, coming to the first landing where the two sets of staircases came together. That was when the first of the guests noticed us: Abigail. Her lips pressed together in a thin line as she eyed Isabela from head to toe. Conversation quieted as we reached the main floor.

Father strode over, leaving Mother to stand alone. "May I present our family spell-caster, Miss Isabela Fuerte."

I was about to remove my arm from hers, but Isabela kept her hold on me as she dipped into a curtsy.

"It is a privilege to serve this family," she stated, "and an honour to meet you all. Thank you for joining us this evening."

Whether she meant it or not, her tone and presence were convincing. Even Father had a twinkle in his eye as he introduced the different families: the Collins, the Baskers, and the Smiths. While the Smiths were older, their children already grown and tending to their own lives and families, the Baskers had brought their four boys and two young girls. For the most part, the children remained still during the exchanges.

Finally, Father suggested that we all make our way to the dining room.

Isabela whispered in my ear, "She has been glaring at me."

"I noticed," I said, avoiding looking at Abigail by watching as Caroline and Nathan found their seats near Mother, who sat at Father's left hand... leaving me to sit at his right.

I pulled out a chair beside mine for Isabela before I sat down. The long table was elegantly decorated with flowers and leaves from Mother's garden, making the dishes seem like they had grown right alongside the vegetation. I noted that the fine china was being used.

Abigail decided to take the chair next to her sister. It might have been my imagination, but I thought I saw the corner of Isabela's mouth twitch upward.

"Miss Fuerte," asked Lord Smith, cutting his chicken, "how long have you practiced spell-casting?" His thick grey moustache moved as he spoke, looking like a furry creature on his lip.

"Practically my whole life," Isabela answered.

"Are you known as talented among your people?" Lady Smith added on.

Isabela took a moment more than necessary to chew and swallow. "Quite, although there are others with more skill than I."

"Then why is your arm injured?" Lord Smith inquired. "Surely your uncivilised magic has remedies for such things."

I wanted to shrink away as Isabela bared her teeth in a way that qualified as a smile by the minimum requirements.

"Uncivilised?"

"Yes. I thought it a better word than 'heathen.'"

"The words carry the same meaning." Isabela stared at him, took a long drink from her glass, and set it gently back in its spot on the table.

"Miss Fuerte," Father warned.

"To answer your question," she continued, "there are things my magic can do for it, but it requires a lot from me, which would defeat the purpose."

"Could you give her a healing rune?" Lord Baskers asked from the other end of the table as his wife scolded their children for accidentally hitting the glass against the edges of their plates. "Do runes work on spell-casters?"

"They do," Isabela confirmed, lifting her arm to show off her wrist. Our guests leant this way and that in their chairs to see better.

"Looks like he did it in blood," a younger Baskers boy said to another.

"Shush," their mother chastised. "Children are to be seen, not heard."

I fought the urge to roll my eyes by looking to Father, like everyone else who was waiting for an answer. At least Abigail had torn her hate-filled looks away from Isabela and me for the time being.

"Some lessons need to be learned," Father answered, waving his hand in the air like he was dismissing the idea.

"And what lesson would that be, Lord Grahm?" Isabela challenged in a calm, even tone. When he narrowed his eyes at her, she added, "I can't very well learn my lesson if I have no idea what it is."

Father's face reddened; he white-knuckled his fork.

"Apologies," I interrupted. "There are some differences in customs that we are all adjusting to."

Dinner went on with a painful lack of conversation—although not quite as painful as the previous conversation had been. Thankfully, Mother suggested we go to the parlour to listen to Caroline play the piano while Abigail sang. The servants set to cleaning up, and we migrated to the other room. Behind me, I heard my father whisper, "You will not continue this blatant disrespect."

"Of course not," Isabela whispered back. "I had no intentions of disrespect, Lord Grahm."

I peeked over my shoulder to see Father nod and walk away. Isabela caught me looking and shrugged.

Everyone settled onto couches and seats to listen to the Collins sisters. Just as lovely as before, Abigail's voice filled the space, captivating each person within its range.

Until I noticed the lyrics spoke of lost love. A heavy sigh lodged in my chest, but I held it in. I appreciated that Abigail kept her eyes closed as she sang, that way I did not have to avoid her gaze.

Caroline's fingers danced gracefully across the keys. Whenever I had tried, I could never coax the same sounds from the instrument— whatever I played sounded more like someone clomping around trying to look for something.

We applauded when they finished. Abigail's eyes gleamed with unshed tears, which she dabbed away with a lace-edged handkerchief.

"Lord Grahm," Lord Smith suggested, "why don't we have Miss Fuerte demonstrate her capabilities in spell-casting? Under your watchful eye, of course."

"That would be permissible." Father motioned to Nate and me, and we stood, retrieving knives from our pockets to cut the backs of our wrists. With practiced ease, we drew runes on the floor surrounding the parlour, even as Mother tried to cover a frown by fanning her face. I furtively checked on Isabela, noticing a tightness in her jaw.

"Well, Miss Fuerte," said Father, "it is time."

Chapter Nine

Isabela

Demonstration

During the time it took them to write the runes, my mind had been scrambling for ideas on what to "demonstrate."

Who treats magic like a cheap circus act?

If they knew what it took to use my magic, would they care? By the way they watched me expectantly, I doubted it. The atmosphere in the room shifted as the runes worked together to create an invisible barrier.

"Well, Miss Fuerte, it is time."

I swallowed and tried to keep a pleasant expression on my face. "What would you like to see?" If I did something too simple, Lord Grahm might think me ineffective and hand me over to *los cazarrecompensas—*

Bounty hunters, I reminded myself.

But if I did something too powerful, they might tag me as dangerous. Better that they underestimate me.

"Is it true you can make fire and hold it in your hands?" Lord Baskers inquired, focusing on me with his beady eyes.

I cupped my hands together in front of me and relaxed my mind, lowering the defences slightly. Wild heat trickled in until I cut it off and maneuvered what I had. It resisted, but eventually the magic flowed out of my palms to turn into small flames.

"Does it hurt?" Nathan asked amidst the murmurs and gasps. Lady

Grahm put a hand to her mouth, her brow knotted.

"No." Inhaling, I absorbed the magic once more and, exhaling, shoved it back out the way it came before it could linger too long near my mind.

"Can you make a flower?" asked one of the little girls.

"Hush," said her mother.

Smiling at her, I repeated the process, this time taking in more magic. A bud rose from my hand, growing and producing leaves as small blue flowers took form. I felt the snap of magic, and I handed the little girl the flowers.

"Beautiful!" she squealed. "Forget-me-nots, Mother!"

"I want one!" the other girl whined.

"There's enough to share," chided Lady Baskers. She plucked a few from the small bunch for her youngest daughter.

"Certainly, she can do more than that," Lord Smith scoffed, "if she is your spell-caster, Gerold. Such creatures are not kept for mere parlour tricks."

"What would you have her do in such a confined space, Reginold?" Lord Grahm asked. "Would we put our loved ones and my house at risk out of mere curiosity? Let not jealousy put a wedge between us. We are still equals, all lords with plenty of respect and admiration."

For the first time, I saw a grin on his face, but the glint in his eyes sent shivers down my spine. He chuckled, and the others joined in like he had just made a joke.

"It has been a lovely evening," Lord Grahm said. "I'll be sure to have more spectacular things in store for the ball next month."

Ball? I was unsure I heard him correctly until the others commented on how they looked forward to it and Lady Grahm promised to send out invitations with the theme within the week.

The Grahm men leant down, licking their thumbs to wipe at the runes. The moment they were smeared or separated, I felt the magic snap and dissipate. Servants entered the parlour, scrubbing at what remained.

As the others said farewell, I was surprised that Abigail approached me, head held high, blue eyes surveying me up and down. With her not dark brown hair and fair skin, she was a beauty—although her expression soured her attraction.

"I did not expect such civility from someone from Isouldia," she commented. "And a spell-caster, no less. I suppose miracles do happen. I look forward to more of your parlour tricks at the ball, Miss Isabela Fuerte."

My eye twitched. I donned an overly sweet smile and said, "Have a wonderful evening, Miss Abigail Collins."

When the last of the goodbyes were given, Lord Grahm strode to me. "I knew you could be civil and useful." I forced myself to keep smiling; he continued, "We'll begin working on what magic you will display for the ball in a few days after I have some things sorted." He left without waiting for my response, humming to himself. Lady Grahm bid me a brief goodnight and hurried after him.

"That was fascinating," Nathan said as soon as they were out of earshot. "Can you show me again?"

"Another time, Nate." Thomas patted his shoulder. "It's late: we should be going to sleep. I think we've had an eventful day as it is."

"We can put the runes back up so Father and Mother don't notice."

"Another time," I parroted. "Then perhaps you can show me how your runes work."

"You don't know?" Nathan raised a single brow, something I'd never been able to accomplish no matter how long I practiced in the mirror.

"Do you know how my magic works?"

He had the decency to blush and rub the back of his neck. "Well, I... No, not really."

"Then do we have ourselves a deal?"

"Yes," Thomas answered for him, "and Nate can participate as long as he actually goes to bed and doesn't try sneaking out to see one of his 'friends' again."

Nathan grinned. "That might actually keep me in this prison of a house. That is, until you beg us to take you out again."

"Beg?!" I gaped, taking a step toward him. "I'll have you know—"

Thomas put himself between us. "Nate, stop. The servants have already cleaned enough blood off the floors tonight. Better scurry upstairs before she spills some of yours."

Nathan winked at me. "I'm holding you to the deal, Isabela."

"Goodnight, Nathan."

With a smirk, the younger Grahm made his way toward the staircase. The older one stood near me, his hands in the pockets of his suitcoat.

"Yes, Thomas?"

He could not seem to meet my gaze as he said, "I imagine tonight was neither pleasant nor easy for you. I am finding myself apologising to you plenty in the short time I've known you, but I want you to know that I am sorry for all of it: the way they spoke to you, the way—"

"You do not need to apologise on their behalf," I interrupted. That drew his attention to my face. "You only need to apologise for what you do or say."

Thomas stared at me, his eyes flitting back and forth between mine, reminding me of the way he looked at me on the stairs before bringing me down for dinner. For some reason, that alone made me feel pinned to where I stood, but at the same time, I felt an invisible tug that nearly made me take a step closer.

"Very well."

The way we were, just a few feet away from one another, gazes locked, a magnetic force pulling us… I was so certain he had to feel it, too, but I was terrified that I was wrong. If Camila were here, she would have told me that I was letting the fairy-tales I read get in my head.

I cleared my throat. "Goodnight, Thomas."

"Goodnight, Isabela," he said softly.

My shoes clicked against the floor as I walked away, but all I could hear was his tone replaying in my head. Pausing, I turned around to see him still standing there, still watching me.

"Thomas…"

"Yes?"

"Thank you for the sentiment. You are a kind person."

Thomas looked down at his shoes. Something fluttered in my chest, and, for a moment, I considered crossing the distance between us to kiss him on the cheek. The thought jolted me. Before I could act on it, I said, "Goodnight."

"Goodnight. Sleep well."

I forced myself to take the steps one at a time, all too aware of his eyes on me.

Chapter Ten

Thomas

I did not sleep much that night. Every time I closed my eyes, visions of a brown-haired beauty danced through my mind, fire and flowers in her hands. My dream self kept his distance, watching. Then she would smile and beckon me closer. As if in response, the rune on my chest would warm, and I would walk to her, mere breaths away before I'd wake and stare at the darkness of my ceiling.

Light finally peeked through the curtains when I decided to give up. As I dressed, I heard voices and footsteps passing my door: Father and Isabela. They were just quiet enough for me to not be able to understand what they were saying. It took me all of a few seconds of wrestling with my conscience to decide what I was going to do.

I eased open my door and slipped out, pausing at the top of the stairs. Based on the softness of their footfalls, I made my way toward Father's office, but instead of going to the door, I entered our practice room, making sure to shut and lock the door behind me. Cutting the back of my wrist, I outlined some complicated runes in a circle on the adjoining wall to the office. The circle was not as neat as I'd normally like, but time was of the essence, so I left it as is.

Like I was looking through a hole in the wall, the image of Isabela and Father sitting in his office appeared in the circle. They were across from one another, the wide and long design of the desk separating them. Without the help of the servants, Isabela wore one of the simpler gowns, her light brown hair loose in soft waves. Despite the plaques, bookshelves, and maps covering the walls, Isabela had her focus on Father, her expression neutral save for the set of her jaw.

"Because I will not tolerate insubordination," Father said, the runes now capturing the sound for me. Their actual voices were muffled by the wall between us. The way he was fully dressed and shaved made me wonder how long he'd been awake, no doubt planning this meeting. "I do not know how things are run in Isouldia, but here you will be nothing but pleasant, proper, and obedient. There is no reason for you to speak unless directly spoken to." When Isabela said nothing, he added, "I am protecting you in this. Women especially are often taken advantage of—let me represent you and keep you safe. Your job is simple, just doing as I say. I am the one to live with the responsibilities, decisions, and repercussions." He leant forward on the desk, his hands folded in front of him. "I am doing what is best for you, for all of us."

Isabela's fingers fidgeted in her lap, out of Father's sight. "Understood, Lord Grahm. Thank you for your hospitality and kindness."

"You are most welcome, dear." Father smiled, sitting up straight. "Now then, anything else we need to clarify?"

"I do have a question."

I searched her face for a clue to what she might be thinking but found nothing other than submission and meekness.

"What was the purpose of inviting the woman who broke Thomas's heart? Surely you could have invited just the lords and ladies to save him some grief."

Father's knuckles turned white; his right eye twitched. "That is not your business," he answered slowly. "However, I will have you know that our families have always been close. We must deal with the consequences of our decisions, no? That is why I tell you that the man's job is always so much more difficult than the woman's. I suggest you count your blessings." Something softened in Father's face as he tilted his head. "I do appreciate your concern for my family's wellbeing. I know one burden of womenfolk is a tender, delicate heart, easily troubled by the pain of others. If it eases your heart, know that I have personally given Thomas a love rune on his chest so that romantic love may find him soon. It is high time for him to find a wife and give his mother the grandchildren she so desperately wants."

I took a half-step back to regain my balance. *He told her...* But why? Father never revealed information without a reason behind it, but there was no way he, a well-respected, prestigious rune-writer, would ever approve of a romance of any sort between me and a lowly, uncivilised spell-caster.

Studying Isabela's face gave me little indication as to what she was thinking other than the slight widening of her eyes and the soft frown that disappeared quickly. "That eases my heart," she said, her hands twisting together.

"That being said," Father continued, "eligible women from the most prestigious families will be in attendance at our ball—the royal family might even be in attendance, if they can spare the time to grace us with their presence. It would not do well to reflect poorly on

Thomas and hurt his chances at a perfect match."

Isabela put on a pleasant expression that looked a little flat in the eyes. "Of course, Lord Grahm. I would not think to hurt Thomas or his happiness. What do you have in mind for the event?"

The rune on my chest itched; I could not help but try to read her face, her posture, her still-fidgeting hands.

"I knew you were up to something," a voice said from behind me, sending a jolt of panic down my spine.

"Hush!" I hissed at Nate as he stepped into the room and closed the door behind him. "How'd you get in?"

"You're not the only one who can use runes." He shook his head and locked the door once more. I should have used runes to keep him out. I doubted he had a bottle of the removal solution on hand to get rid of my runes, and he wouldn't have been able to reach them anyway with them being on my side of the door.

"Just don't get us caught," I warned him.

Nate rolled his eyes and ran a hand through his dishevelled sandy blonde hair. At least he'd had the presence of mind to get dressed, even if the buttons were open at the top of his shirt. He looked closer to a ragamuffin now than he had yesterday, like Father had said, but still nowhere near. Sloppy was a better term. "I'm better at mischief than you give me credit for, Tom." He manoeuvred his way beside me so that he could spy with me.

"Then why am I always left to clean the messes you leave behind?"

Nate flashed me a grin. "We both have our strengths." He put a hand on the wall next to the runes, leaning against it as he surveyed the scene. "How unfair is it that the Maker made a gorgeous spell-caster? Why make something so alluring that's off-limits? It's like He *wants* us to fall into temptation."

"Hush."

"You're thinking the same thing, admit it."

"I want to hear what they're saying."

Out of the corner of my eye, I could tell Nate was smirking.

"Understood?" Father asked, and I mentally cursed for having missed that bit of conversation.

"I will do my best, Lord Grahm," Isabela said.

"Very good. Now then, run along and tell the servants to dress you in something more elegant. We are meeting with the Queen: she has taken quite an interest in making your acquaintance."

"She's meeting the Queen," breathed Nate. "Wonder how that'll go over."

I shrugged, my only show of irritation that I, again, missed Isabela's response because of Nate.

Father and Isabela stood as he said, "I'll have Archibald wake Thomas and Nathaniel so that we can have breakfast and leave for the capital as soon as possible."

In a frenzy, the two of us used our spit to wipe at the runes, which smeared them more than anything. I mopped up what I could with my handkerchief and shoved it back in my pocket.

"It's good enough," Nate stated, tugging on my sleeve. "We've got to get out of here."

Chapter Eleven

Isabela

Queen

After the early-morning meeting with Lord Grahm, everything else seemed to pass by me in a whirl until the carriage ride to the capital.

Which

Dragged

On.

I adjusted my gloves, noting that between the end of them and the length of my sleeves they left enough room to show off my wrists, exposing the rune that marked me as property of the Grahm family. The lines were harsh and black, a stark contrast to my white gloves and the soft colour and cut of my green gown. I tried to keep my skirts as close to me as possible; I shared a side of the carriage with both Thomas and Nathan, which had my side flush against Thomas. Nathan made a few complaints about being pressed against the wall until Lord Grahm demanded that he cease.

Lady Grahm said little, idly fanning herself as she stared out the window. I might have done the same if I'd had the room to move my arms without elbowing poor Thomas. As it was, I was thankful that Priscilla had managed to wrap and pin my hair into a bun, keeping it out of my face and off my neck. It would not do to meet the royal family all covered in sweat. If Camila had seen me in such a sorry state, she'd have laughed and insisted I go to her rooms to freshen up.

The thought of my friend sent a pang through my heart.

Camila, I hope you are doing well. Maybe someday I will be able to send you a letter explaining what has happened.

I had done so well not thinking about her, instead focusing on what had to be done. If we had traded places, I would have been pacing the floors of *el castillo* waiting for news. Thankfully, she was surrounded by her family and others in the royal court, so there were plenty of distractions to hold her attention. *Princesas* rarely had time for themselves, just like all other royalty.

But what would she think of me when she found out what happened? She had risked enough to get me here, and the idea of her trying to help me when I was this far away did not sit well with me.

"You can see the palace from here," Lady Grahm said to me with a smile.

It was true: as we rounded a path that led to the city gates, the palace stood higher than the rest of the buildings, just peeking over the tops of the tallest ones.

When we stopped at the gates, a gentleman in a grey uniform approached the window. "Good morning. May I inquire as to who is seeking entrance to the capital?"

"I am Lord Grahm," he said, leaning forward on a cane with a bird head carved into the top. "I am bringing my family and my spell-caster to meet with Her Majesty Queen Eleanora."

The guard did a sweep of the passengers, his eyes landing on me particularly. I met his gaze and bowed my head slightly in greeting. He looked me up and down, not bothering to return the gesture. "Is she marked?"

"She is," Lord Grahm confirmed, motioning for me to show him.

Satisfied with the evidence, he said, "Very good. Welcome to the capital, Lord and Lady Grahm. I hope you enjoy your time."

I lowered my arm, resisting the urge to hold it against my ribcage, to hide the rune from the world. *Will it ever stop feeling like a chain?* I wondered and immediately answered myself, sounding a lot like Camila, *Yes, it will, as soon as you find a way to remove it.*

It took another ten minutes to reach the palace, or so Lord Grahm muttered as he checked his pocket watch when we arrived. The entrance was grand and wide, the size and amount of guards out front reminding me of *el castillo* back home.

Not home, I corrected myself as I exited the carriage and accepted Thomas's awaiting arm.

"Thomas, she is a spell-caster: she can walk by herself," Lord Grahm said, placing a hand over his wife's.

"Isabela is also a woman, Father," Thomas pointed out. "Proper etiquette dictates that a gentleman never leaves a woman to walk alone."

I bit my bottom lip to keep from laughing. Lord Grahm paused before saying carefully, "You would not want any young women thinking your affections are not available."

"The right young woman will appreciate any courtesy she sees."

I dared to look up at Thomas. All of the Grahm men wore matching attire, the same dark clothes they had on the day they took me from the chapel. The only difference between theirs and their father's was that Lord Grahm's had the silver stitching of a prowling lion on the left side of his suit jacket. Right now, the same dangerous look in the lion's eyes could be seen in Lord Grahm's, but Thomas kept his expression calm.

"I will walk with her," Nathan offered.

"What kind of appearance do you want to give everyone about the Grahms and the future of our family?" Thomas asked his father, not bothering to look over at Nathan, who had taken a step closer to me. Briefly, I considered using magic to calm their emotions, but who knew how that would go over? Given that Thomas had a rune on his chest, there was no telling how many others they had hidden under their clothes, likely ones that would prevent against anything my magic would try to do.

"I am a gentleman," Nathan insisted. "There is nothing to sully our reputation, regardless of who walks with Isabela."

"Miss Fuerte," Lord Grahm corrected.

"I asked them to use my given name," I interjected gently and instantly wished I'd kept my mouth shut.

Lord Grahm turned his attention to me to say something, but Thomas said, "Father, this is a rather ridiculous thing to bicker over, and you know I mean you no slight. If you wish, we can discuss this further at a later date. We should not keep the Queen waiting."

Without another word about it, Lord Grahm pivoted and strode toward the steps leading up to the entrance, his wife clinging to his arm to keep up with him.

"Maker's beard, Tom, I didn't know you had a backbone when it comes to Father," Nathan whispered with a chuckle. "I'll not forget the look on his face for a while yet. Perhaps not ever."

Thomas gave a small smile, showing off hints of his dimples. "You'd best not take the Maker's name in vain in the presence of royalty."

As we ascended the stairs, I noted the statues of men in similar outfits as what the Grahm men wore, every countenance bearing the utmost seriousness. They also kept mostly the same posture, so the only reason I realised that they were of different men was that I noted a moustache on one of them.

Tilting his head toward me, Thomas said, "These are of noteworthy rune-writers in history, a few of them still alive. Father hopes to have one made of him before he dies."

Any replies I could have given were abandoned as we made it to the top, caught up to Lord and Lady Grahm as well as a man whose suitcoat was edged in purple, matching his bowtie and gloves.

"Welcome to the palace," the man greeted. "The Queen is expecting you."

"Thank you, Waylon," said Lord Grahm.

Waylon brought us through carpeted halls lit up by gas lamps. Paintings of various people decorated the walls, making me feel like the figures were watching us. Thomas put his hand over mine, gently squeezing. I looked up at him, and we exchanged small smiles. Behind us, Nate made a noise.

Everyone glanced back, and Nate said, "My apologies. I had something in my throat."

I faced forward again, hoping that the heat in my cheeks was not noticeable; Thomas did not move his hand away until just before we reached a glasshouse with a sitting area shaded by large parasols stuck in the ground.

"Your Majesty, may I present the Grahm family and their spell-caster," announced Waylon as he stepped aside.

"Welcome," said a woman with more blonde in her hair than grey. The beginnings of wrinkles formed at her eyes and around her mouth, as though years of grinning had left their mark. Instead of a crown like I had expected, Queen Eleanora wore a sun hat, which did not quite fit with the aesthetic of her dangling onyx earrings and dark grey gown, even with her sleeves rolled up once or twice. She finished watering a plant and set the can aside on a table. "Thomas, Nathaniel, you two are even more handsome than before, if that's possible."

"Thank you, Your Majesty," they replied, although Thomas was a little more soft-spoken in his response.

"You must be the spell-caster," Queen Eleanora said, stepping forward.

"I am, Your Majesty," I answered, trying to decide if it would be too odd a moment to curtsy.

"What is your name?"

"Isabela Fuerte, Your Majesty."

"Isabela Fuerte," she repeated, pronouncing it more accurately than most. "That is a beautiful name."

"Thank you."

"Unfortunately, Isabela, my sons are all out on business, otherwise they would be here to make your acquaintance. August promised me he would try to make it, but his intentions do not always align with his actions."

The name sounded familiar to me, and I tried to remember what Thomas and Nathan had said about him. All I could recall was Nathan talking about how unattractive and boring the princes were. Oh, and that Abigail had left Thomas for him.

"Please, take a seat," the Queen urged us as she sat on one of the padded outdoor chairs. Servants brought small sandwiches and tea for us.

"Would it not be better to meet inside?" asked Lord Grahm.

"Pish posh," the Queen replied, waving a hand. "This is not a meeting of a serious nature, but rather of friendship and meeting of an acquaintance who hopefully will be a friend in the future." She smiled. "Besides," she said, looking at me, "it is rather stuffy inside. Why waste a perfectly good day in there when we can have fellowship amongst some of the Maker's lovely creations?" She winked, and I could not help a grin.

"It is lovely here," I agreed, looking over the array of various plants and flowers that surrounded us like a wild garden grown over its limits, the glass walls and ceiling the only things containing them.

"You look like you could fit in with the flora with your green dress, although you might outshine the flowers with your beauty," the Queen complimented but did not give me time to reply. "Do you take your tea with sugar and milk, Isabela? We also have honey if that's more to your liking."

"Just honey, please."

One of the servants prepared a cup of tea for me and then stepped back into line with the other two.

"I've sent in the paperwork stating that she is my spell-caster," Lord Grahm told Queen Eleanora. "She also has the rune on her arm."

"I can see that," she said with a sigh, eyeing said rune. "It sticks out. Your linework has always left your runes looking bold and brutish. I wonder, could you redo it and make it look less like a prisoner's tattoo? Perhaps Thomas or Nathaniel could do it: their linework, from what I remember, is much neater and flows better."

"Mine is messier than Thomas's," Nathan amended. "His is almost good enough to be a woman's writing."

"Then it's settled." The Queen nodded at Thomas. "Before you three come visit later this week, I expect you to have made her rune look more presentable."

My jaw went slack for a moment as my mind tried to catch up.

"We will be returning?" asked Lord Grahm. Lady Grahm hid her expression behind her cup of tea, taking a long sip.

Queen Eleanora cocked her head in Lord Grahm's direction. "Come now, Gerold, I am sure you and Marjorie have things to tend to, and I would not dream of taking more of your time. I am extending an invitation to your sons and your spell-caster. If we are to have spell-casters in our realm—one belonging to such a prestigious family—I think it best we start a friendship and get to understand one another, that way we do not go down the same route as history, do you not agree?"

The way she referenced the war surprised me. Spell-casters had ruled my home country until rune-writers and non-magics got together to dethrone them, claiming that my kind had been tyrannical in nature. And yet, here we spell-casters were, slaves of one type or another no matter where we went.

And friends? That was not what I'd expected, and I wasn't sure what her definition of that word was.

"Of course, Your Majesty," Lord Grahm said. "Very wise of you, if I may say so."

"You may." She dabbed at her mouth and turned to me. "Isabela, would you mind telling me more about yourself?"

I fidgeted, nearly spilling tea onto the saucer. "There is not much to tell," I said, trying to sound nonchalant. "What would you like to know?"

"Everything, really," she said with a wink. "Let us start with your childhood. Where did you grow up?"

I took my time swallowing, making sure I didn't choke. Very aware of all eyes on me, I said carefully, "I worked as a servant girl at the... *castillo.*" I winced, trying to remember their word for it and failing. "My mother and I cleaned." *Please do not ask about my father.*

Everyone looked confused, and I scrambled to figure out why.

"I would not have imagined using a spell-caster as a serving girl," Queen Eleanora said finally, brows furrowed. "Though I suppose your magic might help tidy more quickly. Did they give you any other tasks?"

"Oh, no, Your Majesty. They did not know about... what I am."

Lord Grahm interrupted with a huff, "Someone does: you had quite a few bounty hunters after you."

My cheeks burned, and I wished I could use magic to disappear from sight. As far as I knew, it could not be done, and if it could, I feared losing my mind to magic's control. "I do not know who does," I said in all honesty. I had been careful for so long...

Lord Grahm looked incredulous.

The Queen took control of the conversation again, asking, "Is your mother a spell-caster as well, or your father? Or both?"

"My mother was." The twinge of pain in my heart was slight, lessened by time but still very real. I thought I was prepared for their pity, but when I saw Thomas, I had to look away. My eyes stung.

"I am so sorry, my dear," Queen Eleanora said and patted my arm.

I blinked quickly as my eyes welled and put on a smile. "Thank you, but I did not mean to sadden the conversation."

"I asked the questions! You merely answered them." I thought that was the end of it, but the Queen continued: "What of your other family? Your father? Siblings?"

I cleared my throat. "None to speak of, Your Majesty."

"No father," Lord Grahm said and shook his head as though it answered something about me he'd theorised.

"Is something the matter, Lord Grahm?" I asked before I could think, my words terse.

"Nothing is the matter," he responded with a self-righteous expression that made my skin crawl. "I've often found that the lack of a good father figure is the reason behind many shortcomings."

It's a wonder how well Thomas and Nathan turned out then. I bit my tongue and was glad when the Queen spoke up.

"Enough of that." She waved a hand in Lord Grahm's direction. "What brought you to Glennad?"

"Freedom." If the Grahm men were hoping for another answer than what I'd given before, I had nothing to offer.

Queen Eleanora squeezed my hand. "I think you will enjoy life here." I had no idea how to respond without offending or challenging her, so I said nothing. She finished her sandwich and tea. "It was a pleasure to meet you, Isabela. I look forward to seeing you later this week. You young men as well."

"Would you like to see some of Isabela's magic before we leave?" asked Lord Grahm.

"Another time," the Queen declined, standing. "If we want Isouldia to take an alliance with us seriously, we must first show that we can be as civil and dignified as they are, even with spell-casters. Besides, I would prefer to get to know Isabela more before I ask anything of her." She leant forward and kissed my cheeks, leaving the lingering smell of lavender. "I do hope we become good friends, my dear."

"I hope so too, Your Majesty," I responded sincerely.

"Take good care of her," she said, looking at Thomas and Nathan. "Enjoy your day."

Chapter Twelve

Thomas

Blood

The carriage ride home was filled with Father ranting about the nerve of Queen Eleanora and saying that she absolutely needed to get remarried as soon as possible so that someone could help her carry the responsibilities of the Crown. I stopped listening almost as soon as he started talking, every so often nodding in his direction so that he did not turn the rant my way.

Nate pushed me as much as he could to give himself more room in the carriage, pressing me against Isabela. He'd noticed the look she and I had exchanged in the palace: he'd smirked, letting me know that there'd surely be teasing to come.

That, I had resigned myself to, along with a scolding from Father for standing up to him. I was prepared. What I was not prepared for was writing a rune on Isabela.

It'll be like writing one on Nate, I told myself. That did nothing to cool the rune on my chest or slow the pace of my thoughts.

When we finally arrived, Father ordered Nate and me to take Isabela to the saferoom, telling us that he would be there to oversee the rune-writing momentarily. Isabela's fingers dug into my jacket sleeve; my free hand twitched but stayed at my side. We walked inside, overhearing Father tell Archibald to retrieve his keys.

Nate and I exchanged brief wide-eyed looks. Once we were out of earshot, Nate said, "I'll meet you there."

Are you going to need my help? I wondered, hoping it came across with an arched brow.

Nate shook his head and picked up the pace toward the stairs.

"Is he all right?"

"He is fine," I assured Isabela in a more confident tone than I felt. She pursed her lips but said nothing.

The back of the manor was our destination. Using a cut on the back of my forearm, I drew an unlocking rune on the wallpaper. Moments later, part of the wall swung in, revealing a series of circular steps descending into darkness.

"This was not part of the tour of the manor," Isabela commented dryly.

"Consider this a special tour." I reached out, lighting a gas lamp. Its area of effect was little, but it was better than nothing, and there were more at the bottom.

The stairwell was thin enough that we had to go down one by one, so I went first.

"These are the kind of places you read about people being killed in horror stories," Isabela said.

A few responses ran through my mind, but I decided on, "After what you did to Nate's face, I pity anyone who'd try to do anything to you."

Isabela made a sound of amusement. "I've noticed the servants have been covering the bruise with makeup."

"The Grahms always have an image to protect." I ran a hand along the wall, knowing that the final step was coming soon. My thumb brushed against the knob, and I turned it, lighting up the room.

Isabela took the last few steps slowly, her eyes scanning over the cement walls and floor with runes etched and drawn into all sorts of places. She white-knuckled the banister.

I held out my hand. "I promise, no harm will come to you."

Brow furrowed, her dark eyes sought mine. The servants had not covered the mole next to her left eye this time.

"This is where we create new runes and practice old ones," I explained. "The marks are meant to protect us from destroying the manor."

Her demeanour lightened. "I did not know you had runes to prevent stupidity."

"Not prevent: contain."

We exchanged smiles; Isabela let go of the bannister and placed her slender hand in mine. Even with her gloves on, I could feel her tremble slightly.

"Coming down," Nate announced, walking more heavily than necessary. We pulled away, and I walked toward the back table, fixing some books on the shelf that had shifted.

"Here I thought you might be—" Nate started with a grin.

"Did you get it?" I interrupted.

"We're in the clear," Nate answered, rolling up his sleeves and running a hand through his hair. "He's none the wiser."

"What did you do?" Isabela asked.

Nate put a finger to Isabela's lips, which she smacked away. "You have your secrets, and we have ours. But you might be able to get them out of Tom." He winked.

I promptly looked away, straightening papers and removing my jacket so I could roll up my sleeves more easily. Usually the safe room was cooler than this. Much cooler.

"Do you have everything ready?" asked Father as he made his way to us.

"Just about!" Nate called. He came beside me and pulled out a small knife from the drawer. "Try to work some leniency into it. I have a feeling Father wants to shorten the leash."

That had already been my plan, so having Nate come to the same conclusion strengthened my resolve.

"I'll distract him if need be," Nate promised and then turned around. "We have everyth... Why do you have that?"

I looked, trying not to seem too eager, and a cold chill ran through me at the sight of the medical tools in my father's hands. Isabela paled.

"We have the chance to study spell-caster blood," Father answered. "It is our duty to research and learn all we can as rune-writers." Isabela shook her head, so he added, "My dear, we will limit how much we take at a time. You would be no good to us if we took too much."

She looked to me, and my promise of no harm came back to nag at the back of my mind.

"Have you received permission from the League yet?" I asked, grasping for anything to delay this.

"I will soon," Father replied shortly.

"We should wait," Nate spoke up. "Just to keep things legal. That's why you haven't brought her along to meetings yet, because you need her to be registered as legally yours first, right? You're so close to being promoted: why risk it over a little impatience?"

Father stopped in his tracks, his eyes on Isabela. The silence thundered in my ears, making the passing of time feel like an eternity.

I could get between them in three steps. But then what? A scene played in my mind of me scuffling with my father while Isabela and Nate fled. Where they would go, I had no idea. Father's reach was not limitless, but the League—and Queen Eleanora herself—would be loathe to lose a spell-caster. Police and rune-writers alike would scour all of Glennad to find her, might even risk angering the royalty of Isouldia by seeking her there too.

"You make a fair point, Nathaniel," Father said, easing the tension in my chest a little. He handed Nate the tools. "Leave these on the table for later. Thomas, we should not tarry in fixing the rune any longer."

He used his own blood to trace over his work, dissolving his rune. It bubbled and dissolved, leaving nothing behind but blood for Nate to wipe off. Isabela inhaled through her nose, no doubt feeling freer than she had in a while. Father stepped aside, and I allowed myself one moment to look at her before I took the small knife and made a cut on the back of my wrist. Red welled; I held Isabela's forearm still while I took my time carefully constructing the new rune, adding a few flourishes here and there.

"This is not a painting for the art gallery," Father snapped.

"The Queen wants something more presentable and sightly," I

answered, my tone softer than I'd intended. The rune on my chest pulsed, heating, but I managed to ignore it as I finished my work.

Isabela's fingers fluttered; the rune set, morphing from red to a glittering gold, sinking into her skin like it was a part of her. Father leant in close to inspect it, checking my linework.

"Passable," he sniffed. "Come, Miss Fuerte, we have to start your training for the ball."

Without waiting for her, Father started up the stairs. Before she followed, Isabela smiled at me. "Thank you," she said quietly enough that Father could not hear. "I am not sure what you did, but thank you."

"I'll explain another time," I told her, watching her leave. Then I took a jar of powder and applied it to my arm to speed up the healing process.

Nate said, "So, which room are we using to spy on them?"

"That depends on which room Father chooses to train her."

"Then we'd better hurry."

Chapter Thirteen

Isabela

The first day of magic practice found me alone with Lord Grahm in the room where I'd found the boys duelling. Any servants who interrupted quickly turned tail and fled after receiving a tongue-lashing. I'd hoped Thomas and Nathan would have joined us, but I did the best I could with what I had. Thankfully, we only had a few hours before we were called to dinner.

A mere night's sleep was not nearly enough to rid me of fatigue. I loathed leaving my bed the next morning, my head aching enough that I wished I could lower the barrier in my mind without consequence.

You are stronger than that. That is what Camila would have said as she hit me with a pillow and insisted I hurry to make her presentable for breakfast.

Even with tea and food in my stomach, I found my mental processes slow as Lord Grahm demanded that I, yet again, knock over the dummies staggered in a semicircle twenty paces away. I glanced over at Thomas, grateful that today Lord Grahm had requested his sons' assistance, claiming he intended to test my limits and needed all the safety measures in place. According to him, the safe room was far too small a space to experiment, so this room ended up littered with runes. Given there were many, Nathan had retrieved bottles of what I assumed was blood. Each bottle was labelled with a letter: G, T, N.

I rubbed at my temples, willing my mind to work. *They are giving you an excuse to strengthen your control on magic—take advantage of it!*

His brow knotted, Thomas said, "Perhaps we should call for a pitcher of water? Magic always has a cost, and we wouldn't want to leave Isabela weak."

Exhaling through his nose, Lord Grahm rang a bell. A servant came running not too long after but stood in the doorway, scurrying off the moment the orders were given.

I wiped at my brow with the back of my hand and stared down the target dummies, wooden things that vaguely resembled the human form, held together by rope hung from the ceiling. They reminded me more of scarecrows, although straw would be terribly messy if I were to break one open. I'd cracked a few of them while knocking them over, hoping that would satisfy Lord Grahm.

Not in the slightest.

The servant returned with water, and I downed a glass before returning to the spot marked on the floor with a red X. Staring down the dummies, I planted my feet and rolled back my shoulders.

If you fear you will not be able to do it, then you will fail. You have to believe in yourself, mija.

The words gripped me—suddenly I was a little girl again, standing in the orchard while my mother fixed my stance and tapped my chest.

Don't let the magic sense your fear, or it will take control of you. Show it you are fearless. You are powerful. You are strong.

I repeated the mantra in my head, same as I had many times since then. *I am fearless. I am powerful. I am strong.*

Inhale. I cracked open my mind. Magic seeped in, this time cool but refreshing like river water in the middle of summer.

Exhale. It rushed out of me in mighty waves. Ropes snapped; pieces of the dummies shot at the walls and fell to the floor; something shattered behind me.

"Stop!"

The command could barely be heard over the roar of magic, sounding like he was speaking through glass. In the back of my mind, I could vaguely recognize the voice and understand what was happening to my surroundings. I tugged the magic back. It resisted, whipping around in a whirlwind that tore at my hair and clothes while the magic still inside of me threatened to rip through to escape.

"She's lost control! Find something to knock her unconscious!" *Lord Grahm.*

"We don't know if that'll stop it!" *Nathan.*

They kept arguing, and I could see someone come to me from the corner of my eye. He gripped my shoulder, shouting over the noise, "I'm binding us together. Hold on. We'll fix this." *Thomas.*

He reached up with shaky hands, smearing something wet across my forehead.

I am fearless. I am powerful. I am strong.

The magic within me reared and struggled, then clawed at the opening in my mind, permitting more to leak in. I slammed my will against it, feeling like someone trying to plug up holes in a sinking ship. The magic ran through my body, laying siege, filling me with visions of limitless power.

What if I gave in?

Clarity hit me like a bucket of cold water dumped on my head. Another presence joined mine, something warm and strong. I could see what was in front of me, but I could also see myself from the side, eyes glazed over and hair thrashing about me. Lord Grahm and Nathan crouched by the door, rewriting runes that had been split by cracks.

'Use my strength.' His voice entered my mind. I saw my lips press together, saw my brow furrow and jaw set.

I am fearless. I am powerful. I am strong.

Grasping his strength, I yanked the magic. The whirlwind shuddered, losing ground.

Again.

And again.

And again.

I strained against it, giving a final tug and a shove before sealing my mind completely.

Dizziness swept my feet out from under me, and I saw myself tumble onto the floor, taking Thomas with me. We gasped, panting as we lay there in the mess. I noticed fissures in the ceiling—saw it double, as if there were two ceilings next to one another.

With a grunt, Thomas rolled toward me, propping himself on his elbow, and I saw myself sprawled on the floor, looking up. Messy red runes covered my forehead. When he leant over me, it was clear the runes were the same on his forehead. Thomas retrieved a handkerchief from his pocket and wiped at my face, releasing me from seeing double. I blinked. His presence was gone, leaving me feeling rather empty.

"How do you feel?" Thomas asked, locking eyes with me. "Are you hurt?" He sat up, pulling me up with him.

Up close, I realised that his eyes were hazel, not brown, a light green near his pupils. *Is that a scar in his eyebrow?*

"Isabela."

I blinked again, my movements feeling sluggish. "I need to rest. Are you hurt?"

"No." He helped me to my feet, letting me lean on him as I surveyed the aftermath. The dummies were mere splinters now, scattered about the room along with shards of the pitcher and drinking glasses. The bottles of blood had shattered as well, painting part of the room and spattering our clothes.

Pain registered the same time fatigue did. I swayed, and Thomas kept me steady as I checked my hands: a few of the small shards had embedded themselves into my palms.

"Leave them," Thomas said gently. "We'll call the doctor."

My hands trembled. I turned to face Lord Grahm and Nathan. Like Thomas, both had cuts, and their hair and clothes were tousled. Self-inflicted gashes ran along their arms, no doubt what they used in a hurry to fix the runes I had cracked. A bigger piece of glass, slightly longer than the span of Nathan's hand, stuck out of his shoulder, and he yanked it out with a grimace and tossed on the floor.

"You are definitely powerful," Nathan said, trying to run his bloody fingers through his knotted hair out of habit and giving up.

"I am so sorry," I said, my voice faltering. *I hurt them. I hurt them. I hurt them.*

Lord Grahm, for once, did not have much to say. Shoulders hunched, eyes alert, he mumbled something about having a discussion after calling the doctor, and then he left the room.

He would not look directly at me.

Chapter Fourteen

Thomas

 octor

I could not feel anything other than my heart beating wildly in my chest and Isabela's shaking shoulders as I led her away from the aftermath of the chaos. By the time Doctor Cornelius arrived, I'd slumped down onto a chair in the parlour, watching as he stitched Nate's shoulder. Isabela watched as well, leaning forward in her chair, her hands fidgeting every so often. I considered reaching out to her but thought better of it: Father stood near the edge of the room, a glass filled with amber liquid dangling from his fingertips, and Mother paced, wringing her hands. Normally, Father would have snapped at her, telling her to retire to their bedroom if she was going to be overdramatic. Instead, he said nothing as he nursed his fourth drink.

"I'm fine, Mother," Nate said again, as if this time it would snap her out of her panic. "Just a few nicks here and there. Nothing a few runes cannot fix."

"You are receiving *stitches*, Nathaniel. I saw the room: you could have died in there."

"Mother," I cut in, going to her and pulling her into an embrace. She shuddered, the only signal before she burst into a sob against my chest. I rubbed her back and kissed the top of her head. Her perfume filled my senses, so I lifted my head away to avoid having to sneeze. She gripped my shirt, clinging to me like I was keeping her together.

I very well might have been in that moment.

Doctor Cornelius turned to face us but did not leave his seat. "Lady Grahm, if it eases your heart any, Nathaniel seems to have received the worst of the injuries, and he will make a full recovery in a few weeks, less if you use runes. I will schedule a time to return in a week to check the progress of the healing."

Mother quieted and pulled away from me. I offered her my handkerchief, only too late remembering that it was the one I'd used to wipe the evidence of runes from our spying. She stared at me, and I shoved it back in my pocket. Doctor Cornelius gave her his, and she dabbed at her face.

"I would appreciate that," she said. "Thank you, Doctor."

To Nate, he said, "I suggest you rest now."

Father finally spoke up, saying, "I'll give you the runes."

Mother was at Nate's side before he'd even properly stood. "To bed! Gerold, you can give him the runes while he rests."

"I am not sick, Mother."

"Hush! I will have none of your sass. You heard Doctor Cornelius: rest."

Nate shot me a pleading look over his shoulder as Mother whisked him away and Father ambled behind them, swaying a bit.

"Miss Fuerte, you may sit here." Doctor Cornelius scooted his seat back so that Isabela could occupy where Nate had just been. She moved slowly and hesitantly, a stark contrast to the way she normally strode with confidence.

"I had planned on visiting soon to check on your wound," the doctor said, his eyes flitting back and forth between hers. "Did you hit your head?"

Her eyes narrowed. "No, Doctor."

Doctor Cornelius frowned. "I am going to test you regardless. Follow my finger with just your eyes." He went into a series of movements until he was satisfied. Turning to me, he said, "Thomas, be sure to call for me if she seems disoriented, faints, or takes ill."

I nodded.

He started with removing the glass from her palms and bandaging them. Isabela barely flinched, her gaze downcast. When it came time to check her shoulder, I closed the curtains and made to leave the room.

"Thomas." My name came out like a small plea. "Stay."

I could not quite bring myself to smile in an attempt to assure her, so I nodded, and the tension in her face eased. Doctor Cornelius helped partially undo the back of her dress so that he could tug it low enough to work on her shoulder. I averted my eyes, trying to focus on the intricate details carved into the wood of the grandfather clock, just as I'd done as a child whenever Nate and I had been forced to sit through Mother gossiping with her friends.

"It is healing nicely," Doctor Cornelius stated. "I'll check it again when I come next." To me: "Perhaps you could give her a healing rune?"

If only I could. "I'll speak with Father about it."

Understanding dawned on him, and the doctor said, "Very well." He helped Isabela fix her dress. I studied the loops and swirls of the woodwork, painfully aware of what was happening in my peripherals.

As Doctor Cornelius took his leave, he said, "Remember: if anything seems wrong, call for me."

"I will."

Archibald came in and saw the doctor off, but not before scheduling another appointment. Then he checked on us.

"We are fine, thank you," I told him.

Noting the chair still in front of Isabela, Archibald moved it back into place. "I will be in your father's office if you need me, Master Thomas."

Alone, I finally locked eyes with Isabela but did not dare move, knowing that the urge to pull her into my arms was too much for me to fight. Looking like a ship with the wind taken from its sails, she seemed so far away, and I wanted to bring her back here, to see that spark in her eyes and that quirk of her lips, to hear her speak with self-assurance and say words that I found beautiful even though I did not know their meanings.

"Are you all right?" I asked quietly.

Her eyes welled. "No," she managed, her voice giving out. Her throat bobbed. "I hurt Nathan. I could have killed you." Tears rolled down her cheeks.

One heartbeat I was at the edge of the room, and three heartbeats later I found myself kneeling in front of her, my hands cupping hers with care. "But you did not," I said, my mind searching for what I could possibly say to make this any easier, to take the load from her. "Magic has a mind of its own. Father pushed you, and you did the best that you could to stop it. You saved us."

Isabela shook her head. "I almost gave in," she admitted, her lower lip trembling. "You stopped me. You gave me the strength."

I had felt the rush of power in her when our minds connected. It had been so disorienting that I'd had to hold onto Isabela for fear of being swept away by it. "I would not have been able to resist it on my own, let alone stop it. You are powerful... and very strong."

More tears. I went to retrieve my handkerchief but remembered it was bloody. Instead, I tentatively wiped them away with my thumbs. Her skin was smooth and warm, inviting my touch to linger. My gaze drifted down to her mouth, her lips parting infinitesimally. My thumb twitched, and I looked back into Isabela's eyes, realizing I was holding her face in my hands. The rune on my chest pulsed in rhythm with my rapid heartbeat, which seemed so loud in the silence between us.

You've just been in a traumatic experience—let her recover.

Swallowing hard, I forced myself to stand and take a step back, feeling that something like gravity was desperately trying to pull us together. "We should get cleaned up. I'll send Priscilla to draw you a bath."

Isabela lowered her head and bit her bottom lip, nodding. I left before she could look at me that way again, knowing that would certainly break the last bit of my will.

Chapter Fifteen

Isabela

Favour

Thomas and I did not speak of the moment between us, even though I let it replay in my mind repeatedly. His touch on my cheeks remained, even after I'd washed the blood and tears from my face. I made eye contact with him in the following days, but he kept at a distance that left an ache in my chest. Nathan, at least, remained his same self, cracking jokes meant to rile me and then shooting me smirks to whatever witty retorts I could come up with. They were, admittedly, half-hearted, but I appreciated him trying to pull me back into some level of normalcy, nonetheless.

Practicing was postponed, Lord Grahm taking his sons to the safe room for reasons unexplained. I had a sinking feeling that whatever they were working on had to do with what happened. I could not bear to bring myself to that part of the house, but I had been informed by Priscilla that there was no evidence left of what had occurred. The way she said it made me wonder if she even knew what had occurred.

A few days later came time to visit the Queen again, so Thomas and Nathan met me at the front door, dressed in their rune-writer attire. Their hair brushed back out of their faces, I noticed that the cuts were, indeed, healing nicely.

Thomas caught me staring; pink rose in his cheeks as he called to Nathan, "You have to give me some room in the carriage."

Sure enough, Nathan lounged across one side. "I need to keep you from bumping my shoulder."

"I'll sit on the other side of you then."

"You'll still bump it into the wall. You have plenty of room with Isabela."

This time my face flushed, and I settled into my seat before either of them could notice. Thomas hesitated.

"She doesn't bite, Tom," Nate said. "Although she does punch, so do try to keep your hands to yourself."

As Thomas got in, I lifted my chin, praying the burning in my cheeks was not visible. "I'm glad you have learned your lesson, Nathan."

He flashed me a toothy smile.

"Trust me: he has not," Thomas stated, exchanging a small smile with me.

"I did too: I learned to duck out of the way of punches."

"That should be instinct, Nate."

The brotherly banter and bits of conversation here and there filled the time during our journey to the capital. All the while I limited myself on how many times I could glance to my right.

The guards let us through almost immediately, and Queen Eleanora had us join her inside this time, in what she called the drawing room. It was elegantly decorated, paintings of nature on the walls in gilded frames and statuettes of dancers placed on shelves and tables. A grand piano and a harp waited by the opposite side of the room, where two large dogs lounged on a rug.

"Those are August's pets," she explained, bidding us all to sit with her at a table with five chairs and a tea set already prepared. This time she wore her crown, golden with small diamonds, emeralds, and sapphires in a mosaic in the front. Her high-collared, long-sleeved dark grey gown nearly brushed the floor when she walked, and black lace gloves graced her hands. "I am so pleased I could meet with you again."

"The pleasure is ours, Your Majesty," Thomas responded.

She frowned. "Dears, what happened to your faces?"

Silence.

I took a sip of my tea, noting that it was prepared with honey. "We were testing my powers."

She patted my gloved hand. "Did Gerold push you too hard? That man is relentless."

Choosing my words carefully, I replied, "We have to learn by trial and error."

She pulled away and nodded. "That is true."

"Pardon me for my tardiness, Mother." A blond man strode in and kissed the Queen on the cheek before taking the empty seat. The dogs padded over and flopped down on either side of him. "Good to see you, Thomas, Nathaniel. It's been too long."

"This is my son, Prince August. August, this is Isabela Fuerte," the Queen introduced with a smile. "She is the Grahm's spell-caster, the one I've been telling you about."

So this was the infamous August, the one who had stolen Abigail away from Thomas. I could see why she was smitten by him, his level of attractiveness greatly misrepresented, even with the scar on the right side of his jaw. In my opinion, he was not quite as handsome as Nathan or Thomas, but I could easily imagine women fawning over him.

"It is a pleasure to meet you," the prince said to me, his blue eyes looking me up and down. "Are all spell-casters as beautiful as you? No wonder the League fears you—you do not need magic to lead men astray."

"August," chided his mother, "what a thing to say."

"I merely meant it as a compliment, Mother."

"Not all are," I answered him. "Otherwise we might have total rule over both Isouldia and Glennad."

Nathan released the laugh he had been holding in, and August joined him after he got over the bit of surprise. The corner of Thomas's mouth moved, showing off one dimple; the Queen raised her brows at me.

"Indeed," she said. "I need you around to put August in his place more often." She took another sip of tea. "May I see your new rune?"

I placed my forearm face up on the table. She traced the gold with a gentle touch. "Incredible linework, Thomas: it could almost pass as art."

"My thanks, Your Majesty." Thomas dipped his head in acknowledgment.

"How are you enjoying your station at the Grahm manor, Isabela?" the Queen asked.

I folded my hands in my lap. *How do I like being owned like a piece of property?* "It has taken some getting used to… for everyone involved."

"I can imagine," she said, her eyes drifting to Thomas and then back to me. I fought to keep my expression even. "I hate to be too blunt, my dear, but we need to ask a favour of you."

The abrupt change in conversation unsettled my stomach. "What is it?"

"Some princesses from your country are coming here soon to meet my sons and hopefully choose which of them to wed."

Camila, I thought, although I knew that they could be any number of her sisters or cousins. Still, my heart clung to hope.

"What Mother is trying to say," August said, taking over, "is that we would like this potential alliance to go smoothly. We could use your help in learning customs and history and even, perhaps, a few phrases in your native language."

"I can speak for myself, thank you," remarked Queen Eleanora. "If you agree, I will ask Lord Grahm permission to borrow you for a few days each week until either the princesses decide to marry my sons or return to your homeland."

If one of *las princesas* was Camila for certain, I would have agreed instantly. As it was, I took a moment to think it over so as not to seem too eager. "I agree, Your Majesty."

"Very good," she said, clapping once in excitement. "More time for us to become friends."

"Good friends," August amended as he raised his teacup to his lips, his piercing blue eyes pinned on me.

Chapter Sixteen

Thomas

Trouble

Prince August's eyes rarely left Isabela during our visit to the palace. I had seen that same expression many times over the years, and the women almost always fell for him. The thought of her returning on a regular basis, spending lots of time with him…

I pushed those thoughts aside. Isabela could take care of herself, could make her own decisions. She had certainly put Nate in his place when he tried something. A dark part of me wanted to see that happen with August.

The Queen had duties to attend, so she left, but August insisted that he walk with us to our carriage. He lifted his arm to Isabela, so I refrained from doing the same.

She could make her own decisions.

And that she did: with a pleasant smile that might have fooled me if not for the glint in her eyes, Isabela took my arm. "You are too kind, Prince August. Please, do not trouble yourself on our behalf."

He cocked his head slightly, a bemused look on his face; I bit the inside of my cheek to keep my expression neutral. Nate, on the other hand, smirked for a split second before schooling his features into nonchalance.

"No trouble at all, Miss Fuerte," he responded, resuming his air of confidence. "I prefer to give my friends every courtesy within my power."

The urge to laugh transformed into the urge to roll my eyes.

"How very generous of you," Isabela said.

"Not at all." The prince strolled beside us, keeping a respectable distance from Isabela and no farther. "Is it not normal practice to treat one's friends as they would wish to be treated?"

Nate and I exchanged quick glances.

"Perhaps among some," Isabela answered.

When we reached the main entrance, August ordered one of the servants to fetch a parasol for Isabela.

"No need," she declined. "I can see the carriage from here."

"I insist."

Isabela's brows raised. "Prince August, if you wish to be *good* friends, may I suggest learning to take 'no' for an answer? It will do you well for when speaking with *las princesas.*"

"Of course," August replied, recovering from his surprise fairly quickly. "Although, if I may? A little more tact with those in authority will keep you from trouble, *Miss* Fuerte."

I waited for her to make a biting remark, but Isabela widened her smile. "Of course, Prince August. I meant no offense." She gripped my arm tighter.

Nothing else was said until we reached the carriage. August brought Isabela's hand to his lips, leaving a lingering kiss on the back of her glove. "Until we see each other again, Miss Fuerte."

Isabela waited until the prince was a small figure in the distance before she said, "What a prick."

Nate burst out laughing.

"But he isn't boring or unattractive like you said," she pointed out. "Although he acts like he thinks he's more attractive than he actually is."

I kept my mouth shut.

"To each their own," Nate said as he unbuttoned his jacket. "Just wait until he talks about all of his 'achievements.' That's three hours' worth of rubbish that might change your mind. When he did it to me, I almost jumped into the river just to get away from him."

"You might have if it hadn't been frozen over," I said. "And he is not as bad as you make him out to be."

Nate looked at me pointedly. "I have a hard time believing you still consider him a friend after he took Abigail away from you."

"Abigail made a choice, and I am glad we did not end up together."

Nate glanced back and forth between Isabela and me. I readied myself for one of his embarrassing quips, but all he said was, "I'm glad you are past it."

I looked out the window, watching the grand city turn into countryside as far as the eye could see, trying not to overthink why Isabela had nothing to comment on that conversation.

A shot rang out—the horses shrieked and bolted. We gripped to what we could of the inside, trying not to be jostled around. An explosion—the carriage careened sideways, throwing us left, Isabela colliding with me. The thunder of hooves reached us, and from what we could see outside, masked riders with guns formed a circle around the now-stopped carriage. They wore all black, obscuring their faces and covering their hair.

"Bloody hell!" Nate pushed himself up to see what was happening.

A bullet flew right by Isabela's neck and through the wall behind her.

"Get down!" she commanded, yanking her hand away from me as I tried to bring her into cover. The atmosphere shifted, and suddenly the men and horses alike launched backward, and the roof of the carriage tore off like a tornado had broken it free. Now exposed, Nate and I scrambled to retrieve our pocketknives. As I pulled the blade across my wrist, I saw our driver face down on the road and one of the horses half under the carriage. The other screamed and bucked against the constraints still holding it.

Isabela hoisted her skirts and climbed out of the wreckage.

"Help her," Nate told me as he tossed his gloves away and tore his sleeve to cut his forearm. Before the blood could drip, he had it smeared across his fingertips, hurrying to catch up to her as he scribbled on the back of his hand. His steps quickened, and a glimmer of a protective barrier reflected in what little sunlight there was in between the thick layer of clouds. He reached into his jacket, pulling out a pistol.

The first of the men were recovering when I reached Isabela. The air seemed to crackle around her, her hair floating slightly as though she were underwater. I drew a hasty protection rune on the side of her neck—the next shot skittered across the barrier and landed in the grass behind us the second after I'd finished.

A wry smile twisted Isabela's mouth. The ground shook violently, causing all of us but her to stumble. Vines covered in thorns burst free from the earth, scattering everything in their way. They twisted around the attackers, digging into their flesh and holding them in place. I counted five of them, three already dead or dying out from Nate's shooting.

"Thomas," she said in a voice not entirely her own, "I do not know how long I can hold it. What do we do with them?"

"We need to interrogate them, find out what they want."

"They want us dead!" Nate shouted like it was obvious.

"We need the why, Nate!"

The attackers struggled, which made the thorns wrap tighter around them. One managed to awkwardly saw at the vines with a dagger, barely making progress with the way his upper arm was pinned. Nate strode over, easily knocking the weapon away. While he kept his gun at the ready, I hurriedly yanked the mask off the man and put a truth rune on his cheek, hoping the scruff on his jaw would not interfere. The rune did not activate. I put another on his forehead. Still nothing.

Using the end of his pistol, Nate pushed open the attacker's shirt collar. "Tom, he has a silencing rune." He tore open the man's sleeve, exposing a rune that shared the same basic structure as Isabela's. "These arseholes belong to someone."

The man looked normal, like someone I would pass in the streets of the capital, other than the fact that his eyes seemed slightly dazed. I had to wonder if he was fully aware of what was happening.

"Thomas... Nathan..."

We looked at Isabela and then back at each other.

"We cannot let them go free," Nate stated.

"We need to bring at least one of them back. Maybe Father knows something we can do to loosen their tongues. They might be a part of those attacks the League and police have been looking into."

"What do we do with the rest?"

What could we do? "We're not killing them, Nate."

"We cannot let them go free," he repeated.

"Hurry," pleaded Isabela with a grimace.

Nate shot me a "you-know-I'm-right-about-this" look. "We don't even have a carriage anymore—how are we going to keep even one?"

"We're not murderers."

"They tried to kill us!"

We stared one another down. In my peripherals, I saw Isabela beginning to shake.

"Isabela, let go of the magic," I said, trying to keep the panic from my voice.

She inhaled sharply; the vines hung limply to their victims, the thorns barely holding to flesh and clothing. Wobbling, she fell to her hands and knees. I forced myself to focus on the attackers. As Nate's next shot rang out, fire set one attacker ablaze, and then another, their mouths open in silent screams. We looked at each other in horror and confusion, then back at Isabela, who jerked her head up, mortified.

"I'm not doing that!" she cried.

Nate yanked open the shirt and jacket of the attacker closest to us, buttons popping and flying about. There, in dark linework, was a giant rune that took up his entire chest and stomach.

"Get back!" I sprinted, pulling Nate and Isabela with me. We managed to get behind what was left of the carriage before the explosions happened. Heat wrapped us in a heavy blanket and then ebbed away, the overcast day smothering it.

We panted, waiting there crouched for who knows how long.

"Everyone all right?" I asked finally, receiving nods in response, and then braved the wreckage. Scorched earth marked where the attackers had been, pieces of the thorny vines and shreds of clothes all that remained.

So much for bringing one home to question.

The carriage's front left wheel and part of the axel had been blown to bits. The live horse had minor bleeding on his rump.

"Easy now," I said, approaching carefully with outstretched hands, gently petting its neck. Nate saw what I was doing, put away his pistol, and came from the other side, quickly writing out a few runes. The terror in the horse's eyes dimmed.

"We need to go for help," said Nate, already fixing the reins and mounting the horse. "I'll see what I can find up ahead."

"Be careful," I advised.

A hint of a smirk crossed Nate's mouth, and he urged the horse down the road just as the sky began to drizzle.

Chapter Seventeen

Isabela

Rain

I stood a few feet behind Thomas as Nathan galloped away. There were a few tears in my light blue dress as well as my gloves, and I was sure my hair was a mess, pieces of it having fallen out of the pins and into my face, but I was unhurt, so I could get past my appearance. For having just been in a fight, Thomas bore little evidence of it other than a few strands of hair curling at his forehead and his clothing being rumpled.

When he turned around, I blurted, "I did not do that. I did not burn them alive."

He drew near, and it was then I noticed how tall he actually was, making me wonder if he'd made a habit of slouching. If I had not been wearing heels, he would have towered over me even more.

"I know," he assured me. "Someone set runes to do that."

I barked a shocked, bitter laugh. "Why are spell-casters so feared when rune-writers can do that? At least be afraid of both of us. If I were to try something like that, it would almost guarantee I lose my mind completely, yet that rune-writer can do that as much as he wants."

"As long as he uses his own blood," he reminded me, taking off his jacket to wrap it around my shoulders. The rain picked up, ready to drench us within minutes, and we had no shelter. "Magic always takes a price, no matter which way you use it."

"Does it always have to be blood?" I asked, pulling his jacket closer.

Drops caught in his hair and long lashes. He blinked, pink blooming in his cheeks. "No—it can be any bodily fluid. Blood is the strongest bond and the easiest source."

I heard the implication in his voice: also the most proper. Before my mind could travel down that gross train of thought, he asked, "How are you feeling?"

"I'm fine. I cut off the magic before it could control me."

"That's good."

Our clothes soaked up the water, making my dress feel heavy. Thomas's wet white shirt clung to his skin, showing off the red rune beneath. He followed my gaze.

"My father told you about it," he guessed, although by the way he said it, it sounded like he knew.

I nodded, not sure what to say. Bringing up Abigail felt like a bad idea, and the rune itself seemed a little too personal, like crossing into territory I had not been given access to. Even now, Thomas kept some distance between us. I had to snag his arm when leaving the palace—he hadn't even offered it like before.

"What is it?"

Digging my fingers into his jacket, I asked, "Are you afraid of me?"

Thomas furrowed his brow. "No, of course not. Why would you think that?"

"You started avoiding me." I hated how raw and delicate my voice sounded, hated the way I felt completely exposed when he studied me with those hazel eyes.

Tell me what you see, I wanted to beg him. *What does that look mean?*

"After I almost lost control," I continued instead, the words spilling out of me before I could stop them. "You've been keeping your distance. I... I liked having you around, Thomas. You've been so kind to me, and I cannot bear the thought that you see me as the monster everyone thinks I am. I am so sorry, I—"

Thomas crossed the distance between us so suddenly that all I could do was stand there, his arms wrapped around me, my head against his chest. His heart beat loud and rapid against my ear, and I could have sworn that I felt a warmth radiating from his rune as it pulsed in shimmers. Without thinking, I put my hand over it, and his breathing hitched. Suddenly I could not feel the rain, or the cold, only Thomas. I dared not move, fearing I could break whatever fragile thing held us together in this moment... and yet, I so badly wanted to look into those beautiful eyes, to study the curve of his jaw and find that little scar in his brow, to see if he had any more of those lovely imperfections that were now engraved in my mind's eye and inhabited my dreams.

"I am afraid, Isabela," Thomas said so quietly that the rain would have drowned him out if we were not so close. "But not of you."

My heart rate matched his, showing no sign of slowing.

"I am afraid to be without you."

My eyes widened; my heart stopped before stuttering to a start again. I let the words run through my mind once more, twice more, to be sure I'd heard correctly. Those words, so precious, I held onto, let them flicker inside of me to bring life to a hope I'd dared not speak of. "Then why have you kept your distance? Is it because I'm a spell-caster?"

"No." His answer came immediately, no hesitation.

"Then what?" My heart wanted to soar but felt like it was caught on something that needed to be cut away first.

"I wanted to be sure of both of our feelings first."

This time I pulled away enough to lift my gaze to his. "And?"

His throat bobbed. "I am sure of mine. …I care for you, Isabela. Deeply."

I grinned, adding those words to the others so that the flame could grow stronger. Blinking the rain from my eyes, I said, "I care for you too, Thomas." Then added, "Deeply… and truly."

One hand still at my back, his other cupped my face, his thumb running along my cheekbone. I leant into his touch, my eyes still on his. The rain plastered a lock of his hair against his forehead, so I reached up and brushed the curl back into place, letting my fingers run down the side of his face.

Kiss me, I thought impatiently, but was afraid that voicing that would ruin the moment. Instead, I barely nudged my nose against his.

That was all it took—Thomas kissed me softly, like he was unsure if this might be a dream. His rune thrummed under my palm, adding to the exhilaration running through me. My fingers worked their way up to his hair, winding themselves in his loose, wet curls in hopes of keeping him there forever. As if in agreement, he deepened the kiss, his hands moving down my arms. I peeled off his jacket without missing a beat, and he wrapped me in an embrace once more.

Thomas pulled away, and I made to complain until his lips trailed, sending shivers through my spine. He paused at the crook of my neck, resting against it and inhaling deeply. I touched his back, feeling the muscles tense beneath his shirt. We stood there a few minutes, just holding each other, unbothered by the rain drenching us out in the middle of nowhere.

"How will we do this?" I asked. "Has there ever been a rune-writer and spell-caster together before?"

"I'm sure there has," Thomas answered, pressing his lips to my collarbone before looking at me. "We will find a way."

We shared a grin; I could barely contain my elation. It was better than any fairy-tale I had ever read, because it was real and it was mine and it was with Thomas.

"We will," I agreed. "Nathan's bound to return soon."

"Hopefully not too soon," Thomas said before drawing me close for another kiss.

Chapter Eighteen

Thomas

It took everything in me to stop touching Isabela, to stop kissing her, to stop holding her. By the time Nate returned with another horse, we managed to pull apart, and I nearly forgot to scoop my jacket and Nate's gloves from the muddy ground. Isabela made a pained face, to which I shook my head with a smile. A dirty jacket was a small price to pay for what just occurred.

Nate eyed us as he pulled to a halt and offered the reins to me. Something sparked in his expression, but all he said was, "I found a farm a little way ahead and paid him for this mare. We should hurry back to the manor and tell Father what happened as soon as possible." He rubbed at his shoulder after I took the reins from him and returned his gloves.

It no longer rained, but I felt water dripping down me, my clothes and hair clinging to my skin, which would itch as we dried, but none of that seemed to matter much at the moment.

"Thank you," I said, helping Isabela onto the back of the mare so that she sat sideways. Her skirts would not allow for anything else. Facing away from Nathan, Isabela smiled; I fought the urge to kiss her again as I let go of her hips and took my place in front of her. Isabela twisted, wrapping her arms around my midsection. When Nate took off once more, I felt Isabela graze the back of my neck with her mouth.

I inhaled and dug my knees into the mare's sides. Isabela tightened her grip.

How will this work? I wondered as we made our way back down dirt roads Nate and I had traversed thousands of times over the course of our lives. I meant what I'd said to Isabela: we would find a way, no matter what, for as long as she wanted to be with me.

The rune on my chest pulsed with warmth, a mildness to it that was a stark contrast to the wild heat of when she'd put her hand over it.

We will find a way.

Giddiness and warm feelings were dampened as we arrived at the manor more quickly than I'd anticipated. Father came outside mere seconds after we dismounted, Mother on his heels.

"The farmer sent word," he explained, taking in the messes we were. Now would have been a much more appropriate time for him to call us ragamuffins, but no such words left him, to my surprise.

Mother hurried forward to inspect Nate, touching his face and smoothing his hair back as it tried to curl, covering one eyebrow and nearly reaching his eye. He pulled her hands away, holding them.

"I am fine," he insisted. "But we must speak inside immediately."

"Only after you wash and change into something dry," Mother replied authoritatively. "I'll not have anyone in my house sick if I can help it."

"Then meet me in the study," Father ordered. "All of you. Go now."

Servants took care of the horses for us, and we hurried to do as we were told. I did not bother to slick my hair back after I'd dried it, the way Isabela brushed back my loose curls and skimmed down my neck still lingering on my skin… although that was not the only touch I could still feel. Looking at myself in the mirror, I ran a finger across my bottom lip.

Focus, Thomas. There are more pressing matters right now.

I took a breath, hoping it would clear my head. When it did not work, I decided to head to the study anyway—making Father wait was not a wise option. No sooner had I left my room than Nate had pushed himself off the wall to step in time with me.

"You kissed her."

"I did." There was no point in denying it to him. "How did you know?"

"It was rather obvious: anyone else would have been miserable, possibly in shock, standing there in the rain with nothing but the wreckage of our carriage and the bodies of the horse and driver nearby. Not to mention we just survived an attack, yet I see the two of you trying to keep distance and not smile at one another." Thankfully, he kept his voice low as we walked down the stairs. "It was about time. Any more of those lingering, lovesick glances, and I was going to take actions into my hands so I didn't have the urge to either smack some sense into you or vomit. Or both." With a sly grin, he said, "I would have kissed her the first week if I were you. You two were already circling each other, hearts intertwining, after that day in the park when we went to see the priest."

"You tried to do more than that to her the first night we met," I reminded him, unable to keep a smile completely off my face. All that was left of the bruise was some lightly yellowed skin.

"Different tactics for different men," Nate said, shrugging it off, his mouth quirked into one of his signature smirks. "I'd even considered trying to kiss her soon to get you to make a move."

We had slowed our descent, but having reached the main floor, we paused.

"I would have wanted to give you a matching black eye," I told him, "but I'm sure Isabela would have before I could get to you. That is, if she did not take more drastic measures this time to ensure that her stance on the matter is clear."

Nate chuckled. "Well, we have no need to worry about that now, do we?" The merriment in his expression dulled, and his voice went almost inaudible. "I'll not say anything, but do try to keep any romantic excursions secretive and quiet. You might want to keep them away from the manor to keep anyone from hearing."

"Nate," I hissed, my cheeks stinging.

He lifted his hands and flashed me a grin. "I'm here if you need anything."

I spent the rest of the walk to the study trying to keep his words from inspiring images in my head. I had it in control by the time we sat with Father and Mother in the study, but I almost lost it again the moment Isabela walked in. The simple pink gown brought out a rosiness to her cheeks, the fabric swaying with each step she took. Her long, light brown hair hung down to her waist, still drying, barely forming thick waves.

Isabela took the seat next to mine, and my hand twitched as it rested on the arm of the chair. A ghost of a smile crossed her lips, but she did not look in my direction, instead taking in the walls of bookshelves and the fireplace on the far side of the room, where two more cushioned chairs were, our designated spot for reading whenever it struck someone's fancy. An ornate wood clock ticked upon the mantle, its rhythm bringing me back to the present.

"Start from the beginning," Father said. "Start with your visit with the Queen."

Of course he would want to be in the know about all of it. No matter that we had been attacked—start with soothing his ego and keeping him informed on something to which he had not been invited.

"If I may, Lord Grahm," Isabela said, speaking with enough respect to get Father's attention. He dipped his head, and she explained about the princesses coming, about the need for her help. "Queen Eleanora said she plans on asking you and compensating you for the time she borrows me."

I had to wonder if she was catering to him to keep us in his good graces, to make him feel like he was being included. If she and I were to find a way to be together, this was a good start.

"Most excellent," Father said, nodding. "You will be sure to mind your words and your actions so that they reflect upon the Grahm family with dignity and honour and respect."

Her smile tightened ever so slightly. "Of course, Lord Grahm."

Father lit a pipe; Mother's nose wrinkled at the smoke tendrils that crept from his mouth as he spoke. "I'll have a seamstress outfit you with some gowns more suitable for being in the presence of royalty."

I tried not to think about Father's ledger in his office and how this would affect it.

"Father," I said, "perhaps we should speak about more pressing matters."

He raised a brow in my direction. "Such as why you returned home without a carriage and one of my horses?"

Chapter Nineteen

Isabela

Annoyed

I inhaled through my nose. It seemed that no amount of bowing to him and his pride would bring him any closer to acting like a decent human being. I could understand him not worrying about my welfare, but what about the lives of his sons?

Before Thomas could answer, Nathan said, "Father, we were attacked by rune-writers. They tried to kill us. They destroyed the carriage and killed both the driver and one of the horses."

"Then how did you manage to survive without so much as a scratch?"

I nearly huffed in annoyance. There were certainly bruises and scratches from the ordeal, and we counted that as luck. Instead of releasing an improper string of names to call him in my native tongue, I kept a neutral expression and held my chin up and back straight. It was too much for me to put on a smile, so neutral was what I settled into—although Camila had always teased me that I had a mean resting face, something about having a glint to my eyes that could send anyone squirming in their seat.

"We worked together," Thomas clarified, "Isabela, Nate, and I. We were planning to bring at least one of them back for questioning, but they exploded into flames before we could."

"Tampering with evidence?" Lord Grahm looked at me from the

corner of his eye.

"Why would I try to cover for rune-writers?" I asked, and when he frowned, I added, "Unless they were part of the Grahm family?"

"They had runes on their skin," Nathan said, drawing his father's attention back. "Someone sent them to kill us and put those runes on them to ensure they could not live to give any incriminating answers or evidence if things went poorly. Which they did."

"How do you know they were rune-writers?"

We all paused, exchanging looks.

"We assumed," Thomas admitted. "It is possible they were non-magics, but the point remains that there is at least one rune-writer behind this. It has to be someone who knows us and knew where we would be going and when."

Lord Grahm stared at his sons, puffing lazily at his pipe. I had to wonder how his hazel eyes could be so cold and sharp when Thomas's were so warm and friendly. The colours were the same, and yet Lord Grahm's were not as bright as Thomas's, seeming almost subdued, iced over. Like staring at him too long could cut me to the core or freeze me where I sat. "What would be the reason?"

The brothers looked at one another.

"We have a few theories." Thomas rolled back his shoulders. "I know there are those who would not take kindly to finding out we have a spell-caster."

"Why would someone kill from a place of jealousy?"

I blinked. I did not know the statistics, but I would have imagined that a good portion of murders stemmed from jealousy. Pointing that out would do us no good, so I kept my mouth shut. I had done my part—I let Thomas and Nathan deal with their father for the rest of the discussion… partially because I did not want to be held accountable for what might come out of my mouth after I had spent a decent amount of time smoothing over the rifts in the bridge between us.

"Do you have another idea of why we could have been attacked?" Thomas asked.

"Why would I?"

It was really a good thing I let Thomas and Nathan talk with him—all of the answering questions with questions would be a good way to set me off. As it was, I squeezed my hands together in my lap and bit my tongue.

"There are a number of things," Thomas said slowly. "What about debtors?"

Lord Grahm pulled away his pipe, sat up, and lifted his chin in one quick motion. "What makes you think we have debt?"

A wrinkle formed in Lady Grahm's brow; she kept her gaze on her sons, studying each of them in turn. For a moment, I could see the cracks in her façade, the fear peeking through, trying to find a way out.

"You have taught me how to put together a ledger, Father. I believe it is time to stop pretending that we are living within our means."

"You have to spend money to make money," Lord Grahm snapped, bringing his pipe back to his mouth. "I am on good terms with everyone, and, with Miss Fuerte here, I am certainly set to become one of the leaders of the League."

I had heard that name before. From what I knew, it was comprised of self-righteous rune-writers like Lord Grahm who served their country and, more importantly, the Crown. What all they actually did, I was unsure, so I tucked that question away for later, hoping Thomas could give me better insight.

"Even if debtors were after payment," Lord Grahm added, "it would not make sense to send anyone to kill my sons and spell-caster. There are better, legal, more civilised ways to get what they want."

"Then we have very little to go off of," Nathan sighed. "Our best guess would be that someone is after Isabela, but with the men nothing but piles of ash, there is no lead for us to follow. Do you believe that they could be part of the string of recent attacks?"

"Perhaps." Lord Grahm blew smoke rings as he exhaled. Then he stood up and put away his pipe. "Come, boys, let us investigate what is left of them, see if we cannot find something to give us a lead."

That is the most sensible thing I have heard out of your mouth.

Chapter Twenty

Thomas

arden

I waited until everyone else was asleep before I slipped out of my room from the balcony, hanging from the bottom before allowing myself the drop. I'd made it enough times over my life to know how to fall and roll back onto my feet to avoid injury. I unlocked one of the sheds with a rune and took a ladder with me to a balcony window a few down from mine. After climbing up, I gently knocked on the glass, hoping it would be loud enough.

I heard the padding of feet before the window opened.

"Thomas," Isabela whispered, a smile creeping onto her face. Most of her was blocked by the curtain, but I could tell that she was wearing a thin nightgown. Any more thought on that, and I would be too distracted to remember why I came here in the first place.

"Grab some shoes and come with me." I gestured to the ladder.

Puzzled, Isabela did as I said, and I waited for her at the bottom, holding the ladder steady. It took her a little bit longer than I had expected: she came outside in a simple dress, shawl, and boots, her hair still undone but a little less mussed than it had been just a few minutes ago. I took her hand in mine and started walking.

"Where are we going?"

"To the garden," I answered. "If that is all right with you."

She squeezed my hand in response, surveying our land at night.

There was enough moonlight to be able to make out the silhouettes of most things, but it did not matter much since I knew where I was going regardless. I took her to where the rose bushes were, careful not to get too close. The white petals seemed to want to take in whatever light the moon offered, almost appearing to glow.

"Beautiful," Isabela breathed.

"I thought you might like to see them."

She looked sideways at me. "You know, you still have not shown me the library."

It took me a moment to recall what she was talking about. "Ah, yes! I apologise. I did promise you that, didn't I? I'll have to remedy that soon."

"All is forgiven," she said. "We've had a lot happening as of late. You three came home later than your mother and I thought you would. How did the investigation go?"

Trying not to grimace, I replied, "Not well. There was too little left, so we took samples and are hoping to send them to the League for investigation. We also brought back the driver's body for his family and buried the horse. The carriage we are hoping we can either keep for extra parts or fix back up at some point."

Isabela frowned. "That was kind of you, bringing back his body… What does the League do?"

"They mostly think of themselves as researchers and scholars who are above the law," I answered. "Sometimes they investigate things for the Crown that are beyond the capabilities of normal detectives. Largely, I find it to be more of a symbol of status than anything else, something to lord over the rest of the population." My shadow covered part of her face, so I moved to stand in front of her, still holding her hand. "We will find out who is behind it and why," I promised her.

Isabela nodded, the hard edge to her expression melting away. The moon cast a soft light on her skin, somehow making her look even more beautiful. Thoughts of earlier swirled in my mind, and suddenly just holding her hand was not enough. Yet, it had to be, at least for the moment, because I had to ask, "How are you feeling?"

She looked at the rose bushes as though she could see through them. "There is a lot to think about and process," she admitted. A grin crossed her features, and Isabela locked eyes with me. "But that can wait for later." She reached up to rest her hands against my chest. I leant down and found her mouth with mine. Without a corset, I could feel her back through the thin fabric of her dress, and when her front pressed against me, I inhaled sharply as my body reacted.

Isabela pulled back, her brows knotted. "Did I hurt you?"

I let out a husky, shaky laugh. "No, not at all."

Understanding dawned on her. "Do you…"

"Give me a moment." I inhaled more slowly this time, trying to clear my mind.

"Do you not want to?"

My attention snapped back to her, noting the hint of uncertainty in her voice. "Trust me: I want to. But we just met each other not too long ago, and I want to do this right, to give our love time to grow and to honour you by making you my wife first."

She blinked, a mixed expression on her face I was not sure how to read. "You… you see a future for us where we are… married?"

"If you would have me," I said. "If that would make you happy, yes, possibly."

"Are you proposing to me in this moment, Thomas Grahm?"

The way she said it drew a chuckle from me. "No, I am not yet. You and I still have a lot to learn of each other, and I want to get to know everything about you." Taking a step forward, I put my hands on her shoulders. "Is that all right with you, sitting under the stars with me while we get to know one another better?"

"Will there be more kissing as well?"

I grinned. "If you would like."

"Then I accept."

I sat in the grass, and, after grabbing her shawl, which had fallen onto the ground, she settled next to me. I suddenly wished I had thought to bring a blanket for us to sit on.

"Where would you like to start?" I asked, moving her hair off to the side so that I could see her face and slender neck. Leaning over, I pressed a kiss to her temple, then noticed the set of her jaw. "What is it? Is something wrong?"

Her gaze drifted down to her lap. "There is a lot you do not know about me."

"Is that not why we are talking?" I knocked my knee against hers teasingly. "Take your time, share with me what you are comfortable sharing."

Her lips pursed. "I am afraid of what you will think of me."

Those words made my heart ache. I shifted and gently turned her face to mine. "There is nothing to fear. Will it ease your heart if I speak first?"

Isabela gnawed on her bottom lip. "No," she said finally. "If we are to pursue a romantic relationship, you should know who I am first."

My stomach twisted.

Isabela turned a little more so that we were facing one another. "My name is just Isabela," she said slowly. "I do not have a surname because my father has not claimed me as his child, and my mother was a servant in *el castillo* where she raised me."

She had given the barest of truths she could get away with when the Queen had asked about her past. I was curious to hear more. "You chose Fuerte for yourself?"

She nodded, offering a sheepish smile. "It is the word for 'strong' in our language. One of the things she taught me to be when using magic." A wistfulness crossed her features. "She caught a fever a few years ago, and it won."

I put my forehead against hers. "I am sorry, Isabela."

She swallowed hard. "She was a good woman, always seeing the best in people even when they treated her poorly."

"You got that from her."

Isabela brightened at that, and then pulled away to play with one of my curls. In a nearly inaudible voice, she said, "My father is the king's brother." She continued to mess with my hair. "After spell-casters were dethroned, it is seen as a shameful thing to wed one, so my father never asked her. Do not misunderstand me: he has never been cruel. He knows I am his, and he kept our jobs in *el castillo* secure for us, made sure we had plenty. But my mother never told him that I inherited the gift—or curse, as some see it—because she knew that, by law, he could claim me as his property, use me as he desires."

I listened, letting the details fill in the gaps about who she was that had been intriguing me.

"After my mother left, Camila, one of *las princesas*, helped me escape so that I could start a new life on another continent, hopefully in a place where they do not judge me for what I am. The night you and Nathan met me was when I was trying to get passage onto a ship. The innkeeper figured out what I am and told the… bounty hunters, so I had to flee. The chapel was the only place of sanctuary, especially since I'd been shot."

So, she had been escaping when we found her and bound her into service to our family. Instead of freedom, she got servitude. "Do you still wish to leave?"

She stared at me for a long time before answering, "I do not know. I want to be free, and I want you to be with me."

I kissed her softly and sweetly, not intensely like earlier, but something to savour, nonetheless. "Thank you for telling me. You have me as long as you want me."

This time, she initiated a kiss. "Thank you for not judging me."

"There is nothing to judge." I ran my fingers down her long hair, enjoying the silkiness of it. "If your father ever did claim you as his own, would that make you a…" I tried to remember how she said it in her language but gave up. "A princess?"

"Doubtful. Even if it did, there are plenty of true-blooded *princesas* already. All it might get me is an arranged marriage to some lord who wants to feel that the Crown appreciates his loyalty."

"Will you know the princesses coming to the palace?"

"Yes. They might not all recognize me since I was known as a servant, and none but Camila know what I am. If Camila does come, she will know me right away… I had meant to try to sneak a letter to her, but with everything happening, I feared it would not reach her. A lot of the things I want to say are difficult, better to speak about rather than write."

"I take it you are friends?"

"We are." She smiled. "I think she will approve of you."

"I hope so."

We kissed again, holding one another close. I broke it off before the stirrings within me could make me lose control.

"I am sorry," she said, her brow furrowing.

"No reason to be sorry," I assured her.

"I admit, I am not sure of your customs here regarding courtship. Nathan seems to be rather handsy."

I chuckled, shaking my head. "Nate does what he wants, although part of me wonders if he acts a certain way to get attention and make people assume things about him just to spite our father. Here, it is customary to wait until after marriage."

"It is in my country as well," Isabela said, her tone a strange mix of relief and discontentment. She toyed with the collar of my shirt. "I feel better with you knowing who I am."

"I am glad you trust me." We exchanged a few more caresses before

I pulled her to her feet. "It is late. We should get back inside and go to sleep."

In between kisses, Isabela made a sound in her throat that sent shivers through me. "Do this again tomorrow?"

I beamed. "Absolutely."

Chapter Twenty-One

Isabela

Lessons

"Are you quite well?"

I put on a smile, snapping to attention in my mind but unhurriedly reaching forward for my tea. Thomas had intended for us to get plenty of sleep, but I had found sleep was far from me when my emotions ran wild. Now that I was at the palace with Prince August, my eyes kept attempting to slip shut, and the prince's droning about his achievements was making it more difficult. Even his hounds were asleep at his feet. Out of the corner of my eye, I could see Nathan giving me an "I-told-you-so" look. "Yes, I apologise. There has been a lot happening as of late."

"So I have heard," August said, his eyes following my cup and then staying at my lips even when I returned my teacup to the saucer. "Gossip says you were attacked. I am glad you are unharmed."

"Thank you. We were lucky this time."

His brows raised. "This time?"

I pretended to tuck a stray hair behind my ear, trying to get his attention back to my eyes. At least it was better than when he had been studying my low neckline and commented on how he appreciated the dark lace edging. Thomas stared at August, the muscles in his jaw tense and his knuckles white against the handle of his cup. Had August not been the prince, I wondered if he would have said or done something by now. Nathan seemed to be taking enjoyment out of watching the two of them, although that was probably because there was nothing else to occupy his mind—or anyone else's, for that matter.

"It would stand to reason that they would try again," I answered. "Someone clearly wants us—most likely me—dead."

"And we will not let that happen," August said, shifting in his seat, sitting up taller.

"No, we will not," Thomas agreed, his tone surprisingly civilised. "Will the Queen and the other princes be joining us for the lessons?"

August spared a brief look for Thomas. "They should be here shortly, although I do not know if Mother's schedule will allow her to stay long. I was merely making conversation to pass the time."

"What would you like to focus on first?" I asked, grasping for something to keep the tension between the men from snapping. "Language, culture—"

"Let us wait for the rest to join," August suggested with a tight smile. "Get a general consensus."

I had to wonder if he looked at all women this way and if it worked for him. If he got Abigail, then it must give him some amount of success. Suddenly I missed being a servant in the shadows, unseen and unimportant. If the prince did try anything, I prepared myself to retaliate in a remarkably similar way to how I'd responded to Nathan's advances. Granted, it looked like Thomas might beat me to it.

I tried not to grin at the thought, but something must have slipped because August blinked those long pale lashes at me and asked, "May I ask what is so amusing, Miss Fuerte?"

"You seem to be in a state of unease," I replied. "I do not find it amusing, but rather odd, given all of your great accomplishments. If you are nervous about learning in time for the arrival of *las princesas*, I can understand, but you need not worry." The last bit nagged at me, knowing that Camila would certainly be someone for him to worry about if he fell for her. Most of the others would more likely than not be charmed by his tall, elegant frame, bright blue eyes, and blond hair. For his sake, I hoped he did not fall for Camila, although I would be lying if I said I would not enjoy watching his attempts at wooing her go up in flames... possibly literally. I had seen her toss hundreds of flowers from unwanted suitors into her fireplace, and that was the least of what she was capable of.

The prince regarded me with a calculating stare that I did not break. Surprisingly, he lightened up. "Yes, I am a bit nervous," he admitted. "Mother has continuously stressed the importance of this visit going well. Besides, some of us princes might even find ourselves wedded soon."

Before I could respond, the doors to the drawing room opened, and in came Queen Eleanora with three more men dressed just as impeccably as August. Even though August was the most attractive, there was no mistaking the family resemblance, all of them tall and various shades of blond or light brunet.

But none of them compared to Thomas.

We all stood, even the hounds, and I was keenly aware of the men's eyes on me.

"Thank you for coming," Queen Eleanora said with a dazzling

smile. "Miss Isabela Fuerte, these are my other sons, Prince Robert, Prince Herbert, and Prince Claude."

I could only imagine how it was to raise four boys—Thomas and Nathan seemed to be a handful in and of themselves, getting into enough trouble. But Nathan had called them dreadfully boring, so perhaps keeping them from trouble was not the issue.

The Queen did not stay long, leaving me to teach all of these men. I decided to start with greetings and farewells, a few basic phrases to at least give them an air of courtesy. To my surprise, even Thomas and Nathan joined in when it came to repeating phrases and gestures back to me. Their accents remained apparent even when trying to mask them, but I was glad that they were getting close enough to the pronunciation that their speech was understandable.

"Any questions?" I inquired with a passing glance over them. Standing before six sitting men and teaching them was strange but gave me a thrill I was rather enjoying.

Claude adjusted his spectacles and asked, "Can you repeat how to say 'princess' in your language? Slowly?" He was the only one to bring paper and a pen, constantly making notes as I spoke. From what I could see, his handwriting swirled elegantly across the page, but even if I were close enough, I still would not be able to read it. Learning to read in their language was on the list of things I wanted to do at some point, especially if Thomas and I were going to end up together.

After Claude was satisfied, Herbert spoke up: "Will the princesses look like you?"

I blinked in surprise and tilted my head to the side. "Do I look so different from people in this country?" No one seemed to notice that I was not from here until they heard my accent.

"He was asking if they will be beautiful like you," August clarified, making it more of a statement than a compliment, like it was a fact that could not be argued with.

"We are, after all," Herbert added, "possibly going to be marrying some of these princesses. It is natural for us to be rather curious about them."

"Curious," I repeated, drawing out the word. Even the hounds at August's feet looked up at me as if waiting for my response.

But how was I supposed to answer that?

"They all look different, like people do here," I said. "They have had many marriage proposals, many songs and stories told about their beauty and charm, if that answers your question." *Not all of them true, but no need to tell them that.*

Out of all of them, Nathan's eyes lit up the most, leaving me feeling like I had just informed a pack of wild dogs that there was a wounded animal nearby. I was unsure whether I felt more badly for *las princesas* or *los príncipes*… and Nathan. Time would tell, I supposed.

This was going to be quite the show… and I was ready for it to begin.

Chapter Twenty-Two

Thomas

"How do you think it went?" Isabela asked as we walked arm-in-arm out of the palace.

"They might not have remembered much other than the fact that you told them that the princesses are beautiful," I replied with a small smile. "Well, except for Prince Claude. I am sure he will be studying all those notes and practicing to make sure he impresses the princesses when they arrive."

Our new carriage, new driver, and new guards all waited at the gates. I was glad that at least Father took this seriously enough to make sure we had more protection. None of the three of us had said anything about it, but from the silence in between our words and the way even Nate glanced around, it was obvious that we were waiting for the next possible attack.

Isabela tightened her grip on me, and I patted her hand reassuringly.

"I'll definitely be practicing," Nate chimed in, a spring in his step.

"The princesses are not coming to get to know you, Nate."

"Let him try," Isabela said with a smirk. "I'd love to watch."

Nate met Isabela's look with a determined, confident one. "Tell me, Isabela: how would you say my name in your language? Nathaniel, not Nate or Nathan."

Her brows rose, but she said, "*Nataniel*," the earlier vowels softer and the later ones more defined. Nate repeated it a few times while Isabela corrected him.

"And how would you say my name?" I asked as we arrived at the carriage.

"*Tomás*," Isabela said, her voice so smooth that I wanted to ask her to say it again.

"Quit staring at one another," Nate complained. "Some of us would like to return home at a decent hour."

We climbed into the carriage before Nate said, "I am fine with whatever you two have between you, but you have to remember that no one else knows yet."

Isabela stiffened next to me.

"It was obvious," Nate said to her. "All I am saying is that you need to have a plan before someone finds out in a way you have no control over."

Isabela and I exchanged looks. Of course, Nate was right. This problem had been consistently pressing on the back of my mind, reminding me that it had to be dealt with and soon.

"What would you do?" I asked.

At first, I thought Nate was going to give me a flippant response... and I was right: "I do not fall in love with just one person, Tom. There are too many beauties to settle on just one." Still, the words fell flat, subdued.

"What about a serious answer, Nathan?" Isabela's voice was barely above a whisper.

His grey eyes took us in; he sighed. "If I had fallen in love with a spell-caster, or—well, really anyone I thought Father would be vehemently against—I would marry her in secret, that way Father would have no say in what happens. He would just have to come to terms with it all."

Everything seemed to still save the scenery passing us by through the window.

"You pressed for a serious answer, and that's it," Nate said with a shrug. "I never said it was a good idea, but that is what I would do."

Whether it was a good idea or not, it was, at the very least, something. No matter which way I thought about it, there was no good way to move forward and not get resistance.

"If you do take that route," Nate added, "I would suggest getting married as quickly as possible but waiting to tell Father or anyone until after the ball."

"The ball…"

The corner of his mouth twitched. "You two forgot, didn't you? Father still plans on hosting a ball to show off his new spell-caster so that the League will have to consider him one of their Elite."

"He's said very little about it since…" Isabela trailed off.

"Mother is still making preparations," Nate explained. "The Queen agreed to host it at the palace next week, and it should nicely coincide with the arrival of *las princesas*."

I found myself rather impressed with how well he pronounced the words, even though I wanted to wipe that smug expression off his face. I hoped the princesses were prepared for Nate.

"Why would you wait?" I found myself asking.

"Because if Father has already made the public display that she is his spell-caster, he will not try to sell Isabela to keep you apart."

"I am not an object to be sold," Isabela snapped.

"No, you are not," Nate agreed. "But to him, you are his property." After a beat, he leant forward, resting his elbows on his knees, and continued, "Tom, I know you always want to do things the right way, to keep the peace. But sometimes people will not see reason. Sometimes you have to beat them at their own game, to do things your way and let them deal with their pettiness."

It took me a moment to process what he said, my mind still stuck on my little brother giving advice that made sense, no matter how uncomfortable it felt. "Is that why you do what you do?"

Nate shook his head. "I'm a selfish arse: I do what I do because I want to. You are not: you will do this for the love of someone else, for Isabela's happiness and wellbeing."

I met Isabela's gaze; my heart twisted in a mix of joy and anticipation and fear of the unknown. She held my hand, a small, hopeful smile on her lips.

"I will do this?" I asked Nate.

"I would be surprised if you didn't." He sat back up. "Now don't you two get cosy and handsy. I'm still here."

Isabela snorted. "You got handsy with me in the middle of a busy tavern."

"See, those kinds of places are made for that kind of thing. You have to know what is appropriate for your surroundings." He winked and ran his fingers through his hair. "Just keep your hands to yourselves and let me know if you need any more life-altering wisdom."

Chapter Twenty-Three

Isabela

Suggestions

Thomas took longer than usual to retrieve me from my room. Had I not had thoughts forming and swirling in my mind, I might have assumed he was not coming and fallen asleep.

Marriage... that word did not scare me like it had before. Before it had meant that I would be lawfully bound to someone, almost the same as ownership. But to Thomas...

I did not know what he was thinking. As soon as Nathan had given the idea, Thomas had become pensive. It was not something for us to discuss in front of Nathan, or Lord and Lady Grahm, or anyone else. Speaking at night was our only option.

But what if he did not wish to discuss it?

The soft rapping on my window had me nearly flying out of bed. Slipping my feet into slippers I'd left nearby and grabbing my shawl, I went to Thomas.

"I thought you might not come tonight," I said quietly, greeting him with a kiss. I noted that he had freshened up, reapplying some cologne and changing his shirt before seeing me.

"I'll always come for you," he replied with a smile that made my heart swell. That was the kind of thing a knight would say to the princess in the books I liked to read, and I always wondered if words like that would work in real life. Now I had my answer.

Just as before, we slipped away into the night, the moon and starlit sky our only witnesses as we stole kisses and eventually made our way to our spot near the white roses. Blankets covered the ground, giving us space to lounge without leaving conspicuous grass and dirt stains on our clothing. We stretched out beside one another, Thomas propping himself up on one elbow. His eyes appeared darker at night unless the moon caught them just right—either way, they pulled me in, making me their willing captive.

He traced the edge of my face with a fingertip, his eyes following. "We should discuss what Nate said. He made some valid points about our situation."

"He did," I agreed, my heart skipping a beat and then picking up its pace.

"If we were married, my father would have no say in our relationship, and I would be able to protect you legally should anyone find out your heritage."

That thought had not occurred to me—oftentimes I forgot about it since I was so used to being unseen in my own country. I bit my bottom lip, drawing his attention there unintentionally. "Does that mean you are considering it?" My question came out so softly that I barely heard it.

Those captivating eyes looked at me in a moment of pure vulnerability that made any nerves I carried melt away.

"Yes," Thomas whispered, his fingertip pausing at my jawline. The word hung between us, his eyes dancing back and forth between mine. His throat bobbed. "Are you?"

"Yes."

We shared a grin, and Thomas pressed his lips to my forehead.

"Are we insane?" he asked with a chuckle. "We've known each other for nigh on a month now and yet... and yet I feel as though I have been waiting for you all my life, that I've always known you, that I knew we would find each other."

I turned my head to nuzzle his neck and breathe him in. "Yes, we are, but I know what you mean."

"...Then are we doing this?"

I leant back so that he could see my face. "You, Master Thomas Grahm, have to ask properly before you'll get your answer."

It was not lost on me that I had used the wretched word "properly," although in this case it did not sit strangely with me. It almost seemed natural.

With a laugh, he pushed himself onto his feet and helped me up. "Very well then." He went to the rose bushes, pulling and twisting at one of the flower stems before using his pocketknife to finish the job.

"Careful not to stab yourself with a thorn," I said, wincing.

"I need blood anyway," he said, not bothering to explain as he drew on the bottom white petals, staining them red as they soaked in his blood. The thorns disappeared, and shimmers ran through the entire rose before it softly glowed, looking like an enchanted flower in a fairy-tale.

Before I could ask what he was doing, Thomas sank onto one knee in front of me, glowing rose in hand. "Miss Isabela Fuerte, *La Sirena*," he started, stumbling over the words a little in a charming way, "I love you. Every part of you. I never thought I could feel so completely connected and accepted and understood by someone and be able to give that in return. I do not know what life may bring, but I know that I want to be at your side for as long as you will have me." Taking a breath, Thomas offered the rose and asked, "Will you marry me?"

"Yes." My answer left my lips mere seconds before he had me in his arms and kissed me. Then he held me close and spun me around in a circle, my skirts billowing with the sudden movement. I giggled and held tightly to him, caught off-guard.

"We have some planning to do," he murmured, kissing my temple as he handed me the iridescent rose. It was cool to the touch, thrumming with magic. I twirled it between two fingers, watching it shimmer and sparkle.

"I'll get you a ring," Thomas promised. "I thought this might do in the meantime."

"It's perfect," I told him. "We'll not be able to wear rings until after the ball anyway."

"That is true." He rested his cheek against the top of my head. "I'll have to figure out where we can get married and who will marry us in secret. I suppose the 'who' will determine the 'where.'"

Someone to help us. I watched the colours dance throughout the rose as it spun in my fingers. Beautiful colours that had my attention…

"I think I may know who would help us."

Chapter Twenty-Four

Thomas

Ceremony

Leaving the manor under false pretences proved easier than I thought. Father and Mother believed that we were going to be late coming home because the Queen asked it of us, something Nate corroborated without needing to be told.

Lessons with the princes could not go fast enough that day. I was fortunate that me staring at how beautiful Isabela was could be misconstrued as me paying attention to the lessons—I was doubly fortunate that she did not ask me any questions to check if I was following along. Normally Robert, who was silent as ever, and Claude were the least annoying of the princes, but today Claude's incessant questions and perfectionism had me biting my tongue and checking my pocket watch. Nate threw me a look, so I tried my best to relax in my seat.

After the lessons and on our way to the chapel in our carriage, Nate teased, "You're lucky the princes were so smitten with Isabela that they didn't notice what a mess you are."

Isabela chuckled. "I had to stop looking in your direction because you were making me nervous."

"I think it's a reasonable way to feel on one's wedding day," I said, taking Isabela's hand. *How is it that it's gone so fast yet feels so natural?*

"But no one else is supposed to know that. We'll have to work on your acting skills if you're going to keep all this a secret until after the ball." Nate shook his head and sighed, "I, as always, have my work cut out for me."

"Thank you for being a witness for us, Nathan," Isabela said.

He waved it off and handed me a key. "That's the only thing I'll be witnessing. This is the key to your room at the Iron Rose. I paid for the night, but you'll only get a few hours before this carriage is going home so things don't seem more suspicious than they already are. Consider this your wedding gift." Then he added with a finger raised, "But please, for the love of the Maker, do not tell me 'thank you' or that you enjoyed it. I don't want to know any details. I'm only doing this because if you get caught, my fun is ruined."

The carriage pulled to a stop, and Isabela leant forward to kiss Nate on the cheek. "It's a deal."

Nate grinned. "Go on, let's get you married. I can only stand so much sappiness at a time."

Priest Abel was waiting for us in the garden, already prepared with a bowl of dirt on a pedestal in front of him. A cat lounged in the sun while its kittens played at the priest's feet, one tugging on the edge of his robe. He beamed at the sight of us. "Welcome." He made a line of dirt across each of our foreheads and then had Nate stand back, and Isabela and I kneel in front of him. I was glad we'd brought a change of clothes for later: the dirt stains symbolised that we would go through anything and everything together, and they were an easy way to tell that someone had just married.

Her white dress seemed rather simple in comparison to other

wedding dresses, but Isabela did not seem to mind. We had left early that morning to pick it out from a dress shop, and I had known it would be the one the moment her eyes lit up and she traced the beading at the neckline that matched the patterning on the bust and edges of her sleeves. Her lace veil almost covered the length of her hair; I was pleased to see her wear it down.

One of the kittens found interest in Isabela's veil, so the priest scooped him up and held him while saying, "Master Thomas Grahm, Miss Isabela Fuerte, today you have come to me to be joined together in the sight of the Maker, myself, and Master Nathaniel Grahm. If you still agree to this, say 'let it be.'"

"Let it be," we said simultaneously.

The kitten squirmed in his arms but calmed when Abel scratched him behind the ear. "Do you two promise to put one another first, to love, cherish, and respect one another, to be bound in name, body, soul, mind, and blood from this day until your last? If so, say, 'we do.'"

"We do."

"Very good." Abel set the kitten near its mother. "Would you like to finish with the rune-writing marriage ceremony?"

"Yes," I answered, noting Isabela's curiosity.

"Extend your hands." Abel cut into our palms and squeezed them over the bowl. Blood dripped into the dirt. He mixed it all together before handing it to me first.

Isabela watched as I turned to her, gesturing for her to follow suit. Dipping my finger in the bowl, I drew runes on her chin, her left ring finger, neck, and forehead, saying, "From this day forward, I bind myself to you in name, body, soul, mind, and blood."

She smiled, hesitating when accepting the bowl from me. I helped her with the runes while the priest helped her with the words. Each finished rune sent crackles of magic energy through me, making me feel more alive than I'd ever felt.

Abel took the bowl back after we were done. "I now pronounce you man and wife. Best wishes, Mr and Mrs Grahm. You may now kiss."

We did not know what life would bring or how things would turn out, but we did know that, with that kiss, we sealed our fate.

The hotel room was cosy, but more importantly, it was private. Isabela chattered the entire way from the chapel back to the hotel, saying how lovely and simple the ceremony was, how she adored her dress, how she could not believe that we were married, and I thought she would slow down when we reached our room, but I was wrong.

"What do these runes mean?" She examined the dainty one on her left ring finger. I had taken time and care in designing and applying it, knowing that one, of all of them, would last. I had no ring to give her yet, so it was the best I could do.

"They symbolize binding us together," I answered, covering her hands with mine.

"Do they have any magic? Do they make us do anything?" She briefly looked up at me and then back at our hands, her teeth worrying at her bottom lip.

"They don't make us do anything, but they are said to give us a sense of closeness." I brought her hands to my lips, hoping to draw her attention to me. Pink stained her cheeks when it finally did. "What is the matter, Isabela?"

She gave me a quick peck on the mouth and pulled away, walking toward the painting on the wall. "Nothing is the matter."

I wanted to make her face me and talk to me, but I stayed where I was, unsure what to do. She ran a finger down the design work of the frame, following the pattern on the outer edge.

"Are you having second thoughts about us?" I asked quietly, trying to keep my emotions knotting my stomach from colouring my tone.

Isabela whirled around, horrified. "No!" She took small, slow steps to me, still biting at her lip. "It is just... I have never..." Pink darkened to red, and I smiled.

"Neither have I."

She finally met my gaze, the vulnerability in her eyes making me want to hold her close.

"I am nervous too," I told her, offering my hands. She squeezed them. "We can wait until you are ready." A selfish part of me hoped she'd say she was ready now, but I meant what I said and watched as she processed them.

"But we only have a few hours."

"That does not matter," I said. "If you are not ready, we can wait until after everyone knows about us, after we have our own place—it is up to you."

She tightened her grip. "I don't want to wait."

"Are you sure?"

She nodded.

"Good, because I don't want to either," I said teasingly.

"You're terrible," she said as she swatted my arm.

"The worst." I pulled her into my arms, her feet dangling above the floor—she laughed and only put up enough of a pretend fight to make me grin. She lifted her chin, putting on an adorably defiant and challenging look that made me fall in love with her all over again.

Maker help me, this woman could get me to do anything for her. How did I get so lucky?

Her features softened as she toyed with the edge of my shirt collar. "Thomas, I… I don't know what to do."

I rested my forehead against hers, sure she could feel the wild beating of my heart with our chests pressed together. I could have sworn I felt hers race as much as mine. The rune on my chest burned. "Do you want to?"

Her dark eyes lit up with an excitement that set a fire within me. "Yes."

"Then let's figure it out together."

Chapter Twenty-Five

Isabela

Late Night

Our room in the Iron Rose was perfect. Even though he said not to, a part of me wanted to thank Nathan anyway. I felt a little odd leaving the sheets rumpled and spotted, but we had no time to tidy if we were to make it back to the manor before suspicions arose. Besides, the housekeeping was used to things like this, right?

"Thomas, can you help me with my dress?" I pointed over my shoulder to the stays for him to tighten and tie. He stepped behind me, his fingertips grazing my back as he opened the dress more so he could plant kisses down my spine. "Not what I meant!" I chuckled and turned my head to kiss him. "Neither of us is allowed to get distracted."

Thomas made a low sound in his throat that threatened to pull me into making us late. "You are the definition of distracting." He fixed my gown and secured it, his touches lingering on my skin. Then he twirled me around and pulled me close. "One more week," he murmured against my neck, "and we'll no longer have to hide."

I ran my fingers through his curls. One week until the truth came out, and then we would have to face whatever consequences came our way. This time, instead of running away on my own, I was staying put with someone who would stay with me. "Are you ready for whatever may come?"

Lifting his head, Thomas gave me a smile. "I'm ready for whatever may come if you are by my side."

I leant in for another kiss when a knock at the door interrupted us.

"We have to leave," Nathan reminded us.

Thomas and I exchanged looks.

"Coming, Nate," Thomas said as he checked over the room one more time to be sure we had not left anything.

Nathan was waiting for us in the hallway, resting against the wall with his arms crossed and a smirk on his face. He peered over our shoulders and nodded. "Looks like you did it right."

My cheeks burned while I scrambled for a retort, but he was already at the staircase, taking them two at a time.

"Shall we, Mrs Grahm?" Thomas asked quietly, offering his arm. We walked together through the small, quaint hotel. Out of the few people I saw, I felt a little overdressed. No one seemed to pay us attention except for the lanky man at the counter who told us to have a wonderful evening before attending other customers.

Streetlamps dully lit the roads and walkways in front of the surrounding shops. They had no help from the moon or stars either since clouds blanketed the night sky. As Thomas helped me into the carriage, someone called, "Thomas Grahm! What a surprise to see you here at such an hour."

I froze. Nathan tugged me into the seat next to him, that way I was hidden from the man engaging Thomas in conversation. He put a finger to his lips.

"Lord Basker," Thomas greeted. "What a surprise to see you. I must beg your pardon, but—woah, easy there—I am afraid I must be leaving immediately. Our—"

"Nonsense!" Lord Basker slurred. "Come, bring your lovely lady friend and have a drink with me and the boys! I'm sure we'd all love to meet her." His volume raised a comical amount as he shouted, "Come out, love! Let's have a look at you. Promise we'll behave… somewhat." He cackled, making me want to squirm. "Come now, Thomas, stop blocking the door. Have a bit of fun with us. The boys are waiting at the pub."

"I cannot, unfortunately. Have a good evening, Lord Basker."

"Thomas—"

"What seems to be the problem?" One of our guards strode over to stand beside Thomas.

"There is no problem," Thomas said. "We are saying our goodbyes."

"Ah," Lord Basker said, "so these are the guards Gerold spoke of at the last meeting. Heard you got in a bit of trouble. Well, that's to be expected when you have a spell-caster. They bring trouble wherever they go. Although, I'd be more than willing to have a bit of trouble if I could have a go at your spell-caster—"

"You might want to consider sobering up and returning home to your wife and children," Thomas interrupted. "I am sure they miss you dearly."

Lord Basker said some other things that I could not quite make out because Thomas entered the carriage and shut the door. Our guard and Lord Basker exchanged a few more words before we left. Muffled shouts followed us.

I slipped into the seat next to Thomas, and he grabbed my hand. "Be sure to keep gloves on at all times," he said, his thumb rubbing the back of my ring finger. None of the runes we drew during the wedding ceremony stayed visible, all of them disappearing from the naked eye even though I could still feel them. Except the ones on our ring fingers: like the one on my wrist, those had turned golden.

"Lord Basker saw you leaving the inn," Nathan said irritably.

"Lord Basker was inebriated. Doubtless he'll forget the whole exchange before he even makes it home." Thomas stared at our hands, his thumb still rubbing my finger.

"You can't be sure of that, Tom."

Thomas sighed. "What do you want me to do about it, Nate?"

"Be ready with a story, ways to manipulate what he thinks he remembers seeing." This time, there was no mirth to Nate's tone or expression, no cockiness or playful air about him. "If he does remember any of it, it'll get back to Father quickly. We need to be ready."

"We?" I asked.

"I've been with you the entire time," he answered. "They'll be looking to me to confirm your story is the truth."

I tried to catch Thomas's eye to no avail. When I squeezed his hand, he squeezed back, but the frown remained.

"All right, Nate. What is our story?"

Chapter Twenty-Six

Thomas

League

I did not go to Isabela that night. We had agreed that it was too risky to continue our nightly outings, that we could wait for a week.

A week seemed like an eternity.

Sure that we had our story straight with Nate, all we could do was continue our night and next day like nothing had happened. I caught myself staring at Isabela a few times, at which point Nate was kind enough to kick me in the shin under the table or jab me with an elbow when no one was looking. Luckily for me, Father was distracted with going over what Isabela would do for the ball, and Mother was busy planning it out. After what happened the last time, Father made sure to ask Isabela's input on what she thought would be too much for her to handle, and he even made no arguments whenever she said she needed a break.

"Why don't you remove your gloves," Father suggested one of the days of practice. "Perhaps it's getting in the way of your spell-casting."

My heart leapt into my throat, my mind racing. Nate twitched next to me.

"I feel much more in control with them on," Isabela replied smoothly. "They help ground me to reality so that I do not get swept away by the magic."

After a moment of thought, Father nodded. "We'll just need to be sure to get gloves to match your dress for the ball that do not cover your rune. I will have my wife tell the tailor."

I almost sagged against the wall in relief. Isabela smiled and agreed with him, saying that it was a wonderful idea. Since we had yet to hear anything about Lord Baskers after the run-in a few days prior, my nerves had started to settle slightly. We just needed a half a week more before anyone else found out.

The next day, Father sent Archibald to wake us early so that we could attend a League meeting in the capital city with him. A meeting Lord Baskers would certainly attend, same as the other certified rune-writers. I briefly considered claiming ill, but I would not leave Nate and Isabela to fend for themselves, and I most certainly would not wish for Lord Baskers to make comments or accusations to Father without being there to explain and smooth things over. Lord Baskers' words still agitated me, making me want to defend my wife.

My wife. It still seemed like a wonderful dream, being married to Isabela. At the moment, my hope was that we would manage to keep this a secret until we were ready, and then she and I would find a way to live together, to make our marriage feel real. I had no idea where we would go if Father did disown me and kick us out, but I would figure something out. I had a little money stashed away, so that would have to hold us over until I found work and a place for us to stay more permanently.

We dressed in our rune-writer attire, dark suits complete with gloves and jackets with enough room to hide any small weapons we carried in the inside pockets. Isabela wore an outfit with a button-down white shirt with a high neckline and a floor-length skirt that emulated our style: dark, sleek, and simple. Her black jacket would have been identical to ours had it not been tailored for a woman, had red stitching that matched the red bow tied at her neck, and the fact that her sleeves were hemmed short to expose her wrists. Black gloves hid her hands, and her thick hair had been twisted up into a sophisticated bun and pinned into place.

That was one of the times Nate jabbed me in the ribs while Mother was busy handing Isabela a parasol and Father was reminding her to behave herself in front of his fellow rune-writers. Mother glanced over at us with a curious expression. My pulse raced, but she said nothing and turned her attention back to Isabela.

Too close.

Putting on a smile, Isabela simply accepted the parasol and dipped her head. That smile waned throughout our carriage ride to the capital: Father gave all sorts of rules about not talking unless he gave her specific permission, keeping her gaze down, and abstaining from using magic.

"Do not do or say anything anyone else tells you," he finished. "You belong to the Grahms, not anyone else."

"As you wish, Lord Grahm."

I caught Nate rolling his eyes multiple times. I kept myself from reacting to any of it except for when Father patted Isabela's face—I bit the inside of my cheek as he said, "Very good, love. I know you'll do us proud." Addressing all of us, he added, "Soon, we will be at the top of the League, getting all of the respect and honour due to the Grahm name. Then your mother can have the luxurious lifestyle she craves."

I did not bother to correct him: leave it to Father to desire something more than Mother did but pin it on her like she was the reason he did anything.

The League Hall building stood tall and wide to accommodate a plethora of rooms for research, training, testing, and meetings. Very few rune-writers lived there, namely the ones who did ran the library or taught young rune-writers. Of course, servants also resided there to keep the place running and clean, along with a few of the Elites who, as rumour had it, rarely returned to their estates, instead having others to run them so that they could dedicate their lives to the League.

Isabela's eyes widened as she stepped out of the carriage and beheld the League Hall for the first time. She seemed to take in everything as we crossed the expansive lawn to reach the front doors. Gardeners trimmed the hedges, making sure to pause long enough to bow to us as we passed. The guards at the entrance opened the doors for us and shut them again as soon as we passed the threshold. Paintings of all certified rune-writers both past and present littered the walls of the hallway like an art museum. Our boots clacked against the polished wood floors that led to the meeting room.

There was a spot in the centre of the room where there was standing space enough for a few people, but everyone was already seated at one of the assigned long tables when we arrived, one placed horizontally at the front and four off to the sides so that they faced one another but were slanted to also face the one at the front. At the head of the room were the three Elites, their dark clothes stitched with gold, matching their handkerchiefs and the embellishing on Lord Shirehold's pipe, which he huffed away at as he scrutinized everyone. Stepping before their table, we bowed, and Isabela took note and curtsied, not for one second letting go of my arm. Silence reigned as all eyes focused on us.

"Lord Gerold," Lord Smith greeted, "we Elites welcome you and your sons to this League meeting. Please, introduce your spell-caster."

"Gentlemen," Father said, his chest puffed out and arms wide like an entertainer at the circus, "may I present the Grahm spell-caster, Miss Isabela Fuerte."

Mrs Isabela Grahm. Oh, there was a small part of me that could not wait to see Father's reaction when he found out, no matter how nervous I was about that eventuality.

"Wherever did you attain such a ravishing creature?" asked Lord Cornwell, the last of the Elites. Other than the slight grey hair at his temples, the man looked much like he had when I'd met him as a boy, and ladies tended to notice.

"The Maker's favour shone upon me," Father answered, beaming, with a decline of his head as though to mark his humility. "I will be forever grateful and in awe of the Maker's ways."

"He attained her because the Chantry contacted him after the girl claimed sanctuary," Lord Shirehold stated. "Unless the Maker told the priests to call for Lord Grahm, I doubt any sort of deity had much to do with it."

Father's mouth twitched, but he maintained a pleasant air. "Whatever your beliefs, Lord Shirehold, I maintain that I have been given a wonderful opportunity and will neither take it for granted nor be ungrateful."

"Please, gentlemen, take your seats so we may begin," Lord Smith said. "Your spell-caster may stand behind you quietly."

"Are we not going to see her in action?" Lord Cornwell inquired, leaning forward eagerly.

"Come to the ball, and you will," Father promised.

"We have other important matters to attend," Lord Smith reminded him. "Your seats, gentlemen."

"Is she properly leashed?" Lord Shirehold demanded to know, his brow furrowing as he looked Isabela up and down. "We would not want to be caught unawares if the creature does not wish to behave civilly."

My jaw ached from how hard I gritted my teeth. Isabela tightened her grip on my arm, sparing a brief glance at me.

"She seems rather attached to Thomas," Lord Cornwell stated. "I bet you'll behave, won't you, love?" He winked at her, and I fought to keep a neutral expression. Everything in me wanted to take Isabela far away from here, to hide her away from their hungry stares and hurtful words. Suddenly, I found myself enraged and embarrassed to be considered one of their number. A sickening feeling ate away at my stomach. One peek at Nate told me he felt the same.

"Thomas knows how to keep her and her powers in line," Father explained. "No need to worry. For an uncivilised creature, she has learned quickly how to behave properly and appropriately." He looked to Isabela. "Go on, show them your rune."

Isabela obeyed, and some of the men to the sides of the room shifted to get a better view.

"The linework appears almost artistic," said Lord Smith. "Different than last I saw it."

"The Queen asked for Thomas to redo it that way," Father told them. "You know how she prefers things beautiful in her presence."

"All women do," grunted Lord Shirehold, blowing smoke off to the side. "We men get things done, and they make things look more appealing."

"Speaking of getting things done," Lord Smith interjected, "if you are quite satisfied with how the spell-caster is handled, we would appreciate all seats taken so that we can start this meeting."

Chapter Twenty-Seven

Isabela

Meeting

I had to wonder if, had I not been a spell-caster, they would have either given me a seat or had me leave the room because this was a men-only meeting. They did not expressly say it anywhere, but given that I had yet to see a woman rune-writer, I had to assume it was by design. Magic did not know gender, nor did it care. I couldn't imagine magic would suddenly become fickle when it came to rune-writing.

When they made the comment about me being attached to Thomas, my stomach had dropped. With only a few days left, I wanted to leave little to chance, so I made sure to stand behind Lord Grahm like an obedient pet. I had to admit, them thinking I was dangerous almost made me smile. Perhaps that would keep them from doing anything I would have to defend myself against. Some of the rune-writers sneaked peeks at me. I recognized only the ones from the dinner party… and hoped that Lord Baskers looking at me was not a sign that he was remembering the night he ran into us.

"First things first," Lord Smith began, "it has come to our attention that Master Thomas Grahm, Master Nathaniel Grahm, and the spell-caster were attacked by people with runes carved into their skin. Lord Grahm, you believe this might be the work of one of the rune-writers here?"

"I do not know what to believe," Lord Grahm responded in a

respectful tone that I had not heard out of him before, "although I am inclined to theorise that either it is someone here or an unregistered rune-writer."

Murmurs and shifting glances.

"What evidence do you have other than your word?"

Why they did not ask for statements from someone who was actually there, I had no clue. I knew my word would mean little to nothing to them, but I had expected them to at least consider what Thomas or Nathan had to say.

"The samples of ashes we sent to you are all we have," Thomas said. "I have drawings of the runes used on the would-be assassins if that would help at all."

Lord Smith beckoned him over, so Thomas made his way to the front table, his head up and shoulders back, reminding me just how tall he was. Memories of experiencing our height difference in a more personal way flashed in my mind, and I abruptly cut them off before my cheeks began to burn. A choked sound escaped my lips, just loud enough to have Lord Grahm turn around. I pretended to clear my throat and looked at the floor; he refocused on the meeting.

From his jacket, Thomas pulled out a small drawing pad and handed it over to the Elite. The three of them huddled together, heads bent over the drawing.

"Why were we not given this before?" Lord Shirehold demanded to know, removing the pipe from his mouth so that he could point at Thomas with it. "You should have given this to us immediately, boy."

"I apologise to the Elite. Evidence was demanded before I could,"

Thomas answered. "It took me a few tries to accurately replicate it."

"Do you recognise it?" Lord Grahm asked impatiently.

"It is one of the banned runes from the look of it," Lord Cornwell said, brow furrowed. "Henrietta in the library might have some knowledge of this. May we take this?"

Thomas ripped the page out of the pad and tucked the pad back into his jacket. "Of course. Whatever we need to help with the investigation."

They dismissed him, and Thomas took his seat once more.

"We will keep this investigation open, and everyone in this room will submit to interrogations and possible inspections of property and belongings," announced Lord Smith. "Now, on to other items to discuss."

From there, the meeting dragged its feet. Had I a pocket watch, I'd have checked it multiple times. As it was, my aching feet told me that at least an hour passed. Most of the things discussed were men giving updates on their research and training of their children. I found myself pleasantly surprised to hear that one man said his daughter had a knack for rune-writing and wanted to appeal to the Elite to allow her to train at the League Hall.

"We can do an interview with her next Tuesday afternoon," Lord Cornwell stated. "Then we shall make our decision."

At the end of the meeting, Lord Smith announced, "Princesses from the neighbouring country of Isouldia shall arrive at the palace this week. Queen Eleanora has requested that we rune-writers be there at all times as protection, so we have a schedule posted on the wall outside of this room. Be sure to memorise it and adhere to it. Arrive early to all of your scheduled times to be sure that we have no gaps."

I smothered a smile. Anticipation of seeing Camila and being able to tell her about everything that had happened since we'd last seen one another threatened to drive me to insanity if I had to wait much longer.

To finish out the meeting, all of the men stood and bowed to the Elite. I dipped into a quick curtsy in case they were watching me.

"Bring honour to the Maker and the Crown and our country in all you do," Lord Smith said. "You are dismissed."

Rune-writers filed out of the room, but some paused in the hallway to check the schedule or have a chat. I tried not to lean on Thomas too much as I shifted my weight to give a little relief to my aching feet.

"Master Thomas Grahm!" Lord Baskers caught up to us, a sheepish grin on his face. He lowered his voice as he said, "I wanted to apologise to you for the other night. My behaviour was rather embarrassing for both of us, I assure you."

I hoped no one else could hear my heart pounding. Thomas tensed.

"Think no more of it," Thomas said.

"You were at the palace recently? For what?" Lord Grahm inquired, turning around to join our conversation.

"The palace? No, no, nothing like that. I'd had a few too many and saw Thomas coming out of an inn with a woman. I'm afraid I made an arse of myself." Lord Baskers fussed with his ascot like it needed to be loosened.

Lord Grahm stared at Thomas, whose mouth opened but nothing came out. I would have spoken up, but Nathan's plan on what we were going to say inconveniently slipped my mind at that very moment.

"You just missed me," Nathan spoke up, putting on a rueful smile. "I have a knack for getting myself into situations I should not be in, and Thomas and Isabela had to fetch me."

Both of the lords looked back and forth between Thomas and Nathan.

"I got carried away," Nathan added. "They retrieved me before I could do anything to bring dishonour to the Grahm name, Father."

Lord Grahm eyed us for a few moments longer before saying, "Sounds as if all is well again, Lord Baskers. Do enjoy your day. Thomas, Nathaniel, come along now." He swiped a copy of the schedule before walking to the door.

I mouthed "thank you" to Nathan, and he shrugged.

"We are not out of the woods quite yet," Nathan whispered to us.

Chapter Twenty-Eight

Thomas

 *Banned*

The next day, we were asked to come to the League Hall to discuss with Henrietta the rune I drew. Father insisted on coming along, and he had all of us in our rune-writer attire, including Isabela. The moment we stepped into the library, Isabela grinned, her eyes hungrily roaming over the floor-to-ceiling bookshelves that required ladders to reach the top as well as the rows upon rows that filled the middle sections and the stairway that led to the upper level.

"Ah, good to see you arrived on time," Henrietta said, snapping a book shut as if to emphasise her statement. Despite her seemingly permanent sour expression and the twisted scars across one cheek and her throat, she was quite attractive, her long medium brown hair pulled into a neat braid that reached her mid back. Her green eyes took in everything, although she spent a decent amount more time looking at Isabela than the rest of us. Her outfit looked similar to Isabela's for the most part, save the lack of red stitching and the full-length sleeves of Henrietta's jacket. "This must be the spell-caster."

"You may call me Isabela."

Henrietta raised a brow. Instead of answering, she said to Nate, "If I catch you in here with a girl again, Master Grahm, I'll be sure to give you more than the swift kick to the arse I gave you last time."

"Understood." Nate smirked, ignoring Father's sigh. According to

Nate, Father had told him that they would be having a serious discussion about his behaviour and habits soon. As always, my younger brother shrugged it off, claiming that Father said things like that to him on a semi-regular basis. That still did not ease my gnawing guilt and anxiety.

"Follow me." Henrietta strode away, passing her desk with a mountain of neatly stacked books, heading toward a door in the back of the library. She did not bother to check to see if we were following.

As we entered the back room, she made it very clear that we were not to touch or even breathe on anything. "These documents are ancient and require the utmost respect and care." She narrowed in on Isabela. "You may wait outside."

"If it's all the same to you, Henrietta," Father said, "I would prefer she stay with us. She will behave, you have my word as a lord and a fellow rune-writer."

Without taking her eyes off of Isabela, Henrietta said, "I trust your word, Lord Grahm. It is her kind I do not trust." Her fingers grazed the scar at her throat. "I know which runes to use to take down a spell-caster for good. Be aware that I will not hesitate to use them if I feel threatened."

"Isabela is not dangerous," Nate stated in a tone that did not leave room for argument.

Henrietta huffed a mirthless laugh. "All of them are, boy. You'd be a fool to trust any of them." Before I could say anything in my wife's defence, the female rune-writer pulled on a pair of gloves and began pointing at yellowed, crinkled pages laid out just so on the table. "I found these in the banned section of the archives, just as the Elite suspected." She held my rendering near one of the pages for comparison. Although the ink had faded considerably over time, we could make it out when she pointed to where we needed to be looking. "They are from the studies of early rune-writers, back before many of the laws were in place to protect the general public. The one you drew has to do with fire from what I can translate."

"The attackers exploded," I confirmed. "The runes were carved into their skin."

Her nose wrinkled. "Another banned practice. I would be surprised if the one behind this is a registered rune-writer, given the consequences of such practices if caught, but no unregistered rune-writer would have access to this sort of information, and it is not like it is something self-taught. We could have a case of someone pulling strings to avoid anything coming back to them."

I wanted to huff in frustration. Even with this information, we were no closer to finding a suspect, and there was nowhere else to look, nothing else to do except wait and hope we were ready for whatever next attack may come. If anything happened to Isabela or Nate...

Isabela and I exchanged looks, her expression a reflection of my inner turmoil. I fought the urge to reach out to her, to pull her to me so I could hold her. She stayed near the door, no doubt giving Henrietta some semblance of peace of mind.

"That being said," Henrietta continued, bringing me back to the conversation, "there have been multiple cases recently the police handed over to us when they found runes left at all of the crime scenes.

This rune." She held up my drawing and tapped it. "It's almost like they were using it as a symbol for something. They draw it in blood and let the fire and ashes be the sign that they were there."

"What other crimes have they committed?" Father asked. "Why has there been nothing in the newspapers?"

"From what I can tell, there is not much proven information to share as of yet. Besides, making them front-page news would only stroke their egos and stir them to possibly bigger, more dangerous risks. There have been stolen items, people harassed, buildings burned down, all mostly in the country, away from the capital."

"And they tried to kill us," Nate added, crossing his arms. "Don't forget that. That might be accurately categorised as 'bigger, more dangerous risks' without the front page encouraging them."

"How do you know they meant to kill you? What if they meant to kill the spell-caster?"

"I find it safe to assume that a gun pointed at me means someone is trying to kill me." Nate raised his brows as if challenging Henrietta. "Even if they only meant to target Isabela, they killed the driver, one of our horses, and destroyed our carriage, not to mention the fact that they exploded. That seems to be a lot for just taking out one person."

"And yet, if that was their objective, Master Grahm, they failed."

"Then what can we do?" Father pressed, earning a narrow-eyed look from Henrietta when he leant too close to the table. He took a small step back. "Surely we were not brought here to be told that there is nothing we can do."

"I am merely sharing what I have been told to disclose," Henrietta replied, moving to shoo us out of the room. "You know as much as I about this case, Lord Grahm. The Elite are issuing people on the case and will be sending more rune-writers to protect you, your family, and your manor. We are taking this with the utmost seriousness, I can assure you."

Isabela stepped aside so that Henrietta could open the door for all of us. We filed out, Isabela leaving the room last. I turned to offer her my arm, but Isabela hesitated, meeting Henrietta's watchful eyes.

"I do not know what happened to you," Isabela said softly, "but I am sorry." With that, she took my arm, knowing that Henrietta would not speak to her.

Something softened in Henrietta's expression, but the woman spoke flatly, saying, "Lord Grahm, Masters Grahm, have a good day." Then she turned her back to us, returning to her desk and the piles of books upon it.

Chapter Twenty-Nine

Isabela

Princesas

"You put your hand here like so," I said, guiding Prince Robert's movements so that he stood up straight and lightly touched the middle of my back. "Our dances are not so different from yours, I would imagine." He and Claude were the easiest princes to get along with, and I figured that Thomas would find him the least threatening. Not that he had anything to worry about when it came to my attention, but I was fully prepared to put a stop to anything August or Herbert might try.

Robert merely gave a slight dip of his head to let me know he understood.

"Try relaxing," I urged him with a smile. "The point of dances is to let the music take you away, to have fun. I can promise you that everyone is at least a little bit nervous."

"I am not nervous at all," August countered, pushing his brother away so that he could dance with me. Robert hurried to take a seat near Thomas and Nathan. "You have taught us well, and if it is meant to be, these princesses will fall in love with us from the moment we meet, and we will have our happily ever afters."

Nathan snorted, which was what I was trying to refrain from doing.

"Something amusing, Nathaniel?" August asked, keeping an air of calm as he dipped me in a slow arc, one hand supporting my low back while the other held my hand to his chest. Thomas crossed his arms, watching from the table, August's hounds sleeping near his feet. Blood rushed to my head as August kept me there, his eyes locked onto Nathan.

"Your confidence never wanes, Your Highness," Nathan said with a smirk. "I thought you'd be at least a little nervous at the prospect of meeting women from a different country. What if they do not speak our language?"

"Then I shall have Isabela translate," August answered coolly, finally lifting me and proceeding with the dance. "Women love confidence, Nathaniel. You'd do best to remember that."

"I'll try." Nate reached for a teacup and lifted it into the air. "To your never-waning confidence." He downed whatever was left in the cup and leant back in his seat, legs crossed and hands behind his head, a smug look on his face.

I ended the dance before any arguments could ensue. "Very good. Any more questions?"

"Not about the dance," Claude said. "I was hoping you could go over the hand motions for greetings and goodbyes once more. I'm not sure I quite understand them."

"Your Highnesses," said a young servant at the door, "forgive me for interrupting, but the princesses from Isouldia are approaching the gates. The Queen asks that all of you be in attendance to greet them at the palace entrance." He offered a smile that looked more like he was going to be sick with nerves.

"We'd best be off then," Herbert stated, swiping his jacket from the chair so that he could put it back on as we left. Thomas, Nathan, and I followed behind the princes at a small distance.

"Are they ready?" Thomas asked quietly.

"Let us hope so," I replied; Nathan chuckled. "Don't think for one second that you are ready, Nathan."

"I know I'm not," he said with a grin and a wink. "That's half the fun."

I rolled my eyes but could not help a smile. Hopefully, Camila was among *las princesas*. I could not imagine a reason why she would not be. My heart fluttered. *How will she take the news that I'm married—and to a rune-writer, no less?*

"Are you ready to see her?" Thomas whispered, patting my hand as it gripped his arm.

I nodded enthusiastically. Nathan threw us a questioning look but said nothing. I had considered letting him in on my secrets at some point... but now was not that time.

Guards and the promised rune-writers stood around the royals, parting for us to join them. Queen Eleanora wore a silver dress with a long train that seemed to shimmer in the sunlight and all sorts of jewellery that matched her crown. Long, elegant silver gloves covered past her elbows. She turned to look at me with a bright smile. "Come, Isabela! I want you to stand near me when we meet the princesses."

Her sons stood side by side from oldest to youngest off to the Queen's right, and she motioned for me to be at her left.

"Come, Thomas, Nathaniel, you can stand near Isabela. No reason for you to be behind us like servants." When we were all situated to her liking, the Queen bobbed her head in approval. "Pleasant smiles and voices, everyone. We want to make an excellent first impression."

I held my hands against my ribcage to keep from fidgeting. We watched in silence as the procession of seven carriages arrived. The drivers hurried to open the doors and help the passengers. The first of the princesses was Consuela—I could tell by the flowers braided into her hair, the various pastel-coloured petals that went well with her light pink dress. The number of flowers made it almost difficult to see the silver tiara peeking between them. As the oldest of the sisters, she walked with her head held high, taking the lead with grace and dignity befitting one of her status.

Princesses Francisca and Inés came next with their hourglass figures so flawless that it made my torso hurt just thinking of how tight their corsets had to be. They picked up their pace slightly to catch up to Consuela but stayed two steps behind her.

Trying to adjust her dress, Beatriz followed behind Camila. Although Beatriz was only fourteen, she could have passed for seventeen or eighteen, especially with the help of cosmetics and the choice of a curve-hugging gown that drew the eye.

But Camila naturally drew the eye of everyone regardless of what she wore, and today was no exception: even as a young girl, Camila always fit what I thought a *princesa* from a fairy-tale should look like. Her dazzling smile could melt even the iciest of hearts, not to mention a mere glance from those grey eyes left men speechless and tripping over themselves. I had seen it happen before on multiple occasions and knew, for a fact, that Camila was fully aware of her power over people.

Not only that, she thrived on it.

As I suspected, Camila wore her signature colour: red. This time it was a shade of scarlet, a darker hue than her sisters' bright and pale gowns. Where the rest of them wore more attention-grabbing pieces of jewellery, Camila chose dainty pieces. "I am the one on display," she liked to say. "They accentuate my beauty, not the other way around."

I heard one of the princes inhale as Camila drew closer and take her place beside her sisters.

"Welcome," Queen Eleanora greeted. "It is our pleasure to have you here. *Nosotros estamos contentos de que estés aquí.*"

Consuela beamed. "Thank you for your invitation. We look forward to getting to know you."

"Will the king be joining us?"

"He will be here for the ball," Consuela said in a thick accent, taking time to recall the words. "The last carriage is our…" She looked to Camila, who answered, "It has our belongings."

Camila and I briefly exchanged looks, and I noted the slight widening of her eyes, the only response she showed before settling back into her royal persona.

"Very well, we look forward to his arrival. In the meantime, we shall have servants fetch your things and take them to your rooms." The Queen gestured to me. "May I present a spell-caster from your country, Miss Isabela Fuerte. She will help translate if the need should arise."

If my other cousins recognised me, it was not obvious.

The Queen introduced her sons in turn, and Consuela introduced herself and her sisters. With everyone surveying the others, I started to make mental notes of who seemed interested in whom until I realised that Nathan and Camila had their gazes locked on one another.

"Isabela belongs to the Grahms, one of our most prestigious rune-writer families. These are Lord Grahm's sons, Thomas and Nathaniel. They go where Isabela goes, so they will be present for all activities." Queen Eleanora motioned, and some servants rushed forward to deal with the princesses' belongings. "The servants will show you to your rooms so that you can get settled. I'm sure you wish to rest after your long journey, so there is no need to rush yourselves. I will send attendants to inform you when dinner is ready."

We went upstairs into a wing of the palace I had yet to see. The stretch of halls between the doorways told me that each room had to be as big as a small house in the countryside. When we came to Camila's designated room, she asked, "Miss Fuerte, may I borrow you? I would like to ask a few questions."

"Of course," I answered with a dip of my head.

The princes' eyes lingered on Camila as the servants led them away to find Beatriz's room. Thomas and Nathan stayed, which made Camila raise her brow. "I will return her shortly."

"We go where she goes, as the Queen said and our father dictated," Nathan replied with a smirk. "Just following orders, *Princesa*."

"They know," I told Camila quickly before she could form a reply. "Well, Thomas knows, and Nathan is bound to find out. I was planning on telling him sooner or later."

"Tell me what?"

I threw Nathan a warning look. Sighing, Camila urged us inside and shut the door. "Stay here," she commanded Thomas and Nathan before pulling me from the sitting room to her bedroom. As I suspected, everything was spotless and much larger than necessary, most items edged in gold or made of it. If we wanted, all of us could sleep comfortably on her puffy white bed full of pillows of assorted sizes.

Camila embraced me tightly. "I was so worried," she said quietly in our native language. "When I did not hear from you, I had no idea what to think, what to do." She let go, examining me up and down like a mother checking her child. She lifted my wrist to get a closer look at it. "They marked you?"

"They are rune-writers," I replied. "I would be more surprised if they didn't."

"Are you well? Do I need to find you a way out? I can sneak you out of here when I leave—"

"Camila—"

"I'm serious! Whatever you need, I'll make it happen. They'll have no idea where to find you, and—"

I gripped her hands. "Camila, I do not want to leave."

Camila paused, pursing her lips. "You fell in love with the tall one."

My jaw dropped. "How did you know?"

"What else would keep you here when you so desperately wanted freedom?" She smiled and shook her head. "And I cannot see you falling for the overly confident one..." Her eyes drifted toward the entryway, where Thomas and Nathan waited. "...although I will say that his confidence is warranted. I've never seen such a gorgeous man."

"Camila!"

"What? I'm just looking. There's nothing wrong in that. Besides, he has no clue what I am saying." She held my hands. "I am so glad to know you are safe. If you change your mind, you know I will help you."

"I won't be changing my mind," I assured her. "He and I… got married last week. In secret."

"*¡Dios mío!*" Camila sighed heavily. "What am I going to do with you? You have been gone a month and I find you married to a man you barely know. I told you not to let those fairy-tale books get into your head." She flicked my forehead.

"*¡Ay!* I know what's real and what's not, Camila," I snapped. "I'm not a child, I can make my own decisions. Just because it happened fast doesn't mean it's not real."

Camila crossed her arms. "I just don't want to see you hurt, *prima*."

That took all the fight out of me. "I love him, Camila. And Thomas loves me."

After a moment of awkward silence, Camila hugged me. "You know I will always support you."

I squeezed her gently as though that would make up for all the time we'd lost since I left. "I know. Come, let's catch up out there. Nathan and Thomas should hear everything too."

Chapter Thirty

Thomas

Understanding

"What do you suppose they're discussing?" Nate asked, leaning to look through the entryway. I tugged his sleeve. "Hey! I bet you're just as curious as I am. Do you know how they know each other?"

"That is Isabela's story to tell."

He perked up. "So you do know!"

"She is my wife, Nate: she tells me lots of things." I still was not used to the term, but I liked how it sounded to my ears.

"You've been married for what, a few days?" Nate scoffed.

"Doesn't matter. And don't even consider going after the princesses. They are off-limits."

Nate grinned and stuck his hands into his pockets. "If one of them falls in love with me, that can hardly be my fault, and it would be rude to turn her down or ignore her."

Isabela's voice rose, saying, "Camila!" before continuing in their language. They spoke so quickly that even if they were only using phrases we had used in the princes' lessons, I still would've had no idea what they were saying.

Then Camila cried out something, speaking loudly and rapidly as if ranting, and Isabela returned in kind.

The sudden silence was off-putting.

Finally Isabela responded in a soft tone, and I heard my name briefly, making me wonder what she had told Camila about me. A few more sentences were exchanged, and then the women returned to the room.

"Please, sit," bade Camila, gesturing to the ostentatious couches set around a small wood table with a vase of freshly cut flowers. "Isabela wishes to tell us her whole story so that we are all well-informed." She spoke eloquently, although her accent was slightly more noticeable than Isabela's. Granted, I had spent so much time with Isabela as of late that I had to consider that I started to become used to it.

As Camila sat on the other side of Isabela, I noticed the small features that told the tale of their familial relationship: the shape of their eyes, the slenderness of their frames, the curve of their jaws, the similar hues of their hair. All subtle things for those paying close attention to draw the connection.

Isabela took a few moments to breathe and gather her thoughts. Her hands fidgeted in her lap. She spoke quietly at first, telling of her heritage, and Nate, to his credit, listened without a word, his eyes on her, the raising of his brows the only sign of his surprise. Then, when it came time to explain what had happened since Camila had last seen her, it was the princess's turn to take in everything.

"Someone is trying to *kill* you?" Camila hissed.

"It is a theory," I cut in. "We cannot be certain, but it is a possibility."

"A strong one," Nate added, settling into a more comfortable position on the couch. "One we are not taking lightly."

Camila's soft grey eyes bore into mine. "I should hope that you are taking none of this lightly. Should anything happen to my cousin, I will hold you responsible."

"I cannot bear the thought," I replied. "Should anything happen to Isabela, I would hold myself responsible and expect you to dole out punishment as you see fit."

The corner of her mouth twitched upward. "Perhaps, Mr Thomas Grahm, I may come to like you one day, may even count you as a friend. But you must understand that I will hold you to your word, and as of right now, I do not know you, nor do I trust you. Isabela is my *familia*, and I will do whatever it takes to protect one of my blood."

The gleam in her eyes might have made me more nervous had I had a reason to truly be nervous. "I understand, Princess."

Camila turned her attention to Isabela. "He seems to be a good pick, *prima*. You be good to him."

"I am."

"She can get back to being very good to him once they can publicly announce their nuptials," Nate said, warranting a look from me. "What? I mean to remind everyone here that we have to keep this a secret until after the ball. I figured this was as good a time as any, considering that Isabela wanted everything on the table. It keeps us in the same state of mind."

Pink rose in Isabela's cheeks, no doubt mirrored in my own.

"Then we have a few more days," Camila said. "What is your plan after that?"

I said, "First we tell my parents. Then we figure out which path to take depending on their response to the news."

Camila huffed through her nose. "I take it marrying a spell-caster is as frowned upon here as it is in our homeland." She scowled. "I will not allow you to be homeless. Whatever I can do to help, I will, although I will have to be discreet. My father is not of the mind to help spell-casters. There is a reason we've kept her heritage secret for so long... Although I do ask one request of you."

"A request?" Isabela asked, tilting her head to the side with a small smile. "I should have known there would be a price to pay."

"Come now, *prima*, you must know I want you to have another wedding ceremony so that I can attend and give you one any woman would be jealous of. The first one sounds like it was intimate and sweet, but we must have a celebration and get you a dress to make you look like a princess from one of those books you love to read."

"Camila—"

"Do not argue with me. You will love it, I promise, and I will pay for it. You deserve the extravagant wedding of your dreams, and I deserve to be there to help you celebrate. Besides, it gives me an excuse to have a new specially-made gown—but I'll be sure that it does not outshine yours."

Isabela rolled her eyes.

"I am not sure who all would attend," I pointed out.

"Anyone who is worth knowing would," Camila said. "You are to become a lord at some point, yes? Upper classes show off their wealth and prestige through parties and displays. This is the perfect way to do just that while silently telling everyone that if they do not like that Isabela is a spell-caster, they will have to learn to live with it."

"I'm for the princess's idea," Nate said as if someone had asked his opinion. "Let them grind their teeth to dust and shake their fists until they fall off. Sounds like it will be a grand party."

"Thank you for your help, Princess," I said sincerely.

Camila reached over and squeezed Isabela's hand. "Thank you for making her happy."

I grinned. "I hope I always will."

Chapter Thirty-One

Isabela

Interest

As the Queen had said, an attendant fetched us for dinner a little while later, enough time for Camila to change into a different red dress and freshen up. This one was more fitted all the way down to mid-thigh before the tulle skirts widened in a small circle around her. She painted her lips to match the colour of her dress.

Nathan offered his arm to Camila, who hesitated before accepting it. As we walked to the dining room, Nathan said, "You know, I practiced learning how to say my name in your language, and then the Queen introduced me before I had the chance."

Here we go, I thought, rolling my eyes. Thomas smothered a chuckle by pretending to cough.

Camila raised a neatly plucked brow at Nathan. "Well then, indulge me."

He leant closer to her. *"Mi nombre es Nataniel, princesa hermosa."*

Not quite fluent sounding, but it was not bad… and I did not recall teaching him how to call her "beautiful."

Camila flashed him a smile. "Perhaps we can work on that later, *Nataniel.*" She drew out the syllables of his name, his eyes fixated on every movement of her mouth.

It was a dangerous game they played, and I was not sure who, if anyone, would win. Both of them ending up broken-hearted seemed most likely, even if they would refuse to show it. Thomas gave me a knowing look. If I fell in love and got married in a month and Camila supported me, then I could support her if she chose to pursue Nathan. After all, what were good friends for if not being there for you even when you make seemingly horrible, ill-thought-out choices?

Everyone else was already seated by the time we arrived, all of them watching us. They stood briefly to acknowledge us, all except for Queen Eleanora. The guards and rune-writers waited outside of the dining room—as were August's hounds, apparently moping at not being invited to dinner.

"Did Isabela help you with everything you needed, Princess Camila?" asked Queen Eleanora.

"Yes, Your Highness," Camila answered as Nathan pulled out her chair for her. "You are fortunate to have such a helpful spell-caster in your employ."

"She has, indeed, been very helpful. Are the accommodations to your liking, princesses?"

"Everything is perfect," Consuela said on behalf of herself and her sisters. "Thank you, Your Majesty."

Servants stepped forward to pile our plates with food and fill our glasses with a dark wine. When they attempted to pour it into my glass, I placed my hand over it. "Water for me."

I felt all of the eyes on me, knew the questions forming in their heads even before the Queen asked, "Do you not care for wine, Isabela?"

"Spell-casters use magic with their minds," I answered carefully. "I prefer to keep my wits about me."

"Helpful and wise," mused the Queen. "Get her water," she said to the servants, who had been standing there looking back and forth between Queen Eleanora and me.

They quickly obeyed.

"If I may," August said, "what hobbies do you lovely ladies enjoy?"

Noting the confusion in most of their faces, I opened my mouth to translate for them, but Camila stepped up, saying, "Consuela likes to tend to the flowers in our garden. She has a keen eye for detail, and so *Mamá* often lets her decorate the castle, especially when we host parties."

Consuela nodded as if satisfied with what bits and pieces she understood.

"We like to sing," Francisca said, gesturing to herself and Inés. "Although she prefers the…" She frowned, pursing her lips. *"¿Ópera? ¿Cómo se dice, Camila?"*

Camila shook her head and looked to me for help.

"Opera," I told them, remembering how often Francisca dragged her sisters to the performances. Both sisters had beautiful voices, but the incessant singing of the same songs was enough to drive a person mad.

"Opera," Francisca repeated, sounding out the word. "Inés prefers to sing opera music, and I prefer soft, pretty songs."

Inés huffed, taking a sip of wine. "I also like to paint."

"What types of things do you paint?" asked Robert, taking us all by surprise. He and Inés locked gazes.

"I am sorry," she replied. "I do not understand your question."

Camila explained in our language. They conversed for a moment, Inés asking Camila to answer for her.

"She will paint anything that will sit still long enough for her. Many of her paintings are hung throughout the castle."

"Perhaps we could paint together in my studio," Robert suggested, his face becoming blotchy. Camila translated, and Inés beamed.

"I would love to," Inés answered.

"Very good," Robert said quietly, ducking his head.

Nathan smirked, and before he could make a comment, Camila said, "To finish answering your earlier question, Prince August, Beatriz—"

"I like animals," Beatriz cut off her sister. "Horses are my favourite, and the easiest to train."

"We shall have to make a trip to the stables then," said Herbert. "Mother breeds the most beautiful purebred horses for racing and shows."

Beatriz's dark eyes lit up, and then she schooled her features into more of a calm state befitting a princess as she adjusted her posture. "That would be most delightful."

"And what of you, Princess Camila?" August asked.

"I like fashion and parties, especially balls," Camila replied. "I find they often go hand-in-hand."

"It is a good thing we have a ball soon." He did not look away from her as he took a bite of his food.

"Indeed." Camila turned away from him to sneak a not-so-secret peek at Nathan, who did nothing to hide the grin on his face but at least had the decency to not look at August smugly. If Camila set them up against each other on purpose…

"Are you staying the night as well?" August asked pointedly at Nathan.

"I am afraid not, Your Highness," Thomas said quickly. "We have duties to attend at the manor."

"How unfortunate. Well, we shall be seeing more of you this week, so no matter."

As the rest of the dinner carried on, my stomach knotted, watching as August sized up Nathan while Nathan did not deign to even look his direction. When dinner ended, I tried not to appear too eager to leave. After saying our goodbyes, we three managed to almost make it to the front door before August caught up to us.

"I hope you do not mind if I borrow Nathaniel for a moment."

"Whatever you have to say to me, Your Highness, I am sure Thomas and Isabela can hear." Nathan stuck his hands into his pockets and lifted his chin.

August pressed his lips together in a thin line. Keeping his voice low, he said, "I will ask this of you only once: you are not to get in the way of us pursuing the princesses. Would a friend take another friend's chance at happiness?"

A muscle in Thomas's arm twitched under my hand.

"I will adhere to that rule just as you have," Nathan returned, dipping his head mockingly, a flash of anger in his eyes.

August puffed out his chest as understanding dawned on him, but Camila joined us more quickly than I'd ever expected someone in that type of dress could have.

"There you are!" she said. "Prince August, I was hoping you would give me a tour of the palace, especially the ballroom." She looped her arm through his. "It was good to meet you," Camila said to us, eyeing Nathan with a smile. "I look forward to your next visit."

"Goodnight, Your Highnesses," Nathan said, and we repeated him.

"Goodnight," August said in response, a smile curling at his lips as Camila pulled him away, asking him all sorts of questions. Checking over her shoulder, she mouthed *Go, hurry.*

Outside in the brisk night air, Thomas said, "Nate, you really are about to land yourself in a lot more trouble than I'll be able to bail you out of."

With a toothy smile that reminded me how much charm he had at his disposal, Nathan replied, "I know. But, Maker help me, I can't stop myself, and I wouldn't even if I could."

Chapter Thirty-Two

Thomas

Early the next morning, before we could even dress fully and fix our hair, Father called Nate and me into his study and shut the door. Nate and I exchanged confused glances, and I wished my heart would stop racing as I thought of what could warrant this.

Father did not bother to sit. He paced in front of us for a bit, hands clasped behind his back. I fought to keep from fidgeting, the only sound the ticking of the clock on the mantle.

"We Grahms have a reputation to uphold," Father said finally, stopping to face us. "I have been pondering Lord Baskers's words and all of the stories I hear about my sons and their foolhardiness. I had thought that, with how well you two behave around our new spell-caster, you might be maturing, learning the real meaning of taking pride in our family name."

I sneaked a glance at Nate, who kept his gaze on the carpet. For once, I had no clue what he was thinking.

"Then I hear of you meeting a young lady at a hotel at night? Whatever were you thinking, Nathaniel?" Father questioned, his tone rising. "I cannot even bear to tell your mother for fear of her spiralling into one of her emotional fits."

Nate's throat bobbed. I waited for him to look at me like he always did. He didn't.

"And you," Father said to me. "You cannot even keep your younger brother out of trouble. What makes you think that you will be fit to take on the title of lord when I pass it on to you if you cannot even keep him in line? I cannot imagine how you would run this manor into the ground if you continue in this way. Do the two of you ever think about the repercussions of your actions?"

"I am sorry, Father," I said quietly, and Nate parroted me, his voice barely audible.

Father looked back and forth between the two of us, arms crossed over his broad chest. I supposed with the fact that I was taller than he was by a good head or so, I should not have found him nearly as intimidating as I did, but the presence Father exuded made me want to slink away and disappear.

"Stop slouching, Nathaniel."

Nate straightened instantly.

"Perhaps marrying you off would do you some good, help you mature into men. It's high time we found wives for the two of you."

I blanched; Nate tensed.

"I'll ask your mother to find you suitable matches to speak with at the ball." Father stepped toward me, tapping my chest, a strange look on his face. "I would have thought this rune would have worked by now."

I said nothing, silently praying to the Maker that Father could not see the panic in my eyes.

His mood shifted unexpectedly. "I am sorry about Abigail," Father said softly, almost tenderly, "but it is time to move on. Or, if you wish, you might be able to try again with her. It seemed as though, at our dinner party, she was singing of your lost love. She may be open to courtship once more."

The thought soured my stomach. It took me a moment longer than it should have to realise he was waiting for a response. "I have no desire to court Miss Collins again."

Father patted my shoulder. "Then we shall find you another woman to love you the way you deserve." He placed his other hand on Nate's shoulder and squeezed us. "We will work through this, my sons. I remember what it was to be young and want to be free of rules and duties, but you are boys no longer: you are men, bearers of the Grahm name. I know you will not disappoint me again."

"Yes, Father," we answered in unison.

"Good." He released us and took a step back. "I'll be sure to tell your mother to find you suitable matches at once, and then you can make your decisions at the end of the ball." He opened the door and called for Archibald, telling him to inform our mother to make a list of eligible ladies for us to court. Then he shooed us from the study so that we could get ready for breakfast.

This ball will definitely be one to remember, I thought.

Nate finally locked eyes with me. "Looks like we're getting into more trouble than we can handle together."

"Aye," I agreed. "But you have one saving grace: Father will probably be so furious with me that he'll forget about you."

A small smile. "Let's hope so."

I elbowed him, and he chuckled, doing it back.

"Maker help us," Nate said, shaking his head.

We split off to our bedrooms, and for a moment, I considered going to Isabela's, imagining what it would be like to wake her...

A horrible idea. The temptation to join her in bed would be too great to turn down. Just one more day was all we had left, and we could make it as long as I kept my head on straight and did not let my mind wander to those places.

Any lingering notions of going to Isabela fled when I found my mother sitting at the chair near my window. The only time Mother ever left her room in her nightgown, robe, and slippers was when she had one of her "emotional fits" as Father so delicately put them. No cosmetics—even her hair was loose and mussed, soft curls going every which way about her shoulders. She toyed with something in her hands, the blanket in her lap blocking my view of it.

"Shut the door, Thomas," she said softly.

I had to will my hands not to shake as I obeyed her. "Good morning, Mother. Is something the matter?" My voice came out surprisingly calm and even. With careful steps, I drew closer to her, being sure to keep a little distance.

Her grey eyes left the window to settle upon me, the expression on her face enough to make my heart twist painfully.

"How far has it gone between you and the spell-caster?"

It felt like the floor was being pulled out from underneath me. "What?"

There was no hint of anger in her voice as she said, "I see how you two interact. I know you care for her." A ghost of a humourless smile haunted her mouth. "The new attire for the ball came in—the tailor sent them a few days ago. I thought to have the dress set up on the mannequin to surprise her when you returned from your meeting at the League…" Her lips pressed together. "When I went to retrieve it from the back of her closet, I found the rose you clearly made for her. The runes are yours: I recognize the linework." Her hands stilled. "So, I ask you again, son, and please, be frank with me: how far has it gone between you and Isabela?"

I stood there, frozen, words failing me. Whatever was in her hands was too small, too easily hidden, to be the rose. I could not, for the life of me, figure out what she held, my mind scrambling to figure out what else she could possibly have as evidence that I overlooked.

Nate was so much better at things like this than I ever was.

"Please, darling," Mother said, "do not keep secrets from me. Let me be a part of this. I feel as though I am no longer a part of your and Nathaniel's lives. I do not know if it is that you fear your father so much that you feel it is safer to hide everything from the both of us, but I…" Her voice faltered. "Thomas, I love you. I only want you to be happy, to be a part of your life and your happiness. Whatever is happening, let me help you."

"Mother, I…" I found it hard to swallow, found my mouth too dry. "I promise, I will tell you everything, but please, can you wait until after the ball?"

"The ball," she repeated, her head tilting to the side slightly. I waited, watching her ponder the meaning behind my words. "You fear your father will be rid of her if he knows. He will not be able to send her away if he has already made the announcement." When I said nothing else, she added, "I promise not to tell your father—I will let you tell him. But, please, my darling, tell me how far this has gone. I heard a rumour that one of the lords of the League witnessed you and Isabela leaving a hotel in the capital the night you claimed Queen Eleanora asked you to stay late. Your father is convinced it had to do with Nate, but we both know that he is better at hiding his misadventures than you are."

I glanced at the clock on the dresser, knowing that we would be sought out soon if we were not having breakfast with the rest of the household.

"Did you at least marry her first?" Mother inquired. "Did you make an honest woman of her?"

Unable to find my voice, I nodded. My cheeks burned like they were going to melt off my face.

A mixture of relief and resignation crossed her features. "I would have liked to have been a part of the wedding," she whispered, tears lining her eyes. "To share in the joy with you." She bowed her head. Hesitantly, I went to her, kneeling so that I could wrap my arms around her.

"We shall host another ceremony, and you can help plan it," I promised, my voice so thick with emotion that it was hard to get the words out. "I never meant to hurt you, Mother."

"I know." She kissed my cheek, one hand reaching up to rub my back. "My sweet, darling boy, all grown up and married." She lifted the other hand, and I moved back to see what she had in it: a silver ring bearing a large diamond with small diamonds and sapphires extending out to either side of the band, making them look like little bits of starlight with the sun coming in through the window to reflect off of them. I remembered seeing it as a young boy when Nate and I were told to stop rifling through things we found in our parents' room… and to never *ever* play a game of treasure hunt with real jewellery again.

"This was my mother's ring," she said almost inaudibly, a small smile on her face despite the tears. She looked me in the eye as she put the ring in my hand and closed my fingers over it. "Give it to Isabela after the ball, after we tell your father. Since she is a part of the family, she should have a family heirloom… and a proper ring. Although the rose is beautiful."

I kissed her forehead and managed to say, "Thank you, Mother."

"Anything for you, sweetheart."

It took a few moments for me to gather up the courage to ask, "It does not bother you that she is a spell-caster?"

She smiled again. "What I think does not matter. You have made your choice, and I will love whomever you love, even if it takes me some time to adjust to the idea." Mother huffed a small laugh. "I think you will receive enough of a tongue lashing from your father when the time comes—you need someone in your corner other than Nathaniel. I love the boy, but your father will not hear a word he says, given his reputation." She moved to stand, so I got out of her way, offering her a hand, which she took with thanks. "I should dress so we can get to breakfast before someone is sent to find us." Then she added, "Tell me if you need anything. I will help you."

I pressed a kiss to her cheek, and we hurried to prepare for the day.

Chapter Thirty-Three

Isabela

Charm

"Breakfast this morning was odd," I commented to Thomas and Nathan. Herbert and Claude, dressed in riding outfits, led horses from the stables so that Francisca and Beatriz could admire them up close. They were majestic beasts, with beautiful, glossy copper coats and sleek, powerful muscles evident in each movement.

That still would not convince me to get close to them or ride them unless I absolutely had to.

Robert and Inés were the only ones not with us, instead opting to stay in his art studio to paint. With a rune-writer there to chaperone and guard them, of course, just as we had two of them outside with us. They had been all smiles and blushes this morning as Inés spoke of the piece they were working on together.

"Which part?" Nathan scoffed, his eyes every so often drifting to where Camila and August leant against the horse fence and chatted. "Breakfast with Father is always odd, and the meeting made it all the stranger."

"Meeting? What meeting?" I looked to both of them for answers. They grimaced.

"Father decided that our actions are unbecoming of Grahm men, especially after the incident at the hotel," Thomas answered. "He wants us to choose someone to court by the end of the ball tomorrow. He hopes that will end our misbehaviour."

"Unlikely," Nathan said. "I make no promises." He turned away from August and Camila just as she laughed at something August said. I considered telling him it was her fake laugh but decided to let him figure it out for himself. If Nathan wanted to win Camila's affections, he would have to work for them without any help.

It was more fun that way anyway.

"Oh… well, that makes sense as to why your parents were so invested in talking about potential brides for the two of you. Or, at least, your father was. Your mother seemed to be trying to say whatever would appease him so that she could eat her breakfast in peace."

Thomas cleared his throat. "Mother knows everything."

Nathan and I gaped at him.

"Have you gone mad?" Nathan demanded to know. "What possessed you to tell her anything? We have one day left, Tom. One!" He held up a finger to emphasise his point—thankfully it was his index and not another like I expected.

"Keep your voice down," Thomas hissed. "We don't want to draw attention to ourselves."

"That's rich, coming from the one who just told one of the worst possible people to tell! You are bloody barmy if you think she won't tell Father."

Thomas lowered Nathan's hand. "She promised she would keep it a secret and let me tell Father."

"And you believed her?"

"I had no choice, Nate: she found the rose."

"She found it?" I interrupted. "Why was she going through my closet?"

"What rose?" Nathan asked. "How in the world does a rose clue anyone into anything?"

At the moment, no one else was paying attention to us, so I tried to keep my expression neutral as I awaited Thomas's answer.

"I proposed to Isabela with it, put a rune on it so that it would last forever. Mother went looking for the mannequin to show off Isabela's ballgown, and she found it. I suppose I have not been quite as secretive with my affections as I thought, according to Mother."

"That much is obvious," Nathan sighed, running a hand through his hair. "I'm almost shocked Father has yet to catch on. If he were not so self-absorbed, I'm sure he would have."

"You noticed," I said without thinking.

He smirked. "I may be self-absorbed, but I'm not daft. If you aren't aware of others and what is happening around you, something will come along to bite you in the arse." The tension in his shoulders went away. "Alright, let's have it then: what's the new plan, according to good ol' Mother Dearest?"

"Nothing new to add to the plan," answered Thomas. "She's rather put out that she didn't get to attend the wedding, so she wants to be a part of planning the ceremony and party Princess Camila requested."

"I'll see what I can do to persuade her," I said. I could convince her to relent at least a little control. Maybe. Hopefully.

Nathan shook his head and checked on Camila once more. She

adjusted her parasol, watching as the princes attempted to help her sisters onto the horses. One of the rune-writers ran to aid them while Consuela called out some tips to Francisca, who snapped back that she knew all of that already.

"I would've thought you'd be over there charming Camila," I said to Nathan, open to a change of subject. There was too much to worry about going wrong that I felt I'd end up pulling my hair out if I let myself think about it any more than I had to.

"My charm has no limits," Nathan replied. "It can reach her from over here. Besides, it will be much more satisfying to see the look on August's face when she walks away from him to talk with me."

"You're incorrigible." I shook my head.

"Why change my methods if they work?"

"Your methods only work because you are attractive."

Nathan grinned at me. "You're admitting that I'm attractive?"

"Easy, Nate," said Thomas.

"Don't get your knickers in a knot, Tom. This is all objectively speaking, of course. I'm just curious if I would've had a chance with Isabela had I not been bladdered. Too much alcohol threw me off my game, methinks."

"I doubt I'd have given you more than a bit of conversation had you been your usual charming self," I told him. "If you had gotten handsy with Camila like you did me, she would have knocked you unconscious."

"You nearly did," Nathan said. "Glad to finally be rid of that bruise. Mother made the servants put powders on my face to cover the blasted thing."

I smiled at him. "If you are looking for regret or an apology, you'll find none here."

Nathan chuckled, turning to look at the horses but keeping Camila in his peripherals.

"Pardon me," said a voice from behind us. We turned to see a rune-writer approach, the one who had requested lessons for his daughter. Not very tall, the man barely surpassed my height, but there was a kindness to his eyes and an unassuming nature to his demeanour that made me want to listen to him. "I was asked to retrieve everyone for lunch."

"Why did the Queen not send an attendant?" asked Nathan.

"She has every spare hand preparing and setting everything up for the ball."

"Thank you for telling us," Thomas said. "How did your daughter's interview fare, Lord Johannes?"

"The Elite… agreed to teach Georgiana with some stipulations." His mouth twitched as though he was attempting to smile but his body would not allow him to lie. "She will be housed in the wing with Henrietta, who is not overly fond of the idea. They do not want her to learn to fight, so they think she will be best suited as Henrietta's assistant and eventual replacement. If that does not work, they plan on training her as a healer."

"What does Georgiana think of all of this?" I asked.

Lord Johannes looked me in the eye. "Honestly, Miss Fuerte, she is not happy with their decision, but she is learning to make do with what is given to her."

"Then I hope she changes their minds."

This time his smile was real. "As do I, Miss Fuerte. As do I. If you will excuse me, I must inform the others."

"I like him," I said as soon as he was out of earshot.

"He and Tom are the only good ones out of the rune-writers," Nathan said.

"Not going to include yourself?" questioned Thomas.

"We all know I'm too much of a mischief-maker to be described as 'good.'"

"And here comes more trouble."

I looked over as Thomas spoke, noting that Camila was headed our way, August catching up to her to offer his arm. She waved him off, showing that she could not hold the parasol, her skirts, and take his arm at the same time.

"Right on schedule," Nathan commented, trying to wipe the grin from his face.

"Masters Grahm, Miss Fuerte," Camila said, only making eye contact with Nathan, "will you be joining us for lunch?"

"If that would please you, Your Highness," Nathan said.

"It would." She smiled, one of her dimples starting to show.

"Then we had best not keep Mother waiting," suggested August as he led Camila back toward the palace.

Chapter Thirty-Four

Thomas

Suspicion

It was the day of the ball. Isabela and I had mere hours left to pretend until we could make the announcement ourselves and finally be rid of all of the secrets, to finally live in the open as husband and wife.

Even though I had been dressed and ready for the ball for nearly an hour, I kept checking my appearance and tapping my vest pocket to ensure the ring was still there. I was unused to this suit, given that it had been tailor-made for this event. Tonight, we were not rune-writers—we were the Grahm family, prestigious and proud, looking like we belonged to the upper class. Nevertheless, I hid a pocketknife in my jacket and gave up on finding a space for a pistol. The chance of the attackers coming to the ball was a decent one in my opinion, so I would at least have myself somewhat armed. Leaving our fates in the hands of others did not sit well with me.

Someone knocked on my door, and Father came in, looking me up and down. "You and Nathaniel both readied very quickly." He stared at my face, making my heart hammer against my ribcage. "You have so much of your mother in you—both of you boys do. They say that children look like both of their parents, but I have a hard time finding myself in either of you."

I swallowed hard and tried to put some sort of smile upon my face that did not make me look as ill as I felt.

"Ah, well, cannot be helped." A few micro-expressions crossed his features, none of which I could read, and then his face settled into one of vulnerability as he placed a hand on my shoulder. I tried not to flinch. "I know we can be at odds, you, Nathaniel, and I, but… but I want that to change. I want us to be a united family, to work together and love each other the way we should. I am sorry for the times I have made you and your brother feel like I am not proud to have you as my sons, because I am. Truly."

Unable to think of anything else to say, and still fighting the urge to squirm, I said, "Thank you, Father."

He smiled and pulled his hand away. "We will find you someone more suitable for a wife, I promise."

The words hit me like a dagger plunging into my chest and twisting. Did he know? He couldn't… No, he would be angry, shouting and throwing things against the walls. Was he speaking of Abigail?

"No need to be nervous," he said in what I guessed was supposed to be an assuring tone, but that did nothing to settle my nerves. "Everything will go just as planned, I promise. Now, could you and Nathaniel do me a favour? Your mother is in our room, feeling overwhelmed with everything, and could use her boys' help and support. You reach your mother's heart much more easily than I can."

"Yes, of course." I made another attempt at a smile.

"Good lad." He left, and I went to my parents' room to see Nate sitting on one of the chairs while Mother walked in from the bathroom, fully dressed and ready to leave. She beamed as I entered and hurried to hug me, which was a bit of a feat in and of itself with how wide around her ballgown was.

"My sons will be the most handsome men at the ball!" She took a step back to survey the two of us. "Why are you frowning, Thomas?"

"Father said you were overwhelmed and needed our help."

Her mood shifted, her face falling. "Nathaniel, go check on how the servants are doing with getting Isabela ready, please."

Mirroring the same look of concern on my face, Nate quickly obeyed. Mother shut the door behind him.

"What is going on? Did you tell him?" I said quietly, unable to keep the panic from sharpening my voice.

She went back to the bathroom, asking the servants to help Archibald be sure that they had everything together. As soon as they left, Mother took a deep breath and faced me. "He noticed that something is going on between the two of you and asked if I knew anything. I said I noticed the same thing, but I promise you, Thomas, that is all I said. He let it go, and I thought that was that."

"I have to find her, make sure she is all right."

Mother stopped me with a hand to my chest. "No. If he has not already figured it out, it will look suspicious if you storm through the house to find her. Nathaniel can take care of it."

My fists ached. "What if he does something to her?"

Mother opened her mouth to say something but closed it again, a look of apology on her face.

"I can't stay here and do nothing, Mother. Just let me check on her."

Nate opened the door, sparing her from replying. "Father insisted Isabela come downstairs with him, said there was something that needed to be done quickly before we left. He ordered Archibald to follow behind them."

Not bothering to wait for Mother's thoughts, I pushed past Nate. Without argument, Nate fell into step with me. We went to our practice room, noting on the way that Father's study was, indeed, shut, and no doubt locked. It only took a few moments to draw the spying rune and circle, but it was precious moments I was afraid we could not afford.

"Everything will be all right," Nate said, his tone coming out flat.

I said nothing. We both knew there was no guarantee when it came to Father.

The spying circle swirled into being, showing off Father's study. It looked just as neat as it always had.

With no one inside.

Nate and I exchanged looks. Smearing the wall enough to get rid of the evidence, we bolted toward the safe room. Servants bustled throughout the house, carrying items that we were to bring to the ball, and we dodged them, muttering apologies but not daring to stop.

My knife bit deeper than it should have in my haste. I didn't care, didn't slow down, just smeared my fingertips in the blood. I drew on the safe room door, not caring that my unlocking and opening runes looked like a child's scribbling. I felt the thrum of power on the door—his runes were already in effect, making any I put useless. Still I slammed my fist against the door when my runes faded, already feeling bruises forming on my knuckles.

"Dammit!" I tried again

And again

And again.

"Tom, stop." Nate tried to snatch my hand, but I yanked away to continue my mad scrawling. "Tom, I'll deal with this. You tell Mother."

"I can't leave her like this." The rune on my chest burned like a newly-made brand, and yet it still didn't compare to the agony of not being able to protect Isabela. *What is he doing to her?*

"Tom, you're not leaving her. You're trying to get help and avoid making things worse."

I kept at it. Blood spotted the floor at my feet.

Nate grabbed me by the shoulders and shoved me back, gripping me hard. "Get a hold of yourself! There is nothing we can do right now."

We panted. Stared one another down.

Nate released me and took a step back. "I'll try to fix this while you get Mother."

My body trembled uncontrollably. "I can't lose her, Nate," I said hoarsely.

Nate offered me a sympathetic expression. "I know. You won't. We won't let it happen, I swear."

Chapter Thirty-Five

Isabela

Obedience

The moment Lord Grahm brought me to the safe room instead of his study, I had to shove down my panic. Already I had been unsettled at his insistence and the way he ordered Archibald to walk behind us. Thomas and Nathan were nowhere to be seen, and I doubted that any of the servants would help me when that meant going against their employer.

"I thought we could give you some healing runes," Lord Grahm said as he opened the door to the safe room. "Your bandages take away from the beauty of your ballgown."

My bullet wound had healed well, but he was right: the straps of the gown held around my upper arms, baring my shoulders. With my half up hairstyle, the lower parts of my hair somewhat covered the bandages, but they were still very noticeable.

He gestured for me to go down the stairs first. "If your magic has any adverse effects to the healing runes, this will keep us much safer."

I took in a shaky breath. Archibald put a hand to my back, urging me forward.

"Come now, love," said Lord Grahm. "We do not want to be late to our own ball."

I am fearless. I am powerful. I am strong.

I lifted the hem of my dress and descended the stairwell. When I got halfway down, I heard the door shut, the echo of what felt like my impending doom, the final nail in the coffin.

Everything looked the same as it had before, save that wretched syringe lying near a stack of notes, the same one Lord Grahm had brought down here the last time. That, and a glass of what looked like water.

"Please sit, Miss Fuerte," Archibald said to me, motioning to the chair. "Lord Grahm will only be a moment."

I fought to keep my breathing even as I sat. My mind brushed the mental barrier to prepare myself to use magic. The magic slammed against it in response like a rude neighbour demanding they be let in immediately.

Lord Grahm finally joined us, wiping a bit of blood from his arm onto a handkerchief before folding and placing it in his suit pocket. "Blue is a good colour on you," he commented, surveying me up and down in a way that made my skin crawl. He took a vial of red liquid marked "G" from the table and took off the stopper, dipping his finger into it. "Archibald, remove Isabela's bandages."

Archibald's hands were cold, but my shivers were from something else entirely.

"This will not take long," Lord Grahm stated. Instead of coming to my side to deal with my shoulder, he leant over me. I turned my face away, my body instantly tensing. The scent of his pipe mixed with cologne turned my stomach, but not as much as the closeness in proximity to him. Unlike Thomas's gentle touch, Lord Grahm pressed hard as he drew, making my arm ache. I bit the inside of my cheek and fought against the tears stinging my eyes.

Upon completion of the rune, I felt the flesh knit back together. Lord Grahm straightened, then walked behind me, and I made to look at him. He took my head in his hands, forcing me to face forward, and moved my hair to the side.

"What are you doing?" I asked, my voice strained.

"Helping," was all he said in response as he drew another rune on the back of my neck. When he finished, he sniffed my hair, the sound loud in my ear. I started to stand, but he commanded, "Sit still." The rune on the back of my neck flared, and I stilled, unable to move. From my peripherals, I could see Archibald watching, his mouth closed tightly and his hands folded in front of him.

Lord Grahm put my hair back the way it was, covering the rune, and retrieved the wretched syringe. "Oh, before we get to this, how are your hands? Do they need healing runes as well?"

I tried to speak, but nothing happened—not a muscle twitched.

"Answer me."

This time when I tried, I managed to say, "They are healed," feeling like the words were dragged out of me. Even if my hands were not healed, I would not have allowed him to remove my gloves for fear of finding what was on my ring finger.

Not that I was able to fight back in this state.

"Good." Lord Grahm took my unruned wrist and wrapped a cloth snugly around my arm, making my veins bulge.

I tried to look away as the needle went in. Thankfully, it was just out of sight, but I did see when Lord Grahm raised the now full syringe to inspect it.

"Somehow," he said, "I thought your blood might look different than ours." He placed it into a container and sealed it. "This will be good research for the League." Picking up the glass of clear liquid, he said, "Drink this."

I instantly obeyed, my body not listening to anything I tried to make it do. I wanted to throw the glass, to flee, to use my magic to break the door so I could escape.

It tasted like water, but it left a strange fuzziness in its wake. I could hear a pounding that sounded like it was at the door, but neither of them moved to answer it.

"Lord Grahm, was that necessary? You could just order her."

"I want to be sure I get the truth," he snapped. "Now, Miss Fuerte: you are going to tell me everything that is happening between you and my son."

Chapter Thirty-Six

Thomas

Trapped

There was nothing we could do. Mother made me sit on her bed so she could remove my ruined gloves and put a salve on my bruised and bloodied knuckles. I barely registered the sting, could not feel anything other than an explosive mix of rage and panic.

"We will figure this out and make it right," Mother said.

"He is doing something to her."

She had no response other than the sorrow and fear filling her eyes.

"I cannot protect her."

Mother's shoulders slumped, her hands cupping either side of my face.

Nate came in and made sure to close the door behind him. "I got rid of the evidence of us trying to break in. All we can do is wait and try to undo whatever he's doing when we can." His gaze dropped to my hands but came right back up to my eyes. "I'm sorry, Tom."

"Thank you," was all I could bring myself to say.

"Nathaniel, fetch your brother another pair of gloves, please. Oh, and get rid of these."

Nate did so quickly, and then we three made our way downstairs to the foyer. Father and Archibald stood with Isabela near the front door. My chest tightened; I looked her over for any sign of harm and found none. Her dark blue ballgown fit her perfectly and matched her gloves.

Everything seemed styled just right down to the diamonds in her dangling earrings and the necklace that rested just above her collarbone—not even a hair was out of place. Yet her eyes... there was something off about her eyes despite the seemingly genuine smile on her face.

"Nathaniel, please escort Miss Fuerte to the carriage," Father ordered with a pleasant expression as he peered over at me. "What happened to the gloves you had on?"

"He tore them," Mother answered for me; I clenched my fists, welcoming the pain in my knuckles. "Nathaniel threw them out and found him another pair."

Nate hesitated before following Father's instruction. Isabela went with him without even a hint of disappointment or a glance my way.

Father tapped my shoulder and said, "We will find you a suitable woman tonight, son." He grabbed Mother's arm and pulled her along, leaving me to follow at the back.

I paused, looking to Archibald. "What did he do to her?"

"You know I cannot tell you that. Just know that he did it for your own good, Master Thomas." He offered me a sympathetic, grim smile. "Enjoy the ball."

Chapter Thirty-Seven

Isabela

all

Lord Grahm's orders and rune binding me, there was nothing I could do to warn Thomas or even calm him. I itched to embrace him, to kiss him, to tell him everything and ask him to run away with me. Instead, I sat beside Nathan in the carriage and walked with him into the palace when we reached the long line of those arriving for the ball. Nathan picked up his pace, and I matched it.

"What happened?" he asked in a whisper when we were far enough away from his parents and Thomas.

"Your father used a healing rune to fix my shoulder. It would not do to have a bulky bandage. It would have been rather unsightly." I gave him a smile, wishing I could wipe it off my face, desperately trying to make myself explain the rest.

The words refused to get past my throat.

His brow creased. "Where is the rune, Isabela?"

"Here," I told him, pointing to where my thin sleeves covered what was left of the fading healing rune.

"No. Where is the other rune—or runes—he put on you?"

My cheeks began to hurt from smiling. I was sure I looked like a bloody idiot.

"Nathaniel! Wait for us. We need to make our grand entrance together." Lord Grahm hurried to catch up to us, pulling along Lady

Grahm. Thomas walked behind them, a storm brewing in his eyes.

"I apologise," Nate said with a forced grin. "I might be a little too excited for the event, methinks."

"As we should be," Lord Grahm said. "Smiles, everyone."

Thomas did not bother to try.

"Face forward, Isabela," Lord Grahm urged me. "We do not want to dawdle."

I grit my teeth as we followed the stream of couples and groups making their way up to the entrance of the palace. There were double the normal amount of guards, as well as rune-writers, all very much alert. Attendants met us at the open doors and led us through the dimly lit ivy-covered hallways, the gas lamps turned low to help with the illusion of an enchanted forest. Petals of various flowers lay scattered upon the carpets leading up to the ballroom, which was also covered in them. Those already dancing had the petals dispersing with each twirl. Although it was brighter in there than the hallway, it was not by all that much, making it feel like the sun was setting. Plants and flowers of all sorts decorated the outer edges of the room and up the walls and even the ceiling, making me wonder just how much time and effort all of this took to create.

At the entryway, a herald announced, "Welcome our host of the evening, Lord Gerold Grahm, his wife Lady Marjorie Grahm, his sons Master Thomas Grahm and Master Nathaniel Grahm, and his spell-caster, Miss Isabela Fuerte!"

I found myself surprised that he had pronounced my name correctly, even though it was no longer my name...

Until the paperwork Lord Grahm made me sign went through. We still had time to stop it if I could find a way around the blasted rune on the back of my neck. He now knew about our marriage, our plans, even my identity and paternal heritage. The questions had kept coming, and I had been helpless to stop from answering them. All of them. While Archibald just watched. And Thomas and Nathan had been locked out, unable to save me.

I had no idea how, but I was determined to figure out a way to save myself.

And so help Lord Grahm when I did.

I am fearless. I am powerful. I am strong.

Everyone paused their dancing and conversation to look at us and clap as we joined the ball, resuming moments later, the orchestra segueing into an upbeat tune.

Queen Eleanora watched from her throne, a smile on her face as she checked on her sons and their dance partners. The only ones of the princes and princesses who had yet to dance, it seemed, were Claude, who was standing off to the side spectating, and August and Camila, who were chatting near the tables piled high with food and drink. As always, Camila wore her signature red, this time a gown that made the skirts look like elegant rose petals. She caught sight of us, confusion barely showing for a split second as she eyed me on Nathan's arm. I gave the tiniest shake of my head, hoping, praying, that she would understand that something was amiss.

"Go on now," said Lord Grahm, "revel in the festivities." Nathan released me, and his father pulled me toward him, whispering in my ear, "You are free to use your magic now." As if it could hear, magic railed against the barrier in my mind, threatening to crack it... but at least I now had it at my disposal if I needed it. Then, as he walked away with his wife, he added, "Drink some wine and enjoy yourselves!"

Unable to stop myself, I stalked toward a servant with a tray of red wine-filled glasses. I snatched one and downed it as though it were in a shot glass.

"Isabela!" Thomas hissed, pulling me away. "I thought you said you wanted to keep a level head, that you do not drink alcohol."

"Your father said to drink and enjoy the festivities." I took another, and Thomas managed to get it away from me with only a few drops lingering at the bottom.

"What did he do to you?" His hazel eyes sought mine as though he could find the answers.

"He healed my wounds with—"

"That's all you're going to get out of her," Nathan interrupted, replacing our empty glasses on the servant's tray so they were out of reach. He lowered his voice. "I have a horrible theory as to what could be wrong, but, if I'm right, it'll land dear ol' dad in prison at best and in the ground at worst."

Thomas looked between the two of us and guided me away from everyone else. "Isabela, please, tell us what happened." He cupped my hands with his, but I yanked them away. "What did he do to you?"

Damn all this smiling. My cheeks were really starting to hurt. "He healed my wound. You know, Thomas, we should really go find you a suitable woman to marry. Did you memorise the list your mother made?" The words spilled from my mouth, and I wanted to choke on them, my heart breaking as my traitorous eyes scanned the crowd for said women.

"Are you going to let me tell you my theory *now*?" Nathan asked in annoyance, crossing his arms. "Or are you going to wait until she punches you, tries to drink everything in this place, and sets you up with a new wife?"

Thomas glared at Nathan with an anger that we both knew was not toward his brother in the slightest.

"Obedience rune," Nathan said after checking that no one else was close enough to overhear.

"We have to get it off of her." Thomas reached toward me, and I smacked his hands away.

"She'll keep doing that. And you know as well as I that only he can take it off of her since he's the one who put it there in the first place."

"What is going on?" Camila approached, her steps not quite so quick as to draw attention but still hurried. "I only have a few minutes of Consuela talking August's ear off before he seeks me out again."

Nathan quickly filled her in; Thomas's hands trembled as he stared at me. It was almost as if I could feel his heart breaking alongside mine.

"What can we do to fix it?" Camila asked.

"We would have to turn Father over to the League, and they would make him remove it from her."

"Then what are you waiting for? Isabela's father is here, and he cannot see that his daughter is a spell-caster or else he'll take her back to Isouldia."

My mind whirled from both the new information and the alcohol.

"He cannot take her back—she is married to me, so he no longer has any claim over her."

"Do you honestly believe that the Queen will say no to the King's brother?" She shook her head, her loosely curled hair swaying. "We have to fix this and get her out of here before he notices, otherwise our chances will be slim to none." Camila glanced over with concern. "Is that your father talking with Uncle Esteban?"

"If Esteban is the gaudily-dressed man, then yes," Nathan answered.

"We have to stop them." Camila strode their direction, only to be intercepted by August. He clutched her hand, not letting go as she tried to pull herself free, and half-dragged her back toward the dance floor. Nathan darted toward them, Thomas calling after him to be careful.

My head swam; my stomach churned. I sprinted to the exit, hearing Thomas call my name, but neither stopped nor slowed my pace. Magic seeped in through the crack in my barrier. Glasses shattered, spilling wine all over the poor servant and attendees within a few-meter radius of me. I fled while they tried to clean up the mess.

The more magic that trickled into me, the more suffocated I felt, trying to catch my breath. I made it to the hall, relieved to see the main doors. Just a little further...

Flames leapt from my fingers, catching my dress and a bit of the ivy. I quickly put it out with the magic and tried to shove it back where it belonged, but the effort made me stumble. Hands steadied me; I looked up to see Thomas. I yanked out of his grip and ran.

"Isabela!"

Cool night air hit my cheeks as I made it past the guards and vomited on the lawn.

"Isabela!"

I lifted my hand to tell Thomas to stay away, but a blast of magic shot out and threw him backward. "Thomas…" My heart stopped as he hit the ground hard, his head barely missing the edge of the stone walkway.

The rune-writers and guards stepped toward us, but Thomas assured them he was fine as he got to his feet and slowly drew closer to me. Like I was a wild animal he couldn't trust to remain calm. Tears pricked at my eyes.

I'm not a monster…

Just as Thomas opened his mouth to say something, Nathan rushed out and tugged on his brother's sleeve.

"Camila got them apart. You talk to Father, try to get him to see reason, and I'll take care of Isabela."

I vomited again, falling to my knees as I tried to fight back against the magic and alcohol swirling together to work against me. Thomas locked eyes with me, the war within him apparent. I was not allowed to let him touch me, but Lord Grahm had said nothing about Nathan. Thomas must have come to that conclusion as well, because he whispered, "I love you. I will come back, I swear. We will figure this out."

I love you too, I wanted to say, wanted to beg him to stay and hold me and make me believe that everything was going to be all right.

Thomas reluctantly left, and Nathan neared me carefully. The grass beneath my hands withered, which he did not miss. "I am going to try to help," he said gently, slashing the back of his arm for blood and reaching for my forehead.

Chapter Thirty-Eight

Thomas

Convincing

My heart raced even more quickly than my feet as I made my way back into the ballroom. There had been a small spark of horror in Isabela's eyes when her magic threw me back and nearly made me hit my head on the stone walkway.

She was still in there—I would find a way to free her. Maker help my father and anyone else who dared stand in my way.

The orchestra segued into a serenading waltz, bringing almost everyone into the dance. I scanned the room and found my father quickly. Camila was speaking with her uncle, Isabela's father, while my own nursed a drink with a smug smile as he and Mother watched couples dance the night away.

"Thomas."

I cringed at the voice and glanced over my shoulder. "Pardon me, Miss Collins, but I must speak with my father."

Abigail scowled. "A proper gentleman would not leave a lady alone on the dance floor, no matter the circumstance. Also, since when did I become 'Miss Collins'? You have always known me as Abigail." She reached for me, but I took a step back.

"You have been 'Miss Collins' since your heart chose another," I snapped and walked away, almost feeling guilty about how I spoke to her. Almost.

I nearly collided with my father.

"Whatever is the problem?" he asked, his hand clamping down on my shoulder. "Miss Collins, I apologise for my son's poor behaviour. He would be delighted to dance with you for a song."

"No, I would not," I stated plainly. "I am sorry it did not work out for you and Prince August, but there are other men who would gladly take the opportunity to pursue you. I am not among them."

Abigail lifted her chin, eyes glistening. Before she walked away from our relationship, I would have caved in a second, apologising and doing whatever I could to make her smile once more.

Now, the sight of a full-grown woman in a beautiful green ballgown about to burst into forced tears would have been enough for me to laugh had I been in any other situation.

"Thomas," Father said in warning.

"What is it, Father? Are you going to give me an obedience rune too, that way you can finally have the perfect son you always wanted?"

Abigail's trembling lip stilled, her eyes wide. Mother caught the last bit of what I said as she joined us, her gloved hand covering her mouth.

"Gerold," she whispered, "please tell me that is not true. Please tell me that is not what you did to Isabela."

Father's grip on my shoulder tightened significantly; I refused to flinch or break eye contact.

"Miss Collins," he said without looking at her, "you will have to excuse us. We have some family matters to discuss."

"There is nothing to discuss," I argued, forcefully removing his hand. Abigail scurried away while Mother stayed, having not moved a bit. My voice lowered. "You will remove the rune from Isabela, and perhaps the League will have mercy on you for using a banned rune."

"You would turn in your own father? Perhaps I have failed in raising you." He shook his head and tried to grab me to lead us away, but I batted his hand aside. "She is a spell-caster, Thomas. The laws protect us against monsters like her."

"I find it rather odd that, if she is a monster and so dangerous, you have no issue using her to achieve your goals." From what I could tell, no one was watching us, but at the moment, I would not have cared if anyone did. Father, on the other hand, kept checking. "So which is it, Father? Is she a monster who needs to be rid of, or are you the monster for using her as you please?"

"You are making a scene," he hissed, his fingers digging into my arm.

"Am I? Maker forgive me for speaking my mind for once in my life. I think it's about bloody time I did. I am so tired of keeping secrets and trying to avoid stepping on your toes." I straightened, and for once, I saw a glimmer of fear in my father. For once, I actually felt tall. He released me. "I married Isabela because I am in love with her and I want to spend the rest of my life with her. If you want to disown me, then so be it, but you will release her from the obedience rune now before anything worse happens."

Something wicked gleamed in his eyes. "You will not be married to her much longer. I will not lose my son over an illegitimate monster."

My heart stopped for a split second, his words stealing the wind from my sails. "What does that mean? What else did you do?"

Mother's eyes flitted back and forth between us nervously. I felt some others watching but did not bother to look. The happy music went on as though this conversation weren't happening.

"Your divorce papers should go through soon," he answered. "Isabela was all too happy to sign them."

"After you *forced* her." I clenched my fists, wanting so badly to unleash them on this monster who had the audacity to call himself my father.

Mother tentatively touched my arm. "Do not do anything you will regret later, Thomas."

A dark part of me doubted I would regret it if I gave in.

Before I could, an explosion rattled the palace.

Chapter Thirty-Nine

Isabela

Nathan got part of the rune drawn on my forehead before my magic flared, radiating heat around me like a cocoon. Hissing, he jumped back and shook his finger, blowing on it.

A familiar face, Lord Johannes, approached carefully. "What can I do to help?" The others stood at their posts, watching us—me—warily, hands near their weapons.

"She's been given an obedience rune," Nathan said quickly and quietly enough for only him to hear. "We need to keep her magic under control until the offending party is convinced to take it off of her."

A muscle in Lord Johannes's jaw twitched. I could see the questions and theories forming in his mind, but he spoke none of them, instead turning to the other rune-writers and guards nearby. "Set up barrier runes," he ordered, gesturing in a circle around us.

The men started to obey when a shot rang out and one of them dropped to the ground lifeless.

In the dark of the night, it was easy to miss the approaching group clad in all black. Just like the attackers from before, they wore cloaks and masks that only showed their eyes, strutting toward us like they owned everything in the world.

Nathan cursed, hurriedly scribbling a protection rune on me and then himself.

The guards raised their muskets, exchanging shots with the unwelcome guests while the rune-writers cut themselves to draw runes. One drew something on the back of his hand, and flames leapt from it, catching the nearest attacker's coat on fire and quickly spreading.

Nathan moved to finish marking my forehead, but I swatted at his hands.

"There are too many of them." Bullets ricocheted off our barriers. "You need my help."

He stared at me in concern. Then he gave a decisive nod.

The world swayed as I pushed myself to my feet, my heel catching and tearing through the fabric of my skirts. In the back of my mind, I lamented that I had ruined my dress, first with fire, then with grass and dirt stains, and now tears. At least I had managed to keep vomit off it.

There are more important things to think about right now, I chastised myself, wiping sick from my mouth.

"These protection runes won't last long," Nathan warned. "We have to think of something quickly."

More shots fired—more men down. The attackers took their time, stalking toward the palace. Just when I thought I had an idea of how many, more seemed to slink out of the shadows. My mind reeled as I tried to come up with an idea of how to help without losing control…

There were too many.

I threw a torrent of wind, making them stagger back and trip over each other. The magic leapt at the opportunity, more shoving its way into my mind and body before I could stop it. A wave of dizziness nearly knocked me off my feet, but I managed to find purchase even with my heels about to sink into the grass.

I am fearless. I am powerful. I am strong.

The attackers recovered and picked up their pace, splitting their focus so that more people went after me. A bullet shattered my barrier, and I moved my head just in time for it to only nick my cheek. Nathan moved toward me, ready to draw again. I caught sight of the attackers about to throw explosives and unleashed magic at them—

Magic flooded through me and rushed outward in all directions in the form of ice, blanketing everything and everyone in range. I stared at the wintery landscape, people frozen in place. Horror built up within me as magic seeped in, slowly drowning me from the inside out. I fought to take back control, fought to breathe, fought to stay awake—

My last cohesive thought was the realisation that one bomb was already in the air, and my magic had launched it into the side of the palace.

Chapter Forty

Thomas

Control

I leapt to my feet before anyone else could and tore back outside, consequences be damned. The closer I got, the more the temperature dropped, and I made it to the entrance of the palace, only to find what looked like a horror version of a winter night. Still alive—from what I could tell—were tons of people, most of them dressed in the same black as those who attacked us prior. Some lay dead on the ground, the ice around them looking like coffins. I spotted Lord Johannes and Nate near Isabela, both encapsulated as well...

Isabela jerked and twitched on her hands and knees, her mouth open in a silent scream, her eyes squeezed shut. Waves of magic pulsed from her, slamming me back onto the floor so hard that I hit the back of my head. Stars burst in the darkness before my eyes. Blinking my vision back into focus, I rapidly made a protection rune on myself, pushing back onto my feet and staggering toward her. The magic railed against my barrier, and I replaced the rune before it could fail.

"Thomas!" I heard my father call, and then he cried out as the next wave hit him. Tremors shook the ground, the ice cracking. Our marriage runes flared, burning and tightening on my skin like I had ropes around me, tugging me toward Isabela. I had to retrace the protection rune once more before I finally reached her and fell to my knees.

"Isabela," I said. She lifted her head, opening her eyes—her shimmering, iridescent eyes that held nothing I knew of the woman I loved. Cracks formed in my barrier as the next wave came, but I focused on drawing runes on her forehead and mine. My hands shook so badly it took me longer than it should have.

The moment our minds connected, magic overwhelmed me, trying to break the connection between us. Through her eyes, I saw the cracks in my barrier grow.

There was not enough power within me to both fight the magic and continue making barriers for myself.

I pulled her into my arms and closed my eyes.

I know you are still in here.

The magic lunged at me, surrounding me, threatening to suffocate me to force me from her mind. The swirling of pure power left me breathless and dizzy, almost snuffing out the last bit of hope I had. I felt another tug, and I followed it, seeing a dim flicker of light—a flicker of my Isabela. I grabbed onto her.

Take my strength.

Her light grew a little brighter and a little bigger. We clung to each other, our lights merging in a warmth that made the magic stumble back.

'You came for me,' Isabela said.

Always.

The barrier in Isabela's mind was wide open for magic to come through as it pleased. Together, we shoved back, leaning on each other for support.

The next wave of magic shattered my physical barrier—I did not let her go, burying my face in the crook of her neck.

'The magic will kill you! Hurry, put up another barrier!'

There's no time. We have to stop it now.

I bound myself to her the day we were married, and if this was our end, it would be together. I would not let the magic take her if I could help it. If it took her, it would take me too.

We wrestled with the magic, pressing it back toward the breach in her defences. My strength waned, and I could tell that hers was as well, her light starting to dim.

Keep going! We are almost there. I'll shove, and you get ready to seal the barrier.

'...Thomas...'

You can do this, Isabela.

She paused. *'If it does not work, escape while you can.'*

I am not leaving you. Together until the end.

The words carried a different weight now that it could very well be our end.

'I love you, Thomas.'

I love you, Isabela.

She spoke her mantra, summoning the last of her strength to fix the barrier. I used what I had left to shove the magic out as it struggled against me.

Isabela gasped and shoved me away. I hit the ice, wincing at the pain shooting up my elbow. But that did not matter—those eyes, those beautiful brown eyes, were my Isabela's.

Chapter Forty-One

Isabela

 *Aftermath*

I panted, trying to catch my breath, as I locked gazes with Thomas, who looked utterly relieved. He sat up slowly, and I examined him for any injuries: frost clung to his clothes and tousled hair, his protection rune was gone, and the only blood I could see on him was the bit at his nose and upper lip.

That is when I felt my own trickling down my chin. It dripped onto my gown.

Well, it was already ruined, so there was no use in lamenting over it...

Through Thomas's eyes, I could see that one of the sleeves hung from threads, and the corset and backing felt loose, the stays torn, not to mention where my heel had caught in the skirts. I was surprised there was anything left of it. My hair framed my face in wild waves and slight curls like it could not make up its mind.

But we were here, and we were alive. The magic had not won—we had.

This time my smile was genuine, my vision blurring as emotions rose within me.

Thomas removed the runes from his forehead, breaking the connection. Trembling and lightheaded, I wiped at my face, willing myself not to retch again. Part of me wanted to curl up right there on the ice and sleep for the next week or two.

Ice… Everyone else was still encased in it, including Nathan and Lord Johannes.

"What happened?" Queen Eleanora emerged from the palace, taking in what was left of the crumbling hole near the entrance to the palace and the aftermath of my magic. Guards tried to surround her, but she waved them behind her and lifted her skirts so that she could manoeuvre around the scene more easily.

"My sincerest apologies, Your Majesty," Lord Grahm said, smoothing his appearance and stepping closer to us. "I thought she had better control of her magic. Perhaps I was wrong to think that we could work with a spell-caster."

Thomas stood and spoke out before I could: "I would suggest you give the Queen the respect and honour she deserves by giving her the truth, Father."

More people stood in the entryway—I spotted Camila, Lady Grahm, Lord Cornwell… and my father.

How no one else had figured out that we were related was beyond me. I had always wished that I had my mother's darker hair, but I had received my father's colouring instead, branding me as his for those who were paying attention to a lowly servant girl. He scanned the area before pausing on me. I had expected at least a flicker of surprise or recognition, but there was nothing to see except the unreadable mask.

But why would he be surprised? Lord Grahm had already spoken with him, already told him who I was.

"Go on," Thomas goaded, "tell her about the obedience rune, how it caused all of this. We are lucky that she was able to stop the attackers before they could do more damage." He gestured toward the people for emphasis.

"Lord Grahm," the Queen said, her tone edged, "I would err on the side of candour if I were in your position."

"Your Majesty, would you honestly believe that I would stoop to using a banned rune? I have too much at risk to be so foolhardy."

She eyed him, then looked to Lord Cornwell and Lord Shirehold behind her. "How would you check for it?"

"It would be on the back of her neck," Lord Cornwell answered. "If he put it there, he would be the only one able to remove it."

The Queen pointed in my direction. "Do it, Lord Grahm." When he hesitated, she said, "If you are truly innocent, you have no reason to worry, no reason to avoid this."

I stood slowly, ice breaking as my dress pulled away from the ground. Dizziness hit me, but I managed to stay on my feet while Lord Grahm took slow steps closer, the Queen, Lord Cornwell, Lord Shirehold, and Thomas trailing him at a short distance. I tensed as he positioned himself behind me and moved my hair aside.

Heavy silence.

"Remove it immediately," commanded Lord Cornwell, who positioned himself close enough to make sure that Lord Grahm actually tried.

A few moments passed before his finger traced on my neck, leaving another wet trail that dissipated upon completion. Feeling like I had been unshackled, I sucked in a breath greedily, tears rolling down my cheeks.

"Arrest him," barked Lord Shirehold, and more rune-writers hurried to follow the order, ignoring Lord Grahm's protests.

"Gag him if he insists on blathering." Lord Cornwell walked into my peripherals. "I do not think there are words enough to right the wrong done to you, Miss Fuerte."

"Mrs Grahm," I corrected, my voice raw.

"Pardon?"

I tried to turn to face them and nearly collapsed from fatigue. Thomas caught me, letting me lean against him. My fingers dug into his jacket as I straightened myself. "My name is Isabela Grahm, Mrs Grahm if you prefer formality."

Everyone looked back and forth between us, understanding dawning on them. Thomas kept a supportive hand at my back, giving me strength and confidence.

"Isabela," Queen Eleanora said, "unfreeze my guards, the rune-writers, and Nathaniel first. I want to be aptly prepared to arrest all of the attackers."

I swallowed, trying to relieve the ache in my throat. The thought of even brushing against magic after all of this…

"If I may, Your Majesty." My father strode forward, his spell-caster servant following closely behind. The spell-caster was ordinary-looking, which was to his benefit, considering his talent of being able to blend into wherever he was. It was no wonder I had not seen him at the ball—although I should have suspected he would be. "She looks to be spent. It would be safer if my spell-caster fixed everything."

A nod from the Queen, a few movements with the spell-caster's hands, and the ice melted into water and soaked into the earth. It was as if it had been nothing more difficult than a stroll through the park to him when it had almost cost me my sanity.

The newly released people inhaled and stumbled forward. Nathan looked up at us, a slight smile on his face even as he fought to catch his breath.

"That is enough for the moment, Lorenzo," my father said in approval.

"Thank you, Prince Esteban," the Queen said. "My Elite, take care of this mess. I want a trial set up first thing tomorrow."

"It shall be done, Your Majesty," Lord Cornwell assured her with a decline of his head.

"We need to rune the female spell-caster, bind her magic," Lord Shirehold said. "It has proven to be too dangerous."

"That was my father's fault, not hers," Thomas argued, his grip on me tightening.

"We must take a look at all of the evidence before we come to that conclusion, Master Grahm."

"Mister Grahm, Lord Shirehold," Thomas said. "And Isabela is innocent. She needs to rest—she was just released from a banned rune. You would rune her again so quickly?"

"It is for the best interest of everyone." His eyes narrowed on Thomas. "If you are so worried, rune your *wife* yourself." He nearly spat the word "wife."

Thomas looked to Queen Eleanora, who said, "Do it, Mr Grahm.

We shall get to the bottom of this."

Chapter Forty-Two

Thomas

Binding

An attendant and two rune-writers led us away to a small bedroom in the palace to await interrogation. Isabela leant against me, and I did my best not to falter and show how tired I felt. I had no idea how she was still standing, much less walking.

"We will return to bring you before the Queen and League for interrogation," Lord Johannes told us. "Someone will bring Miss Fue—Mrs Grahm replacement clothing." He began to walk out but paused at the door. "For what it is worth, Mrs Grahm, I am ashamed that a rune-writer did such a terrible thing to you."

Isabela offered him a weary smile. "Thank you, Lord Johannes. I know there are good rune-writers."

"As there are good spell-casters." He returned the smile and dipped his head.

"Where is Nate?" I asked.

"He is being examined by a doctor and then will be held for an interrogation as well. Your mother is with him."

That, I could live with. "Thank you."

Lord Johannes bowed and left.

Alone, I took the time to study Isabela. I didn't see any wounds, just an exhaustion in her eyes and the slump of her shoulders.

"I am here," she said, the corner of her mouth twitching. "I promise, it's not just a wonderful dream."

"If it were a wonderful dream," I countered, "we would not look like we are survivors of a shipwreck... and I would have dreamt up a room with a larger bed."

She chuckled weakly and shook her head.

A knock at the door interrupted whatever Isabela had been about to say. A servant came in with new clothes for Isabela and set up the bath.

"Let me know if you need anything else," she said as she left.

My whole body—even my insides—ached, but I could not bring myself to let go of Isabela. I kissed the top of her head.

"We should probably clean up before we are called in for questioning," she said softly, tugging on my hand. I walked with her to the bathroom and caught sight of myself in the mirror. Dipping my hands into the wash basin, I rinsed my face and hoped that the water would tame my curls at least a little.

Isabela's gown dropped to the floor. She fumbled with the stays of her corset, her hands trembling too much.

"Let me help."

She peered over her shoulder. "So eager to help me undress, Mr Grahm."

"If you knew how beautiful you are, Mrs Grahm, you would understand." My own tired fingers had a difficult time even with the ties having snapped. In exasperation and impatience, I yanked the corset apart.

Isabela laughed in surprise, the sound lifting my spirits. She turned around and kissed me, reminding me with that simple action that we were alive,

We were safe,

We were together.

"Are you going to join me?" she asked against my mouth.

"I would," I said between kisses, "but the tub is too small, and we do not know when we will be called upon."

Isabela sighed, stealing another kiss before stepping into the tub. "Hopefully we will have this sorted soon so we will have real time to ourselves." She dipped her head under, wetting her hair.

"Trust me," I said, pulling a stool to the tub so that I could sit near her, "if I were not so knackered, I might have tried anyway." I pressed my lips to her shoulder and let my knuckles graze her spine. She leant into my touches, her eyelids fluttering closed. "I can only imagine how you feel. I did not realise how greedy magic can be."

Her eyes half-opened, Isabela reached for the soap. "Magic owes nothing to anyone. It is its own master and seeks to take everything it can, offered or not." The blood from her face lightly tinted the water pink and then disappeared. "If I could, I would sleep for a week straight without interruptions."

When she tried to get her back, I took the soap and moved her hair aside. "That was your father and his spell-caster? The one who undid your magic?"

Isabela nodded, her eyes glazed over. "Now he knows."

"We'll get this sorted," I promised her, running the bar of soap along her back in slow, gentle circles.

She did not respond at first. I shifted, moving to her side. With that faraway look, Isabela finally said, "I could have killed you... Or Nathan. I was so terrified..."

I knelt beside the tub so that I could cup her face in my hands and make her look at me. "You did not. We are all alive, and you stopped an attack on the palace."

"I could not have done that without you."

"People can rarely do things alone." I kissed her forehead, glad for the scent of flowers instead of blood. "Come, let us get you dressed before someone fetches us."

The clothing the servant left for Isabela was more simplistic, nothing Father would have allowed her to wear to the palace. I shoved thoughts of him away abruptly. Whatever happened to him, we would deal with it later.

"We still have to bind my magic," Isabela said after she was finished dressing. The gown did not flatter her like the others that had been tailor-made specifically for her, but it was better than what she had worn when we first took her from the chapel. To be fair, almost anything was.

I exhaled through my nose. "I am sorry."

"I would rather you do it than anyone else." She smiled at me, squeezed my hands. "It should only be until they are done with the trial, right? No reason to fret over it." Pulling up her sleeve, Isabela offered her unmarked wrist to me.

"It goes on your forehead," I told her, "since your magic has to do with the mind."

"Oh." She fixed her sleeve. "That makes sense."

I paused, staring into her eyes. "I hate doing this. I feel like I am taking a part of who you are away."

Her hand came up to my cheek. "It's all right, Thomas. It's just for a short while. I trust you."

I took my time drawing the rune, making it as elegant as possible like the one on her wrist. She stayed very still, looking up at me through her long lashes. When the rune was complete, I felt Isabela tense.

"That feels very... strange..." She blinked. "It is almost freeing, in a way, not having to keep up the barrier. It's like you did it for me."

"It's just for the time being."

Isabela stood on her tiptoes to bring her face closer to mine. "Everything will be all right, Thomas. I promise."

My throat tightened, and I could not trust myself to speak. Instead, I pulled her close and kissed her.

Chapter Forty-Three

Isabela

Father

Uncomfortable as the corset made it, I spent the rest of my time on the small bed, my face against Thomas's chest, his arms around me. We fell asleep instantly, our bodies trying to recover from fighting off my magic.

The pounding on the door a few hours later made me stir, but my eyes were too heavy to open, my body too stiff to move.

"Mr and Mrs Grahm."

I sighed, loathe to untangle myself from Thomas and move from the bed. Everything ached, and I nearly tumbled taking my first steps toward the door. Thomas did, with a great *thump*.

"Just a minute," I called, helping him back onto his feet. Thomas ran a hand over his face and into his hair. "You'll be all right."

"I feel like I collided with a charging horse," Thomas muttered.

"Fortunately, you will recover. Unfortunately, you will not get used to it." Because we both knew that, being married to me, he was going to have another run-in with magic at some point.

Thomas stole a quick kiss and then said, "Come in."

Lord Johannes looked us up and down, focusing on the binding rune briefly. "Good, you are cleaned up. I'm sorry to have interrupted your rest, but Queen Eleanora is requesting your presence immediately."

From what I could tell by the lack of light peeking between the curtains, it was very late at night, a time when everyone should be sleeping, not pulled from their beds to be questioned.

But I was not about to argue with the Queen.

Lord Johannes took the lead, and two more rune-writers tailed us. There were more guards posted throughout the halls than I had seen previously, but no one else, no one I recognised. Even with all of the guards, it seemed eerily empty and strange, lacking life. Bits of the decorations still hung on the walls and lay on the floor, although someone had turned up the lamps, leaving little room for shadows. The guards eyed us as we passed.

He brought us to a meeting room, where Queen Eleanora, Lady Grahm, the Elite, my father, and his spell-caster were already seated around a table. Their conversation paused the moment the door opened, their attention turning to us.

"That will be all for now, Lord Johannes."

With a bow to the Queen, he took his leave and shut the door behind him, the soft noise echoing in the small room.

"Sit." Queen Eleanora had not bothered to change out of her ballgown into something more comfortable for sitting in a chair. As soon as we obeyed, she said, "Both of you are to give a complete and honest account of the events of tonight."

Thomas let me go first, his face twitching as I went over what Lord Grahm had done. The Queen showed no emotion and kept her eyes trained on me. I avoided looking in my father's direction, hoping that the only reason he was present was to report back to the King of

Isouldia about the incident.

After I had finished, the Queen looked to Thomas. My heart twisted as he spoke of trying to figure out what his father had done to me, knowing how worried he must have been. Instead of squeezing his hand like I wanted to, I folded my hands in my lap.

Then we waited in silence for the Queen to make the first response.

"If I am correct in my remembrance," she said finally, "using the obedience rune is a serious offense."

"You are correct, Your Majesty," Lord Cornwell confirmed. "It would be up to a judge, but the consequences for using such a rune are severe."

"Imprisonment for life or even death," Lord Shirehold added with a scowl. "I say good riddance to anyone who would dare use a banned rune. They know what they were getting themselves into, knew the risks."

"Do we have a trial scheduled?" the Queen asked.

"Tomorrow morning," Lord Baskers said. "Judge Acker has been notified of that and the other trials for the attackers and…" His eyes flitted to me, and he cleared his throat. "Mrs Grahm."

"What?" I asked at the same time Thomas demanded to know, "Why does she have a trial?"

Lord Shirehold exhaled a plume of smoke and waved his pipe. "We must be sure that she did not do any of the damage willingly and that she is not dangerous."

"Her magic was dangerous because of the obedience rune."

"Mr Grahm," Queen Eleanora warned, "you will keep a civil tone and adhere to protocol. If your… wife is innocent, she will be absolved of all charges."

A muscle flexed in Thomas's jaw. "Yes, Your Majesty."

"Is there not a law against marrying a spell-caster?" Lord Shirehold furrowed his brow.

"I think not—I doubt it has been done here in our country before," Lord Cornwell said, an amused look on his face.

"It may not matter," said my father, turning my stomach to knots. "Lord Grahm informed me during the ball that the spell-caster signed divorce papers yesterday. They should go into effect in the next few days."

I gritted my teeth. "Lord Grahm forced me to while under the obedience rune. I wish to remain married to Thomas Grahm."

"The judge will certainly make the appropriate rulings tomorrow."

I hated the hints of smugness in his expression, his tone.

"Why would Lord Grahm reveal that to you, Prince Esteban?" the Queen wanted to know. "I did not think the two of you knew one another previously. That seems an odd topic for strangers, especially at a ball."

"It makes sense when you understand the context," Esteban replied smoothly, a glint in his eyes. "You see, Isabela is my daughter."

Chapter Forty-Four

Thomas

Nate

I walked into the infirmary wing of the palace not knowing what to expect. In the craziness of the night, I'd had little time to even look at my brother. My chest ached at the realisation that I had not even tried to check on him until this morning. Granted, Isabela had needed me, and I her.

Most of the rooms were open and empty, nurses shuffling past those to check on their patients. No one paid me heed, and I was fine with that.

I found Nate's room and knocked before stepping inside and closing the door. His jacket was neatly folded on a chair, his shoes on the floor beneath. That was the only piece of furniture other than the bed, and there wasn't much room for anything else anyway.

Nate pushed himself into a sitting position from under the mound of blankets, his button-down shirt rumpled.

"Glad to see you. Mother left not too long ago," he said with a grin that waned as he peered past me. "Where is Isabela?"

"The Queen is preparing her for the trials today. No one is allowed to see her at the moment." I shoved my hands into my pants pockets, trying not to worry over the paleness of his skin. "How are you feeling?"

"Better than I was. Is my mouth still blue?" Nate prodded at his bottom lip. "At least I have feeling again. I'm not nearly as freezing as I was. Colder than a witch's tit, that magic. Before I do something bloody stupid again to piss off Isabela, remind me not to."

I smiled weakly. "I'm not sure I'll be able to convince you not to do anything, Nate. You are too stubborn for your own good."

"Ha! That's true." He adjusted the pillows behind him. "Stop looking at me like I'm about to get a visit from Death. He and I have an understanding: I'm not supposed to die until I am good and tired of my fourth wife."

"Fourth wife?"

"Well, I assume the first time I'll wed is because I was too bladdered to understand what was happening and got myself into trouble, so that one won't last. Wives two and three will be passionate love affairs that will force me to marry them so that no one can say for certain that our children were conceived out of wedlock."

"And the fourth?"

"Number four I'll marry so that I won't die alone in my old age."

"Sounds like you have given this a lot of thought."

"I've practiced it," Nate answered, his expression falling. "Was going to give it to Father to tell him to bugger off when he tried to pair me up with a random lass. I suppose I may not have to worry about it any longer."

I looked away and scanned the room, but it was so bare and plain that there was nothing with which to distract myself.

"I was hoping you would help me convince the doctors to release me so I can be there. At the trials, I mean." He stared at me with a seriousness that I had rarely seen out of him. "Mother told me what happened at the meeting. If you want the best chance of proving Isabela's innocence, we will need to use what little time we have left to tip the scales in our favour."

"I was planning on going to the League Hall to talk with Henrietta," I said carefully.

"Then you will definitely need my help." Nate heaved the mass of blankets off and clambered out of bed. At first his footing was shaky, but he managed, smacking away my attempts to help. "Go on, no time to argue. Tell the doctors we are leaving immediately."

Chapter Forty-Five

Isabela

Unwanted

I hated that no one could stay with me in the room, not even Thomas, but I was glad that he was going to check on Nathan. After servants came in to dress me and do my hair, they left. I sat on the edge of the bed, pulling the pillow to my nose. It still had a lingering scent of Thomas.

Someone knocked but came in a split second later without bothering to wait for my answer. A foolish part of me hoped it was Thomas or Camila.

"Isabela."

I stood and faced Esteban, lifting my chin. At least his spell-caster had not come with him, although I assumed he was standing just outside the door with the guards. "They are not allowing anyone in here."

He smiled, his hands clasped behind his back. "You will find that, when you are a prince of another country and negotiations for an alliance are in the works, you can get almost anything you ask." Our native language sounded too sweet on his tongue, the kind of sweet that would make someone sick after just a taste. "No need to be guarded, *mija*. I am only here to talk."

"You do not have the right to call me that."

His brows raised slightly. "You are my daughter. I believe that is the only qualification for using that term of endearment. Your mother loved to call you that."

"She earned the right."

Esteban studied me. "I do not understand the hostility, Isabela. I have done nothing but give you and your mother a life in the palace, made sure you had everything you needed. I would have given you every comfort that your cousins had, but your mother insisted she wanted to remain hidden in plain sight, that you did not want that life." He tilted his head, his silky hair brushing against his shoulders. "Now I see she merely wanted to keep the truth from me."

I snapped, "For good reason. I see how you treat your spell-caster: he is nothing more than a dog, following your every command."

"Come now, there is no need for that kind of talk. Lorenzo enjoys his life and is proud to serve me. You can ask him yourself if you would like." When I said nothing, he sighed, bringing his hands before him like he was offering something invisible. "I want peace between us, Isabela. I do not know what your mother said to poison you against me, but I have no intentions of hurting you."

"Then you are not going to lay claim to me?" I challenged, wanting to take a step back to put distance between us. I could not—that would be seen as fear, as weakness, and I would not give him the satisfaction. "You will allow me to remain married to Thomas Grahm and live my life in peace as I please?"

Esteban did not respond right away. His hands lowered to his sides. "If the judge rules that you are innocent and not a danger, then yes, I will allow it. If not, then I will take you home so that you do not have to endure any punishments they would give you."

"As your property?"

"As my daughter and my spell-caster," he corrected. "I did not make the laws, Isabela. Do not be angry with me."

"I will be angry with whomever I please." My words came out edged, and he flinched. "If you wish to be my father, then you will have to treat me as a person, not as a tool to use at your disposal."

"I did not mean—"

"And you are not to speak ill of my mother anymore. Maker only knows why, but she never spoke ill of you, she loved you until the day she took her final breath, the day you would not even come to her bedside to say goodbye."

"THAT IS ENOUGH!"

Shock kept me from continuing. Agony took over his expression, laced his tone, making it falter. "I loved your mother," Esteban said, his voice fragile. "Believe what you will of me, but you must know that I loved her more fiercely than I have ever loved anyone in my life. I worked to change the laws on marriage to spell-casters, but prejudice is not something easily changed in one lifetime." He was about to take a step forward but stopped himself. "I hope one day I will earn your heart and affections, Isabela. But right now, whether or not you agree with my methods, I am trying to protect you. One day, you will understand."

What was there to understand? If he fought for us, there were no signs of it, no protests, no talks of change. Where was the proof? I'd never seen my parents interact, never heard them speak a word or even look at one another. No, I did not understand his claims—but I understood my mother's heart forever longed for a man who paid no attention to her while he claimed to be fighting for her freedom.

Tears welled in my eyes as I commanded in an icy tone, "Get. Out."

Without another word, Esteban left.

Chapter Forty-Six

Thomas

Help

Nate and I had barely made it out of the infirmary and out the front entrance of the palace when Camila caught up to us. Foregoing her signature red, this dress was grey and simple, something that could have been worn for a stroll in the park. No jewellery, no crown, very little cosmetics, and a hat to keep the sun from her face.

"Where are you going?" she asked, tugging on Nate's arm.

"On a grand adventure to rescue a dear friend," Nate answered. "We already have the do-gooder knight and the handsome devilish rogue, but the position for the beautiful sassy princess is available if you are interested."

"…do those kinds of lines work for you?"

"Generally, Your Highness." He winked and offered his arm. She took it and urged us forward.

"Are you allowed to leave the palace?" I asked quietly, dipping my head to the guards. They eyed us as they returned the gesture. Camila kept her gaze down, letting the hat help hide her face.

"I have not given anyone the chance to order me one way or the other."

I waited until we were far enough down the stairs that the guards could not hear us. "I take it your sisters are confined to their rooms for their safety?"

"Unless they find a way out, not that any of them would take the risk of angering *Tío* Esteban."

Isabela's father. Just thinking about the way he had spoken of Isabela and looked at her was enough to set my blood to boiling. "And you would?"

"For Isabela, yes."

The princess and I exchanged approving nods. As long as she trusted me enough to help Isabela, that was all I cared about.

We took our carriage to the League Hall (Mother would be stuck at the palace for now, unsure where we went, but we would explain later). Camila's eyes roamed constantly, taking in all the scenery like Isabela had.

"What is this place?" she asked when we got out of the carriage.

"Welcome to the main operations building for rune-writers," Nate told her, leading her toward the entrance.

"Why are we here? What is the plan?"

"There is someone who knows more about banned runes than most," I chimed in. "Henrietta, a rune-writer who works in the library of the League Hall. We are hoping to have as much evidence as possible to sway the judge to rule Isabela innocent."

Camila pondered my words before saying, "Should we also talk with the priest who married you? Isabela made him sound very..." She searched for the right words. "...kind and helpful."

"I'm glad to not be the only one coming up with good ideas," Nate said, grinning at me. I rolled my eyes.

The Hall was much emptier than usual, most of the rune-writers at the palace recovering or on patrol. Our steps echoed as we made our way to the library.

"But this rune would keep dust from settling on the books." A young girl's voice.

"We would have to add it to each book, and then take them off every time we wanted to be able to remove it from the shelf and open it. Too tedious, child."

"I am not a child! I am nearly thirteen."

We walked in to see Henrietta and Lord Johannes's daughter, Georgiana, at the desk bickering. Henrietta straightened and snapped her mouth shut when she saw us, swallowing whatever retort she was about to make. Her eyes narrowed on Camila, and she gave a stiff curtsy. "Your Highness."

Georgiana hastily followed suit. With her attire being the same as Henrietta's, the child was a miniature version of the female rune-writer. Georgiana looked just like her father, although there was a determined set to her jaw and a fire in her eyes that left me looking forward to seeing how she changed the League as she grew up and trained.

"What can I do for you, Princess Camila?" Henrietta did not bother to look at us Grahm brothers, probably because she assumed we were here as protection for Camila.

The princess glanced at Nate questioningly, and he nodded. With a smile, Camila said, "We would be most grateful for your help. You see, we need someone with knowledge of banned runes."

"For the spell-caster's trial." Henrietta fixed a stack of books on the desk so that they were perfectly aligned. "Georgiana, sign these back in and put them in their correct places this time."

"My system is better," she grumbled as she opened a record book and dipped a quill pen in a bottle of ink.

"Yes," Camila confirmed once Henrietta's attention was back on her. "Your knowledge and testimony would be most helpful to ensure that Isabela Grahm is proven innocent."

"What makes you think I would want to help the spell-caster?" Henrietta asked, thumbing the gnarled scar at her throat. The princess's eyes followed it briefly before flicking back up to meet the rune-writer's steely gaze.

Georgiana said, "Because Isabela Grahm saved my father and your lover in the attack."

Nate grinned and whispered to me, "I like her," as Henrietta scowled at the girl.

"This is an *adult* conversation."

Georgiana mirrored Henrietta's scowl. "If that is all you can say in response, you have no ground to stand on. You know I am right."

Camila cleared her throat. "We would greatly appreciate it if you would help us. I assume you had a terrible experience with a spell-caster, and I know of the hatred for them from people of both of our countries, but I must speak on behalf of Isabela and say that she is a wonderful person whose only downfalls are that she loves too fiercely and believes in the fairy-tale nonsense she reads in books. Well, that and her fashion sense could use a little more work, but I digress." The princess took a step forward, her expression vulnerable. "The point I am trying to make is that no one is perfect, and not all spell-casters are bad or good, just as not all rune-writers are. Isabela is one of the good ones, and she could use your help."

Henrietta pressed her lips together into a thin line. We all watched her, waited, even Georgiana, who had paused her task.

"I will speak at the trial," Henrietta stated. "I will give only facts about the banned runes and what I witnessed that night, nothing more. If it eases your mind any, I will neither lie nor twist the truth to fit one narrative or another."

"You have my thanks, Henrietta," Camila said. If the woman was surprised that the princess knew her name, she did not show it. "Good day, Henrietta, Georgiana."

"Good day, Princess Camila!" Georgiana beamed and dipped into another curtsy. Henrietta's farewell was not nearly as emphatic as the young girl's.

Back outside, Nate said, "I knew it was a good idea to bring you along."

"You did not bring me along," Camila argued, pinching his arm. "I invited myself, and you were happy to have me." They exchanged smirks. "Now then, shall we visit the priest?"

"I have yet to pick out my wedding clothes."

Camila raised a brow at Nate. "If we were getting married, I would have already picked out your clothes for you."

"Already planning?"

"It is going to take more than pretty words and charming smiles to win my heart, *Nataniel*."

I saw the spark in Nate's eyes, the sign that the challenge had been accepted.

Chapter Forty-Seven

Isabela

The courtroom was full of people, tables, and chairs. All eyes fixated on me as Lord Johannes led me to a squared-off section that looked a lot like the witness stand. He closed the low gate behind us, sealing us inside, and positioned himself behind me. Above, Queen Eleanora and her sons sat in a balcony area as if this were some sort of opera or show. They kept their expressions neutral.

Thomas and Nathan were off to the side with their mother, a few seats away from Camila, Esteban, and Lorenzo, my father's spell-caster. I met Thomas's gaze, and he dipped his head as if to reassure me that everything was going to go well.

I hoped so.

My hands fidgeted, and I remembered that I had been asked not to wear gloves, all of my markings exposed. I traced my wedding rune.

When the judge entered, everyone stood, even the Queen and the princes. When he reached his box, he looked up at the royal family and bowed, then to Camila and Esteban. It was not until he was seated that we sat again.

"I am Judge Acker," he said, fixing his spectacles so that they rested on the bridge of his thin, long nose. "We have three very important trials today. In the interest of time and efficiency, I ask that, when it is your turn to speak, you keep your responses truthful and concise. I will not tolerate unruly behaviour. If I deem you uncivilised, one of the guards will throw you out without a second thought."

I straightened, my heart thudding against my ribcage.

"We are starting with Lord Gerold Grahm. Bring him in."

Still in the clothes he wore to the ball, Lord Grahm held his head high as if he were trying to challenge everyone in the room. Nathan lowered his gaze, but Thomas watched as their father was brought to the front table facing the judge's box.

"Lord Grahm," Judge Acker announced, "you are accused of using a banned rune to force Mrs Isabela Grahm to obey your every command. How do you plead?"

"Not. Guilty."

I had no idea why I expected anything else.

Sitting just behind Lord Grahm, the Elite appeared to be a mixture of annoyed and amused at the response.

"State your case."

"By law," Lord Grahm answered, looking at the different faces in the room, "is it—"

"You are speaking to me, Lord Grahm. This is not a show for you to put on an act. You will address me and answer my questions as clearly and concisely as possible. The truth, Lord Grahm."

Facing forward, Lord Grahm bowed his head. "My apologies, Judge Acker. I merely meant to point out that, by law, the spell-caster is my property with which I can do as I please, especially when it regards the safety and welfare of my family."

"The spell-caster, Mrs Isabela Grahm, intentionally put you or a member of your family in harm's way?"

"She did. She once let loose her magic and nearly killed me and my sons. Thomas stopped her before she could, and luckily Nathaniel was the only one who required stitches. You can ask Doctor Cornelius."

Thomas looked like he wanted to throttle his father. I shared the feeling, wanting to speak in my defence, but kept my silence, not wanting to risk irritating the judge. I doubted he would throw me out since one of the trials was about me... Still, it was unwise to jeopardise my verdict.

Judge Acker looked about the room. "Is the doctor in attendance?"

From the back, he stood. "I am present, Your Honour."

"Come to the witness stand."

I dug my nails into the flesh of my palms as Judge Acker asked Doctor Cornelius to recount the visit. The doctor stuck to the facts, speaking only of what he knew and emphasising that he had no knowledge of what had happened to result in the injuries to Nathan's arm and my hands.

"Did you find Mrs Grahm dangerous in the times you have encountered her?"

"No, Your Honour."

"Thank you, Doctor Cornelius. That will be all. You may return to your seat."

The doctor bowed and walked back, sparing a quick, sympathetic glance my way.

"Lady Grahm, were you present at the incident of which your husband speaks?"

"No, Your Honour," she answered, her voice trembling. She cleared her throat and added, "I saw the injuries and the aftermath of the room, but nothing more."

"Describe them to me."

Peeking at her husband every few seconds, Lady Grahm spoke of that day.

"You are not speaking to your husband—you are speaking to me. If I might remind you, the Maker and I hold much more power than your husband has, so I suggest you speak only the truth."

She tried again, keeping her attention on the judge.

"Thank you. You may be seated. Master Nathaniel Grahm, come to the witness stand."

Nathan reluctantly stood and obeyed, his movements less fluid than normal.

After hearing his version of that day, the judge asked, "Do you mean to say that your father is mistaken about Mrs Grahm's intentions or that he is lying?"

Nathan swallowed. He locked eyes with his father, a strange look on his face.

"Master Grahm?"

In a strong voice, Nathan stated, "Your Honour, it is my belief that my father is lying to protect himself."

Lord Grahm turned red and opened his mouth, only to snap it shut when the judge glared at him in warning.

"Do you find Mrs Grahm dangerous?"

"No."

"Tell me about yesterday, including anything that led up to the incident at the ball."

Nathan explained everything, making me realise that the pounding I had heard while in the safe room had, indeed, been Thomas trying to save me. The more he spoke, the more Lord Grahm scowled.

"Mrs Grahm froze you with her magic?"

Nathan faltered. "Yes, Your Honour. She was not in control of it because of the alcohol my father ordered her to drink. Thomas helped her stop the magic."

The judge pondered. "Thank you, Master Grahm. You may return to your seat."

Nathan ignored his father on his way back.

"Mr Thomas Grahm, come to the witness stand."

Thomas briefly looked at me with a small smile. The witness stand brought him closer but too far away for my liking.

"I will remind you that even though she is your wife, you are to speak only the truth. Is that understood?"

"Yes, Your Honour."

Thomas answered all the same questions Nathan had, his tone respectful.

"You helped stop the magic?"

"I did. I put a mind-melding rune on our foreheads, and we joined our strength to push out the magic."

"Push out the magic..." he repeated. "Explain."

"I believe Isabela could explain it better than I can."

"I did not ask her. I am asking you."

Thomas shifted from one foot to the other. "From what I could understand, she keeps a barrier up in her mind so that magic can only enter when she chooses. It is wild and hard to tame, so forcing it back out of her is a challenge."

"The alcohol inhibited her ability to keep it out and control it?"

"Yes, Your Honour."

Judge Acker stared at Thomas. "Did the spell-caster, at any time, intentionally hurt you, put you in danger, or force you to do something against your will using magic?"

"No."

"You married her of your own free will after having known her for…?"

"A month, yes." Thomas seemed unfazed by the question, sure of himself. "I fell in love with her and asked her to marry me."

"Are you certain there was no magic involved to convince you?"

"I—" Thomas's jaw slackened; my heart stopped.

He could not believe that I magicked him to fall in love with me, could he? After all we had been through?

Thomas blushed. "My father gave me a love rune a week or two before I met Isabela."

"Why is that?"

Lord Grahm interrupted, "I wanted my son to be happy."

"You will hold your tongue," snapped the judge.

"In this case, my father speaks the truth: I had my heart broken, and he had thought it was time for me to fall in love again."

Looking to the Elite, Judge Acker asked, "How does that rune work?"

"It varies, Your Honour," Lord Shirehold answered. "It is meant to speed up the process of creating an emotional bond, to find someone compatible for the person."

"He would have become smitten with the spell-caster regardless, albeit at a slower pace?"

"Yes, as far as we know. The love rune is one of those that we do not yet fully understand as it seems to have different effects depending on the person."

"That will be all." Thomas had barely returned to his seat before the judge said, "Mrs Grahm, come to the witness stand."

I found it rather silly to move so short a distance. Lord Johannes followed behind me, standing dutifully outside of the stand.

"I appreciate your silence during this affair," the judge said. "Although your expressions speak loudly enough."

He prompted me to answer as the others had, so I did, doing my best to school my features and keep my tone even. Judge Acker listened, nodding every so often.

"Mr Grahm runed your forehead so that you cannot use magic?"

"Yes, Your Honour."

"What of the other runes?"

"He did those as well."

I anticipated more questions, but to my confusion, he bade me back to my seat.

"I have come to a conclusion," he proclaimed. "I declare Lord Grahm guilty of using a banned rune, the obedience rune, on Mrs

Isabela Grahm and forcing her to consume alcohol, resulting in her loss of control over her magic. He is to serve a life sentence in prison." The banging of his gavel stressed his verdict.

"I thought my family was in danger!" Lord Grahm protested even as the guards grabbed his arms. "I was trying to keep my family together! She is my property, and by rights—"

"The law is clear that banned runes are *never* to be used, Lord Grahm, on any person, property or not, and she is not your property."

"She has the rune!" Lord Grahm exclaimed, pointing wildly at me. "You saw it!"

"By law, the person who writes the rune holds power and the right to possession," Judge Acker said. "Mr Thomas Grahm owns her." He waved to the guards. "Remove him."

Lord Grahm's curses could be heard up until the doors slammed shut. I inhaled, the tightness in my chest easing a bit.

"Now that that is settled," Judge Acker said, adjusting his spectacles, "bring in the attackers."

Chapter Forty-Eight

Thomas

Henrietta

I was relieved when Judge Acker pronounced jailtime instead of death for my father. From what I could tell of Nate's demeanour, he was too. No matter how complicated our relationship with him was, he was our father, and we wouldn't wish death on him. And... there was a small part of me that clung to the hope that perhaps, one day, Father might change, even if that day did not come for a long time.

I glanced over at Henrietta, who sat towards the back of the room. I had thought of suggesting she give her expertise on the matter of banned runes, but it seemed it was unneeded for Father's case.

But there was a chance it would be needed for the attackers'. I was surprised that there was nothing much to say with Isabela's case, given the importance the Queen and others had stressed importance on it.

She belonged to me. The way Judge Acker had said it, it was as if Isabela were a horse or a pocket watch, not a person. If, for now, that was what kept her from being taken away, then I would not begrudge it.

The guards brought in six of the attackers—mostly men, but a few women—all in chains and bindings that prevented the runes on their bodies from working. Some were stone-faced, while others glanced about the room with wide eyes, as if they were confused on how they ended up here. Their black attire had been replaced with dull brown prison clothes that were thin and looked uncomfortable. The buttons of the men's shirts were undone at the top, showing off the banned rune carved into their chests. Their sleeves were rolled up as well, showing off some legal runes. I found the linework crude at best, making me think the person who drew them had not gone through proper training with the League. Either that, or they were trying to mask their work to keep us from figuring it out.

Once they were all positioned in front of the judge, he surveyed them and then nodded to an attendant nearby. The attendant stepped forward with a tray of flasks.

"These are bottles of truth serum," the judge said, and I noticed Isabela frown. She had mentioned truth serum in her testimony against my father, that he had forced her to tell her everything. "Given that we cannot allow runes to work on your bodies, this is what we must resort to. If you fight back, the guards will force you to take it. We know that you have been given banned runes by someone, and we want to find out who is behind this. Out of the attackers still alive and able to respond, you are what is left, and we need your help to bring about justice. If you are, in fact, innocent and forced to do this, be rest assured that we will release you once we can find a way to reverse the effects of the banned runes."

One of the women and two of the men reached out, accepting the vials and taking the contents without a second thought. Two more hesitantly followed, but the last stared at the judge defiantly. The attendant waited in front of the final attacker, vial ready.

"Drink it, or I can have Samuel assist you."

One of the guards, Samuel, stepped closer. The attacker flinched and took the vial.

The questions started out with their names, ages, marital status, and employment (if any). Their answers were mixed, leaving little to find a pattern from. The only things of worth that they seemed to have in common were that none of them were rune-writers but all had family members who were, family members the judge cleverly ferreted out that they had estranged relationships with, or at least tense ones at best. To be fair to them, I could not imagine how it would have affected my relationship with Nate had one of us not been a rune-writer—Father would have been all the more ashamed and played favourites.

"What is this group you are a part of?"

"We are the Sanctifiers," answered one of the more forthcoming women by the name of Clara. The others grimaced and scowled. "We are on a holy mission to help do what the Chantry cannot: weed out magic and magic-users so that they can no longer tear apart humanity and destroy it. People have come to rely on magic, to believe that they are above the Maker and no longer need Him. We are to burn away all that is unholy, to be sure to save humanity from themselves."

Nate and I exchanged baffled looks. The Chantry taught that the Maker created all things—that would include magic, so why would He make something just to be destroyed?

"And who leads the Sanctifiers?" the judge asked, looking the tiniest bit intrigued.

Silence. Fidgeting.

"We do not know his name," Clara said slowly. "There is a man who wears a mask and refers to himself as the Speaker. He tells us the will of the true leader, someone called the Flame. They refer to us as the Kindling, saying that we are helping to start the revolution."

After a few moments of thought, Judge Acker said, "I have been told there is an expert on banned runes present today. Miss Henrietta Jameson, come to the front."

Henrietta marched, her head held high and her eyes on the judge's. She bowed. "How may I assist you, Judge Acker?"

He waved to his attendant, who came forward with a notebook. "We had these people examined and all of their runes drawn out. Can you tell us what each of these are?"

She took the notebook and flipped through it. "Almost all of them are banned, Your Honour. In fact, the only one not is the claiming rune like the spell-caster has, although that can be considered illegal if these people did sign away their freedom to whomever drew these." Snapping the book shut, she added, "There are silencing runes, explosion runes, obedience runes, tracking runes—even a scrying rune."

"Scrying?"

"It allows the drawer into the runed person's mind and senses to see, hear, and feel what that person is experiencing."

"All of these are suppressed by the bindings?"

"Yes, Your Honour."

"Could we use those runes against the one who wrote them?"

Henrietta frowned. "The risks of removing the bindings outweigh the benefits in my opinion, given that they could explode at any moment."

"Is there a way we could enter their minds to get more information on who is behind this?"

Isabela swallowed hard before speaking up: "Your Honour, if I may—I believe I could enter their minds with my magic."

Chapter Forty-Nine

Isabela

Tricky

"Explain." Judge Acker stared at me, his eyes looking even smaller through his spectacles.

"My magic is of the mind," I said. "I can connect my mind to theirs, and Thomas can rune me so that he can see what I see and draw it for you. Perhaps then we can have some clues to help us find out who the Speaker and the Flame are."

While he pondered, the room waited silently, people looking back and forth between the judge and me.

"What are your thoughts, Miss Jameson, on the risks of what Mrs Grahm is proposing?"

Henrietta locked eyes with me, a coolness to her gaze that was not quite as edged as it had been before. "Your Honour, based on my interactions with her and what I have witnessed of her character, I would have to honestly say that there is little risk involved, especially if she were to be connected to Mr Grahm."

I smiled at her, to which she merely declined her head slightly.

"Your Honour, if I may," interrupted Lord Cornwell.

"You may speak. What concerns do the Elite have?"

He stood, smoothing his jacket. "Several. Firstly, Mrs Grahm has not proven that she is stable. We had her runed because of the incident at the palace, and we do not know if her magic is under control or if she is still susceptible to its seductive power."

Lord Shirehold nodded curtly, hands fidgeting on the top of his cane. I had half-expected him to bring his pipe here as well, even though I doubted the judge would allow smoking of any kind. Lord Smith, on the other hand, showed no emotion and did not move except to look at whomever was speaking.

"Secondly, there is no telling what her magic might do to their minds. Regardless of criminal status, these are *people*, and we cannot subject them to something that could cause irreparable damage or, at worst, death."

I forced myself to breathe in and out slowly. He did, of course, have a point: we had no idea how my magic would work in their minds. However, how was it that he could see them as people but me as property? A similar thought must have crossed Thomas's mind, considering the gleam in his eyes and the set of his jaw. Nathan looked about as amused as his older brother.

"Lastly, Your Honour," Lord Cornwell said, "we worry what could happen to Mrs Grahm after having exerted so much fighting the magic the first time. Prince Esteban of Isouldia has taught us a little about spell-caster magic: too much of it can take a toll on the user's health, even make them mad or kill them if pressed far enough."

Of course my well-being was the last thought, but at least it was mentioned, even if it was not sincere.

"My concern," Lord Shirehold added, "is that if the spell-caster does not keep control of her magic and has to be stopped, Mr Grahm will put everyone at risk for the sake of keeping his wife safe."

I nearly laughed at the look on Thomas's face—he might as well have told the room that Lord Shirehold's speculation was correct and that Thomas would not regret his decision.

"We could have two rune-writers bound to her at the same time," Henrietta suggested. "It is a little more difficult to accomplish, but it would mean that we have twice the strength to deal with her if the need arises."

"Indeed," the judge said slowly. "I have taken your concerns into consideration, Elite, but I must pursue this option if we are to bring this case to rest before more damage is done."

Esteban rose, getting everyone's attention. "Judge Acker, if I may: use my spell-caster. He is more experienced than... Mrs Grahm, and Mr Grahm will have less attachment clouding his judgment." He raised a brow in my direction as if he were gauging my reaction. I kept a neutral expression. What he said made sense, and there was no reason for me to argue—in fact, it would not help my case if I did. Besides, I was in no hurry to use my magic.

"Thank you for the generous offer, Prince Esteban," Judge Acker replied, then looked to Henrietta and the Elite. "Will this amendment suffice?"

Out of the Elite, Lord Cornwell seemed the most ruffled, frowning as he took his seat once more. When he did not speak, Lord Smith said, "Yes, Your Honour. We trust your judgment."

"Then let us not dally any longer."

Chapter Fifty

Thomas

The room watched with bated breath as we prepared to enter Clara's mind. I sneaked a few glances at Isabela, whose eyes never left me. She offered an encouraging smile from where she sat in her box, Lord Johannes still standing behind her.

The sooner this was over, the better.

An attendant waited nearby, holding a sketchbook and ink set in his hands, undoubtedly for me. It had only taken a few moments of the judge asking who would be best suited to draw before the Elite and Henrietta unanimously agreed that I was the person for the job.

I peeked back at Nate, who had slid a few inches closer to Camila. Not enough for anyone else to draw conclusions, and they did not look at each other or speak. The princess lowered her hand to the bench they sat on, keeping her gaze fixed on Prince Esteban and his spell-caster, Lorenzo. Nate lowered his as well, even though there was plenty of space between their hands. He gave me a reassuring nod.

Not for the first time, I wished I had his confidence—or at least could fake it.

Mother had left the courtroom after Judge Acker had given Father's verdict, but now she returned, eyes red, to sit beside Nate. They whispered to one another, Nate surely filling her in on everything else that had happened in her absence. She looked at me with wide eyes, then pulled out her fan, waving it in front of her face more quickly than normal. Nate stopped her and said something into her ear; she bowed her head and resumed fanning herself, slower this time.

"Look at me and stay still, Mr Grahm." Henrietta dabbed at the blood welling on the back of her arm and drew on my forehead. The runes tingled as they were completed, and seeing triple set my stomach rolling. I closed my eyes, suddenly grateful I had eaten little for breakfast.

"Is it necessary to connect all three of our minds?" I asked.

"Better to be safe than sorry."

I could tell Lorenzo's mind from Henrietta's by the sheer amount of magic that made my unsettled stomach all the worse and threatened to make my knees buckle. When I had first connected with Isabela's, I'd brushed against her essence, taking in emotions and bits of who she was, warmth and a wonder toward the world and what could be. Henrietta's mind felt guarded, like a dog with its hackles raised, her essence icy and calculating.

Lorenzo's, on the other hand, seemed hollowed out, like there was nothing left in him but a vessel for power. There was no warmth or chill—nothing until he opened the barrier and magic rushed in. The spell-caster channelled it, making it flow the way he wanted it to, and we connected with Clara.

Uncertainty

Hopefulness

Despair

Faith

Passion

Faith

Grief

Faith

Anger

Anger

ANGER

anger

anger

FAITH

FAITH

FAITH

Flickers of heat and

drips of cold and

patches of lukewarm.

The sensations jarred me, almost made me open my eyes. Her mind was like patchwork, a quilt of contradicting things that gave her essence the appearance of not being entirely her own.

Lorenzo pressed forward, tugging Henrietta and me along as he sorted through her memories in whirls of colour attached by cords of strong emotions. He passed over the bright ones, focusing in on the subdued tones and muted feelings. Panic shot through Clara as Lorenzo lifted one for us to see: a man in all dark attire, including a cloak, his face covered by a mask made of bits of red, orange, and yellow glass that reflected the hundreds of candles around him. His voice was muffled and distorted—in fact, all sound was, as if perhaps Clara could not quite remember exactly what was said.

Luckily for us, what we really needed was visual details.

Clara had been hiding in the wings of the stage behind the curtain, close enough to the Speaker to note the light colour of his skin where the mask did not quite cover his face and the loose strand of blond hair that peeked just outside of the edge of his hood.

But it was the scar at his jawline that had my attention and froze the blood in my veins.

Because it was from the same incident when I had gotten the scar in my eyebrow... back when that man and I used to be friends.

Chapter Fifty-One

Isabela

Thomas's face twisted like he was in pain. I had to clasp my hands together in my lap to keep from going to him. I could only see part of Henrietta's face, and hers was a bit pinched as well. Lorenzo—of course Lorenzo showed no emotion, as always. In contrast, Clara's expressions constantly shifted as if there were dozens vying for control. The poor woman shook to the point where I was almost certain that Lorenzo's hands on her shoulders were the only things keeping her upright.

All the while, Esteban watched intently, glancing down at his pocket watch every few seconds. He caught me looking and offered a smile I did not trust in the slightest. I frowned.

Thomas inhaled sharply, eyes moving rapidly behind his lids. Henrietta's grip on Lorenzo's arm tightened. The Elite said and did nothing, although Lord Cornwell sat on the edge of his seat, his mouth pressed into a thin line. The other attackers fidgeted, some looking at Clara, others not.

After what seemed like ages, they opened their eyes, and Henrietta and Thomas removed the runes, disconnecting themselves from each other and Lorenzo. The attendant came forward and extended the drawing supplies. Thomas waved him off, instead looking at the judge with the same surprised look that was on Henrietta's face.

"Well? What is it?" Judge Acker asked.

Thomas swallowed with difficulty; his hands trembled.

"Out with it, one of you."

Henrietta cleared her throat. "It is a rather… delicate situation, Your Honour. May we speak with you in private first?"

Esteban squared his shoulders and made a subtle gesture. Lorenzo dutifully positioned himself at his master's side. Something dark had passed through Esteban's expression, but it fled as quickly as it came.

"Request denied. You will speak truthfully and plainly for all to hear."

Thomas and Henrietta exchanged a look, their faces pale.

Raw and desperate, Clara's voice amplified the rising anticipation. "They are afraid, Your Honour."

"Of what, Mrs Grayton?"

She licked her chapped lips. "They figured out who the Speaker is and are afraid of the repercussions of exposing that knowledge."

Judge Acker stared at her for a few moments before ordering, "Guards, be attentive. No one is to enter or leave this courtroom without my permission."

They stood straighter, hands at their revolvers or rapiers at their waists.

"I will not ask again: one of you, speak the name."

Weighty silence.

Then Thomas spoke: "Prince August."

"Liar!"

Everyone looked to the prince on the balcony.

"Why would I ever have anything to do with such filth and blasphemy against the Chantry?"

"Your Highness," the judge said evenly, "if you would, join us down here."

"What is the meaning of this?" Queen Eleanora interjected. "Certainly you cannot believe one of my sons is behind something like this."

"I am simply checking all of the facts, Your Majesty," Judge Acker stated. "We must if we wish to solve this case."

August opened his mouth, but the Queen ordered, "Do as he says."

With a huff, August gave in, marching through the curtain behind them and down the stairs. His brothers turned their heads to watch him leave.

"Mr Grahm, Miss Jameson, what did you see that brought you to this conclusion?"

"We saw a man with a mask of broken coloured glass," Henrietta answered. "We caught a bit of blond hair—"

"The hair colour of half the people in this country," retorted August as he stood near the judge's box.

"Do not interrupt," snapped Judge Acker. August reddened. "Please, Miss Jameson, continue."

"Mr Grahm would be the better one to explain. He put together the details before I could."

I held my breath as Thomas briefly glanced at me with disbelief and hopelessness.

"It was the scar at his jawline on the right side," he said in resignation. "I was there when he got it as a boy."

August scowled and took a step toward Thomas. "How dare you! You are the one who gave me this scar in the first place. This is treason. Arrest him!"

Thomas said nothing, did nothing except look at the prince with sadness as August thrust a finger in his direction.

"You will calm yourself or I will have the guards detain you," warned the judge. "Mrs Grayton, is that what you saw?"

"Yes, Your Honour."

"Lorenzo?"

The spell-caster glanced at Esteban, who nodded.

"It is what I saw as well," Lorenzo stated without emotion.

"This is preposterous!" August waved his arms. "You all have gone bloody mad!"

"August!" Queen Eleanora shouted. "No one actually believes it was you. There has to be a way to disprove it. Judge Acker, how are we to proceed?"

The judge exhaled through his nose. "I would suggest a truth rune, but given the circumstances, truth serum will suffice."

"Give it to me," the prince demanded. "I will prove to you that I am innocent."

Judge Acker nodded at the attendant, who walked up to the prince and offered a vial. August snatched it and emptied its contents in one go.

"I—"

"Give it a moment," Judge Acker told him; August glowered but waited nonetheless. "Now you may speak."

"I am not the Speaker. I have never heard of the Sanctifiers or whatever nonsense they call themselves, and I have no blooming idea who the Flame is." He glared at Thomas. "Satisfied?"

Thomas stared at the prince, bewildered, then looked to the judge. "Your Honour, I did not lie. I told you what I saw. What we saw."

"You have wished vindication on me ever since Abigail chose me over you," hissed August.

Thomas shook his head and sighed. "I have no ill will toward you, Prince August."

"And we have no time for petty squabbles," Judge Acker said dismissively. "Something is wrong here."

"Your Honour, if I may," offered Lord Cornwell, "it may be that the spell-caster used magic to tamper with what the rune-writers saw."

"That would mean tampering with Clara's memories," I interjected. "Our magic cannot do anything with the mind like that. All attempts to use magic to change the mind have only ended in disaster."

"That you know of." Lord Cornwell stood, holding his head high. "Your Honour, Mr Grahm and Miss Jameson are honest and trustworthy rune-writers who would have no reason to lie. The prince took the truth serum, so he could not lie. That leaves the spell-caster."

"Or the woman's memories," said Esteban. "It could be that she does not quite remember the details correctly."

"That is a random detail for her to make up."

"I did not accuse her of—"

"ENOUGH." Judge Acker surveyed all of us, his gaze lingering on me before focusing on Esteban. "Your Highness, with your permission, I would like your spell-caster to also take the truth serum."

Just how much of this do they produce? I wondered, although I had to admit that it was helpful. Or, at least, it would be if it got us down to the bottom of this. Just another reminder of how magic could make anything messy and confusing.

"Permission granted." There was a gleam of smugness in his eyes as Lorenzo took it and confirmed that he did not, in fact, use magic to alter Clara's mind in any way.

"I find myself rather baffled," the judge said, and I felt like he was speaking for all of us. "Who else has blond hair and a scar on the right side of his jaw?"

No one had an answer.

Chapter Fifty-Two

Thomas

Ownership

I drew a sketch of what we had seen in Clara's memory, and I was borderline certain that the judge was going to have Henrietta and me drink the truth serum as well. But Lorenzo had, and he confirmed what we were saying, as did the attackers that spoke up. Clara insisted we hadn't lied in the slightest. So, we got out of drinking that nasty concoction.

Judge Acker considered having us try again on the other attackers, only to decide against it, knowing that the others would only have seen the Speaker in the same mask and attire as Clara had.

"If you are quite finished," Queen Eleanora interjected, "I would have my son join us once more."

"Of course, Your Majesty." Judge Acker bowed his head. "Prince August, thank you for your cooperation. You may be seated."

August shot me one last glare before he strode back up the steps to the balcony. Even though there was nothing I could do to explain this away or smooth it over, I still wished things were different. If he thought the distance between us was over Abigail Collins, he was sorely mistaken. That had only widened the gap.

Judge Acker then proceeded to ask us about what else we had seen in Clara's memories, whether or not we believed that she and the other Sanctifiers were in control of their actions.

"There is conflict," I answered honestly. "It feels like there is a lot of magic meddling with their emotions and choices…"

"They are not completely in control of themselves," Henrietta agreed. "While I hold to the belief that they joined of their own free will, it seems that they were manipulated and lied to, that they are no longer able to make decisions for themselves, especially given the banned runes."

Judge Acker took a minute or two to think. "This case will remain open for investigation. In the meantime, the Sanctifiers will stay with the League under surveillance and will be granted every comfort. Mr Grahm, Miss Jameson, you will continue to help with this investigation and report to me daily until this is closed."

"Yes, Your Honour," we said in unison.

"Thank you, Your Honour," Clara said quietly as guards escorted them out of the courtroom. The others maintained their silence, keeping their heads down.

"Mrs Isabela Grahm."

Isabela's head jerked up to look at the judge.

"We have one last case to attend today. Please join your husband and Miss Jameson."

Henrietta took a step away so that Isabela could stand near me. I clenched my fists to keep from reaching out to her. What more could he have to decide when it came to her? He already declared her as mine, much as I hated how that classified her as property.

"Your Honour," Isabela said respectfully, "I do not understand. I thought we cleared my name during Lord Grahm's trial."

"Your intentions were cleared," Judge Acker agreed. "However, it has been brought to my attention that your magic is, indeed, dangerous, and there is the question of to whom you belong."

"You said I belonged to Thomas."

He raised a brow. "You would do well to keep a civil tongue, Mrs Grahm. I said that the rune on your wrist was drawn by Mr Grahm, so you would, by our laws, belong to him. However, you are not a person of our country, and Prince Esteban has made it clear that he is your father, therefore you belong to him by the laws of your country."

A knot formed in my stomach.

"I am married now, Your Honour. Prince Esteban need not concern himself with my wellbeing."

This time Prince Esteban spoke up. "Isabela, I only wish to take care of you. From what I have gathered, you have known this man for barely over a month."

"I have made my decision," she snapped, looking at her father over her shoulder. "Do not pretend to have an interest in me now that you know what I am."

"In these delicate matters," Judge Acker interrupted, "I have decided to hand the final decision over to our Queen." He looked up at her and held up a few official-looking papers in one hand. "Your Majesty, the spell-caster did sign divorce papers while under the obedience rune, so they have not been filed as of yet. I give the final decision of ownership of the spell-caster to the Crown."

I could not breathe. The silence was deafening as we waited for Queen Eleanora to give her answer. Isabela slipped her hand in mine, squeezing almost as tightly as I did.

Slowly, the Queen rose, her eyes flitting between Prince Esteban, Isabela, and me. Every second she waited, panic rose higher within me. How had our plans gone so awry? Was there a chance that Isabela and I could flee and start a new life elsewhere?

As soon as she looked at us with a hint of sorrow in her eyes, my heart stopped.

"Prince Esteban of Isouldia has ownership of his daughter, the spell-caster formerly known as Miss Isabela Fuerte."

"Thank you, Your Majesty," Prince Esteban said. "Isabela, come, let us return home."

"*¡Tío Esteban!*" Camila jumped to her feet, Nate following suit. Then she began rattling something that sounded like a plea in their language. He replied tersely, and Camila looked at Isabela, wide-eyed and mouth slackened. Nate whispered something to her, and she nodded, taking his arm as he escorted her from the benches.

"I am not going anywhere with you," Isabela declared, moving closer to me.

Softly, Judge Acker said, "Unfortunately, Miss Fuerte, you do not have a choice." He banged his gavel, signalling the end of the trials.

Wildness in her eyes, Isabela touched my cheek. "Thomas," she whispered, "you have to remove the binding rune. I might be able to get us out of here and then—"

Guards surrounded us, their hands twitching near their weapons. Prince Esteban said in a calm tone, "Come quietly. There is no reason to make a scene, *mija*."

She looked around and then met my gaze once more, this time with angry tears welling, threatening to spill. My heart broke all over again, seeing her like this, knowing there was nothing I could do to stop it.

"We'll find a way," I murmured. Tenderly, I pulled her to me and kissed her. "I love you."

Letting her go, letting them take her away, letting her father walk her out of the courtroom… all of it was difficult, and letting it all happen was the hardest thing I had ever done in my life. Isabela tried to hold onto me even when the guards pulled us apart, and she refused to look away from me until she was outside and the door to the courtroom shut, its echo like a final nail in the coffin.

Judge Acker passed by me, but I barely noticed his presence until he said, "I am sorry. I have to follow protocol." When I said nothing in reply, he left.

"Thomas, I am so sorry," Camila said, wiping at her face with a handkerchief. She held Nate's arm like he was her only source of comfort. "I will speak with him again, see what I can do to change his mind."

"Thank you," I managed, my words sounding as hollow as I felt.

"Now is not the time to give up," Nate said, keeping his voice low. "Tom, look at me. Look at me. We are going to get this sorted, I promise. Don't lose your hope."

I would not, because that was the only thing I had left, the only thing that was tethering me to my sanity. I felt that, if I lost my hope, I would fade out of existence.

Chapter Fifty-Three

Isabela

"I can walk by myself, thank you very much." I attempted to yank my arm away, but Esteban kept an iron hold under the guise of escorting me like a gentleman. "Let go of me."

"Do not make a scene, *mija*," he said quietly and strode toward an awaiting carriage.

"Let me go, and there will be no scene to make."

"You know I cannot do that."

"Because you have to be in control of absolutely everything or it drives you mad."

His cheek twitched. He stopped in front of the open carriage door and offered me an insincere smile. "Your mother would be mortified to see you speak and act in such a way, especially to a prince."

I glared at him. "My mother would be mortified to know that all of her hard work keeping me from your clutches was all in vain." I refused to blink, to look away. If he wanted to see the fire in my soul, I would show it to him in full force.

"Get into the carriage."

"No. Release me."

"Isabela, this is not a request." His tone dropped to a dangerous low; his dark eyes pinned me where I was. "I am sorry that I was not the father you needed growing up, but I am trying to be now."

I shook my head slowly. "I do not believe you."

To my surprise, he released me. I whirled around to run back to the courthouse but collided with Lorenzo's chest.

Esteban got in and ordered, "Put her in the carriage."

I struggled against the other spell-caster to no avail. Without much effort, he forced me inside and shut the door behind him. Between his bulky frame and the wall of the carriage, I had no room to move.

"You are only making this more difficult than it needs to be." Esteban's smugness stoked my ire. "You will see soon that I am doing this to help you."

"You are doing this for yourself," I snapped.

"The more you struggle and fight, the more crazed you will appear."

"Why would I care what others think?" The carriage had barely started moving, and already I felt like I was overheating. If I had my magic, I might have been able to escape... if I had gotten out of the range of Lorenzo's.

And then what? Found Thomas and asked him to leave everything—and everyone—behind? Granted, I could see Nate jumping at the opportunity to leave, to go on adventures. I would hate to leave Camila behind again—

Camila. She had tried to convince Esteban to see reason and reconsider, and hopefully she would try again. Certainly she would, knowing her.

But was there anything that would change his mind?

Esteban leaned forward slightly. "I would care if I were you. If you wanted people to believe that it was in your best interest that I release you, acting like a mad woman will not help your case."

I stared him down. "Or you could release me."

"I am not going to do that, Isabela." He straightened and adjusted his gloves.

"Why not? Why keep me? You already have one spell-caster. Why do you want to keep me too?" I gestured to my forehead. "I do not have access to my magic."

"That will be remedied shortly," Esteban said with certainty. "First I have to speak with Master Thomas Grahm to be sure he will not try heroics when I have him remove the binding rune."

The title pricked at my already bleeding heart. How had things gone so wrong so quickly? All of the fairy-tales I'd read had their happily ever afters, and I thought we'd been on the brink of ours...

This is not a fairy-tale, you silly girl.

The ride to the palace was short, and Esteban held my arm once more as we walked. It was better than being manhandled by Lorenzo... slightly.

I said nothing but kept a frown plastered on my face so that it was obvious to all of the servants passing by that this was not what I wanted. If nothing else, Esteban did have a point about appearing crazed.

He had no idea how crazed I could be.

Even though it had very similar decorations and furniture selection, Esteban's rooms were even bigger than Camila's, with its own music room and balcony. His trunks of belongings were closed, and I could see nothing of his anywhere. Even his bed looked untouched.

Lorenzo stayed outside of the room, leaving us alone. We stood there, gazes locked like we were two wild dogs circling each other, waiting for the other to attack.

"You did not answer my question."

His brows raised. "Which question is that, *mija?*"

"Why?"

Esteban sighed. "Isabela, you have to understand that my methods are harsh because being a spell-caster puts you in more danger. Look at Lorenzo: magic took almost all of his emotions, he is almost a shell of a man. Even if you can control magic, others will always see you as a threat." He stepped forward; I stepped backward. "I have been looking for you ever since you disappeared. I had *cazarrecompensas* looking for you, but they said you were claimed by a rune-writer family. I had to be careful in finding a way to save you and bring you home to safety without risking our alliance with this country."

I blinked as I took in the information. "You sent *cazarrecompensas* after me? You... you knew what I am?"

"I knew your mother was a spell-caster. The chances of you not having the gift were slim to none."

He knew... and he had let me live my life until I ran away.

As if he could sense my hesitation, he took another tentative step toward me. This time, I flinched but did not move away.

"Isabela, I promise you that I have your best interests at heart. I am trying to protect you."

"I do not want your protection," I said quietly, my anger mere embers that could easily be stoked into flame once more. "I want freedom."

His expression softened. "You were property to the Grahm family, not a person. Is that truly the freedom you sought?"

"That was about to change. I married Thomas, and—"

"And what?" he challenged gently. "Marriage to a lord will do nothing to change how society sees you. You are a spell-caster, and that is all they will ever see, a rabid wolf pretending to be a lapdog. I tried for years to change the minds of my people, my own brother, so that I could marry your mother, so that spell-casters could have more freedoms. Even if Lord and Lady Grahm had accepted your marriage, Thomas could not have taken over the family manor: the League and upper classes would not have stood for it, not if he had a spell-caster as a wife."

"Why are you being cruel?"

"I am trying to get you to see reason."

"Do not pretend to understand," I warned, my tone edged and sharp. "This is not about you. *Mamá* would have married you had you asked her. She did not care about what others thought, but she cared about your thoughts and feelings. She hoped for years that you would change your mind." Traitorous tears rolled down my cheeks. "Thomas loves me and wants to be with me no matter how society treats us. He is willing to give up whatever it takes to be with me."

"And you would let him?"

The question hit me as if Esteban had slapped me. "What?"

"You would be selfish and let him give up his future so that you would be happy?"

"So that *we* would be happy."

"You barely know him."

"You do not know him at all."

Esteban sighed and ran a hand over his face.

"How are we supposed to change how society views us if we let them dictate how we act?" This time I drew closer, leaving a little space between us. "If you want to be my father and you want what is best for me, then release me and let me be married to Thomas. Be our advocate—show society that you support us."

His eyes misted. "If only it were that simple, *mija*."

Before I could say anything else, he left, locking the door from the outside.

Chapter Fifty-Four

Thomas

Hope

I rubbed at my eyes, hoping that would be enough to keep me going for another few hours. Or at least one more. I had no idea how late it was, but the candles were much lower than I remembered them being. Henrietta was in another part of the League's library with Georgiana, looking for any other books that might help us solve the case. Her line of thinking was that if the Sanctifiers were using banned runes, then one of them might help us figure out why the Speaker looked like Prince August.

Around noon, Nate and Camila had come to check on me and brought food. None of the princesses, not even Camila, had been able to convince their uncle to even let them visit Isabela, although Camila was certain she knew which room in which my wife was being kept.

My wife. No longer.

I had tried to come up with some way to communicate with her, even slip her a letter, but she could not read my language, and I could not write in hers. Camila might have helped me, but getting it to Isabela would have been a whole other matter. What could I have said? I was no closer to freeing her than I was when she was prised from my arms.

My eyes stung as I turned the page carefully with a gloved hand, scouring the faded words for any sort of clue. Part of me wondered if I should have gone with Nate and Camila to seek out who else might have blonde hair and a scar along their jawline. But no, it was better to split up and cover more ground. I highly doubted they would find anyone matching the description anyway.

Footsteps echoed in the vacant hallway.

"Thomas?"

I looked up to see Prince August entering the room. I banged my knee on the desk as I hurriedly stood and bowed.

"None of that," he said, waving a hand. "I want to know why you tried to pin this on me. I know we are not the friends we used to be, but… well, I rather thought we had gotten past that nasty business with Miss Abigail Collins." To my surprise, there was genuine hurt in his expression, a vulnerability I had not seen out of him in years.

"You must know I have no ill will toward you," I said softly, meeting his gaze. "I did not want to believe that you were the Speaker, and I am relieved that you are not. Judge Acker wanted the truth, and we told him what we saw." Did he not see how it pained us to speak in the courtroom, that we were asked multiple times before any of us said anything? Even Clara had the presence of mind to know how scared we were to reveal what we had seen.

August exhaled slowly. "I want to believe you, Thomas, but I saw how you treated me with Isabela around."

I winced. "There is a difference between forgiving someone and trusting someone. I did not mean any disrespect."

"You never do." August crossed his arms. "You are so pure-hearted, it's maddening."

"Nate's said something along those lines." I chuckled, although it sounded flat. "August, please believe me when I say that I do not wish any harm or bad fortune to befall you. Yes, I am protective of Isabela, but that does not just have to do with you."

"You really love her."

"With everything I am."

August watched me for a moment like he was trying to puzzle something out. He nodded slowly, unfolding his arms. "I am sorry about how the trial played out. I'm going to miss her."

"I'm hoping to find a way to keep her here."

"Of course you are." The prince smiled genuinely. "Is there something I can do to help?"

"I honestly have no idea," I answered. "Perhaps you could inquire the Queen, see if she will speak with Prince Esteban? I have been wracking my brain for solutions, but splitting my time between that and solving the Sanctifiers case…"

"You seem exhausted," August said, not unkindly. "I will see if I can speak with Mother, although I cannot promise anything."

"I understand. Thank you regardless."

Henrietta strode toward the desk, Georgiana at her heels, taking two steps for every one of Henrietta's. "Prince August." She bowed, and the girl followed suit. "What can we do for you?"

"I came to check on the progress of the Sanctifiers case," August said. "It's rather unsettling, having people second-guess me despite having taken the truth serum. Even my own mother interrogated me."

I flinched at the guilt that accompanied that statement. That was one of the many reasons I had not wanted to speak.

"Our apologies, Your Highness," Henrietta said. "Our intent was—and is—to seek out the truth, not to bring you harm. That being said, you seem to have impeccable timing."

"Why is that?" he asked, eyeing the large book Henrietta carefully set on the desk.

She flipped to a bookmarked page and tapped at a strange-looking rune. "Because, Your Highness, we might have found out why the Speaker looks like you."

Chapter Fifty-Five

Isabela

Magicless

No one was allowed to visit me. Being alone in the room for three days was driving me mad—something that my magic could have done by itself had I let it. "It's for your own safety," Esteban had said, but the irony was not lost on me.

The doors were always locked from the outside, and the windows were sealed shut as if I would have considered jumping from three stories. Or was it four? I supposed I could have tried fashioning some way to escape out the window, but the height would have made it too difficult without magic anyway.

At least we hadn't left for Isouldia yet. Esteban claimed that he wanted to have the alliance ironed out and the engagements between the princes and princesses sorted before he considered returning home. That means I had that long—however long it was—to convince him to release me. So far, our conversations were brief, taking place whenever he deigned to visit, which was at least once or twice a day. He had chosen to take up a new room next to mine, giving me my space.

I am not sure what I would have done if he had even suggested we sleep in the same room.

My body and mind were finally recovered from the magic mishap, so I spent my lonely hours scouring the rooms for ways out as well as planning what I could say to convince Esteban. If his word was to be trusted, he had not yet spoken with Thomas, who, despite whatever Esteban said, was sure to try some heroics to save me. In case that did not work, I had to have a plan.

I was not leaving Thomas under any circumstances.

Thinking and moving around made it easier to distract myself from the constant ache in my chest. Whenever I lay down, I cried myself to sleep thinking of Thomas. How had things gone so wrong so quickly? Every time we seemed to have something under control, something else fell apart. Esteban's words stuck with me, picking at my mind and stabbing at my heart.

I tossed and turned, throwing the blankets off. The thing about thoughts is that you cannot get away from them. I would have gladly listened to Prince August prattle on about his achievements for a day straight if it meant I could get away from the cycle of thoughts that threatened to consume my sanity.

A soft knock at the door jarred me.

I've finally gone mad. Who would come to my bedroom in the middle of the night?

I heard it again. Quickly donning a robe, I went to the door. "It's locked on your side," I said quietly.

A few soundless seconds passed before a click, and then the door opened.

To my surprise, the guards were gone. Prince August was at the door in a dark cloak. He raised a finger to his lips and lifted a drawing book with something written on one page. Trying to recover from my surprise at seeing the prince here, I shook my head. He looked confused.

"I can't read your language," I whispered. I could have used magic to help had I the access.

"Rescue. Hurry." His voice was slightly lower than usual, which I figured was because he was trying to make extra certain no one would overhear. He threw a cloak around my shoulders, fastened it, and put the hood onto my head in rapid succession. Taking my hand, he pulled me into the hallway, which was oddly void of guards as well. Had he ordered them away, bought their silence to break me out?

His steps were muted even though he was wearing boots on the marble floor, which made me think that perhaps Thomas or Nathan had runed him. They had to be working together. Why else would August help me?

His hand was more calloused than I expected, and my mind ran through all of the times we had touched during dance lessons. He had been wearing gloves then, hadn't he?

Isabela, quit overthinking things—he's trying to help you.

Yet there was something off that I could neither put my finger on nor ignore.

You're just surprised that he's helping after all of the bad blood between Thomas and him.

We took the stairway to the bottom floor, where a guard strolled toward us, a candle in hand. August yanked me into the drawing room and behind a large vase. We crouched, my heart beating wildly. I looked at August, but he looked at the door, his hood covering what little of his face I could see.

The eerie feeling grew as I thought of Thomas's description of the Speaker.

But what would he want with me? He sent Sanctifiers to kill me, not to rescue me.

Still, that did little to calm me.

The light passed by the door, shadows stretching and moving in time with the guard's steps. August waited until it was completely dark again before moving to stand.

Twin growls halted us. August's big hounds stalked toward us, hackles raised and teeth bared. I tugged August's hood back to show them their master; he balked, grabbing at it, but the hounds still closed in.

"Tell them to stand down," I urged him, my nerves solidifying in the pit of my stomach.

"Sit," he ordered, his voice still not quite right. "Lie down."

The hounds snapped at him, backing us into a corner. I tried to prise my hand away, but he held fast.

"Who are you?" I asked.

He met my gaze for a brief second. How could someone look so much like another person yet not at all like them at the same time?

One of the hounds latched onto his leg and yanked him onto the floor. He let go of me in surprise, and I leapt back out of the way.

"Help!" I yelled as the man cried out, fumbling with the dagger he'd pulled from his waist. He wrestled with both hounds, who had him pinned. One bit down on his forearm, instantly drawing blood.

I fled, wishing I had my magic to keep them from tearing him apart.

We had to figure out who he was…

I yelled again as loud as I could, knowing full well that I was losing my chance to escape. There was enough noise that someone was bound to hear and come running, so I could leave now while there was a distraction—

High-pitched yelps startled me. I turned around to see the man stumble out of the room after me, his clothes torn and blood-soaked. He said my name and reached for me. I tried to twist out of the way, but he caught my sleeve, tearing my robe. While I tried to get loose of the sleeve, he got a hold of my arm. I whirled around and landed a swift kick between his legs.

The first guard arrived when the man doubled over, still gripping my arm. Two other guards and a rune-writer quickly followed, separating the man from me.

"Prince August," the rune-writer started to say.

"That's not him!" I exclaimed.

They looked between us, me with nothing but my torn robe and a cloak, and him covered in blood and wielding a dagger.

"What is the meaning of all this ruckus?" snapped Queen Eleanora as she descended the stairway. Relief hit me hard at the sight of the real August just behind her, along with Claude, Esteban, and Lorenzo. She gasped. "Arrest him!"

The man attempted to flee, but the guards and rune-writer were faster. There were runes on the man's neck within mere seconds—but they disappeared just as quickly, fading from his skin like they were rejected. Lorenzo lifted his hand; the man fell to the floor, motionless.

"Keep him there," ordered Esteban as he made his way to me and fixed my cloak to cover my bare arm. He kept his hand at my back, and I did not bother to move away.

"Check him for other runes," demanded August.

"Now!" added the Queen.

The rune-writer tore at the man's shirt to reveal messy runes across his chest and stomach as if they were written quickly. August manoeuvred around his mother, getting as close to the imposter as he dared. He pointed at a larger rune near the man's heart.

"That is the one Rune-writer Henrietta Jameson showed me," he said to his mother. "I told you that was what they suspected was happening. It's a banned rune that lets you take on the appearance of someone else."

"How do we take it off and find out who he is?" the Queen asked.

"We could give him a truth serum, which seems to be the answer to everything," August suggested with a hint of mockery.

"If I may, Your Majesties," the rune-writer said, "it would be best if we allow the League to handle it."

After a moment of pondering, she said, "Send someone to inform the Elite. I want to be there when they solve this case."

"As you wish, My Queen."

Esteban smoothed back my hair and whispered, "Let us get you back to bed. I'll be sure to have more guards posted to prevent anything like this happening again."

There were too many guards to run, and I was magicless. So I let him lead me back to my luxurious cell.

Chapter Fifty-Six

Thomas

Suspect

It was very early in the morning when I was woken by Nate telling me that they found the Speaker. In my groggy state of mind, I did not think to question why he was at the League Hall when the sun still had yet to make its appearance for the day. And why, after I straightened my appearance and hurried after him into the meeting room, I stared at Camila in confusion, my brain not quite awake enough to understand what was bothering me. She put a finger to her lips, and I looked away, focusing instead on the gathered rune-writers, royal family, and Prince Esteban with his spell-caster. Where our meetings were normally orderly, everything was in mayhem, people standing and talking over one another. Of the Elite, I noticed only Lord Shirehold and Lord Smith, but they, too, were lost in the crowd, Queen Eleanora and her sons having taken up the Elite's table.

My eyes roamed the crowd for a minute before I realised whom I was seeking out, and my heart squeezed painfully. Of course Isabela was absent. As if sensing my distress, her father looked at me, dipping his head in acknowledgement. I pondered approaching him to ask where she was, but more rune-writers arrived, a shackled man in tow.

The man held a striking resemblance to August, which gave me a bit of relief to have physical proof that I did not intend to slander the prince in any way.

"It is hard to tell them apart," murmured Henrietta from beside me, making me jump. She eyed me with slight amusement. "Did you not realise I was here, Thomas?"

"Still waking up," I admitted. "They captured the Speaker? How?"

"Word has it he tried to kidnap Isabela," Nate said, his gaze checking on Camila in the back corner every once in a while. She kept to herself, and for once, no one other than Nate seemed to be paying her any attention. "She fought him and screamed until the guards found them."

I had left her without magic. I silently thanked the Maker that she was still alive, that nothing terrible happened. If all went well, I hoped I could finally convince Prince Esteban to let me see her, to at least let me unbind her magic. He had yet to speak so much as a word to me since that day in the courtroom.

"She's fine, Tom," Nate said softly. "August himself assured me that she is unharmed. He is still trying to persuade the Queen to reconsider her stance on Isabela."

I nodded, my throat tightening.

"Enough!" Queen Eleanora commanded, bringing a silence to the chaos of the room. "Let us begin."

"We do not have everyone here, Your Majesty," Lord Shirehold pointed out. It made me feel better that, even though everyone here was dressed, no one looked their best, considering how early it was in the morning. Granted, there was no way I was going to look my best when I had fallen asleep at the desk until Henrietta had dumped water on me and insisted I take one of the spare rooms. I had fallen back asleep to Henrietta snapping at me about drooling on ancient texts.

"This cannot wait any longer. Proceed immediately." Her eyes narrowed in challenge; everyone either stepped aside or brought the Speaker forward in preparation. He held his head high, scanning the room, no doubt for any potential escape options. I took note of his bloody, torn attire, wondering if Isabela had done something to him, although it looked animalistic, especially the bites on his arm and legs.

"Your Majesty," said Lord Johannes from beside the Speaker, "we have checked this person's body for runes, and we have found none that would prevent us from undoing them without consequence. However, since he or she has clearly been runed to change his or her appearance, I fear there might be a possibility that they found a way to hide them."

"Miss Jameson?" The Queen wasted no time in addressing Henrietta. "What are your thoughts on this?"

"I know of no such rune," Henrietta answered clearly. "However, there is always the small chance that someone has created a new one I know not of. I would deem it highly improbable, My Queen."

Queen Eleanora turned her attention back to Lord Johannes. "What options would it leave us with if you do not remove the runes? Truth serum?"

As my mind started to clear, I had to wonder if there was a way to make a rune that would leave truth serum ineffective. The thought did not sit well with me.

After some discussion, the Queen commanded that Lord Johannes and two others remove the runes, and that the rest of us be ready in case something went wrong. Despite myself, I cringed, thinking of the lives of the attackers we were not willing to sacrifice, but this man's could be forfeit.

We watched in silence as Lord Johannes and his helpers prepared: vials of opaque brown liquid sloshed against the glass as they unstoppered them and added drops of their own blood. The liquid darkened, a sure sign that it was working.

The Speaker jerked, throwing his head into the nose of one of the men holding him. Then he sprinted toward the back door, knocking over Lord Shirehold and narrowly missing the vials. He did not get far: the rune-writers nearest him made a barricade to force him back. Frantically, the man tried to shove his way out, then resorted to throwing punches when it didn't work. One of the men stumbled back, giving the Speaker a chance to get through. Luckily he was stalled long enough for someone to stab a syringe into the Speaker's neck—after a few seconds, he slumped to the floor, his open eyes the only part of him moving.

Lord Shirehold was helped back onto his feet, and the Speaker was dragged back to the front of the room. The Speaker's shirt was taken off and he was held up so that Lord Johannes and the others could use the brown liquid to coat the runes. They dipped cloths into the vials to avoid contact with their own skin, and I tensed every time they touched the Speaker's. The lone sign that the imposter felt the tearing, burning sensation was the shrinking of his pupils. My stomach twisted, remembering the lesson on the removal solution where our teachers applied it to us so that we would know how it felt. Even though only the League had it (and in small supply), their belief was that, if we ever had the option to use it on someone, we would wait until it was our last resort, that we would not choose flippantly.

The brown liquid bubbled and foamed on the runes, turning into an even darker reddish colour. The imposter's eyes darted back and forth as if he were going to find a saviour. When the rune-writers wiped away the excess, raw blisters were left behind.

His face and body began to change as if my vision blurred and refocused. The rune-writers held up the Speaker so he wouldn't fall to the floor, so that everyone could watch the transformation, strange and unsettling as it was.

Audible gasps filled the space, and I would have joined them if I'd had breath in my lungs.

The Speaker was Lord Cornwell.

Chapter Fifty-Seven

Isabela

News

To my surprise, Camila was allowed to visit the day after the Speaker attempted to kidnap me. When she knocked on the door and opened it before I could say anything, I tensed, reaching for the fire iron near the fireplace.

"It's me! Put that down before you poke my eye out." Camila shut the door behind her. It was her voice, the signature red of her dress, and the way she carried herself that reassured me that it really was her.

I dropped the fire iron and flung my arms around *mi prima*, pulling her close. My eyes stung, and I was helpless to stop the flow of tears.

"I am so sorry, Isabela," Camila murmured. "I tried to visit sooner, but *Tío* refused everyone, even Beatriz. You know how she gets away with almost everything."

My laugh came out strangled, caught in my throat with the emotions that were overflowing. It took a few tries before I managed to clear my throat enough to say, "Thomas?" Not a full sentence, but I knew she'd get my meaning.

Camila pulled back so that she could see my face and dab at my cheeks with a handkerchief. "He is just as much of a mess without you as you are without him, although he has enough presence of mind to do everything he can to change *Tío*'s mind about you."

"They are talking?"

"I believe so. They walked out of the League Hall together this morning."

I gripped her shoulders hard enough that she hissed, pulled my hands away, and held them. "What were they doing there? What were *you* doing there?" My thoughts ran various directions and collided into each other in an epiphany. "You found out the identity of the Speaker."

"And the Flame."

"Then hurry! Tell me everything!"

"I need to sit. I was standing for a long time in that meeting." She led me to the couch.

I sat quickly and tugged her down. "Well? What happened? Who are they?" I felt a small twinge of guilt, seeing the dark circles under her eyes and the fact that Camila was not even wearing cosmetics or jewellery—she must have been in a hurry to be a part of the meeting and was now exhausted from how early it was. I myself was still running on adrenaline from the events of the night before, but it would hit me soon.

Camila explained everything, how they used a brown liquid called remover solution to get rid of the runes disguising none other than Lord Cornwell. I gasped at the revelation.

"That's not all," Camila said to shush me before I could interrupt with more questions. She straightened and locked eyes with me. "While he was incapacitated, they had Lorenzo search his mind for facts about the Sanctifiers and the Flame. Turns out that Lord Shirehold is the Flame, and a few other rune-writers were a part of the scheme."

"Why attack the palace and us?" I asked. "That makes no sense."

"The only way the League could get more power is if the Crown decided that they were in a state of emergency and sought out the rune-writers for help. The Sanctifiers were a way to cause chaos and fear."

"Then why attack me one day and try to kidnap me the next?"

"That part was a little tricky to decipher, according to Henrietta and Thomas."

They had made Thomas do it again. I recalled the look on his face, the way he paled last time. Of course, with his loyalty and good nature, he would not turn down an opportunity to help.

Camila gave me a sympathetic look and squeezed my hand. "Thomas offered. He said he wanted to see the truth for himself, to see this through. What the two of them put together was that the Flame and the Speaker thought that killing you would call our country into suspicion, causing more tension and possible war. After they failed and saw what you did at the palace when your magic went out of control, they thought they could replicate it to destroy part of the capital city and force the Queen to take action."

This time I was silent and processed all of the information. "Then they stopped it? The Sanctifiers are no more?"

Camila shook her head. "They have the Flame and the Speaker, but it may take a while to find all of the Kindling and return things as they should be."

How long would it be until we felt safe again?

We? As of now, I am still headed back to Isouldia.

"Also," Camila interrupted my train of thought before I went into another bout of depression, "a man named Priest Abel approached your father and tried to convince him to let him speak with you. He is the man who married you and Thomas, is he not?"

"Yes." I immediately perked up. "What did he want?"

"From what I overheard—"

"Eavesdropped," I corrected, not at all upset at her for doing so.

With a smirk, Camila said, "The point is, I got the information to share with you if you will stop interrupting me." Her brow raised in challenge; I said nothing. "Priest Abel appealed to your father and asked him to consider other options for your best interest."

"Like?" I pressed, scooting closer.

Camila sighed and grimaced. "I have no idea. Consuela found me and nearly blew my cover. I had to walk away with her before I heard the good parts."

I slumped and gave my own sigh. "Hopefully Priest Abel at least opened Esteban's mind to another possibility where I can stay here with Thomas and Nate."

"And me," Camila added with a sly look.

"You are staying? Did one of the princes propose?" With everything going on, I had forgotten about the alliance and proposals. I doubted that Camila had spent much time flirting when I was locked up, but I could have been wrong. Possibly.

"Prince August proposed," Camila confirmed slowly enough to make me want to throttle her.

"And?"

"And... I declined. Respectfully, of course, and August seems to understand and holds no ill will. Inés already accepted Robert's proposal, and it is rumoured that Herbert will ask Beatriz, but we shall see." She smoothed her dress. "There is no pressure for me to marry one of the princes anymore."

I narrowed my eyes. "What are you not telling me, Camila? Quit baiting me."

With a smug smile, Camila announced, "*Nataniel* kissed me."

I chuckled. "It was a matter of time. Have you spoken of intentions?"

Like the *princesa* she was, Camila waved a hand with a snooty air about her. "His lips and tongue said it all."

More details than I wanted, but it was less than I was afraid she would give. "And they said…?"

Camila looked at me in annoyance and then smiled. "I am sure we will speak of it soon. Right now our focus is on setting you free so that you can be with Thomas."

Chapter Fifty-Eight

Thomas

Unafraid

"How did the meeting with Isabela's father go?" Nate asked quietly, even though no one was close enough to hear us. Who would want to be anywhere near the prison?

"I have no clue," I admitted. "He listened to what I had to say and then dismissed me."

"You could have pressed the issue."

"With the Prince of Isouldia? I'd rather not hurt my chances of setting Isabela free."

We stood side-by-side, neither of us taking a step closer to the prison. The sun hid behind the clouds, and cooling winds passed through every minute or so, leaving me unable to pretend that the sweat beading at my forehead and on my hands was due to the weather.

"Did he at least tell you when you can remove Isabela's runes?"

"Today," I managed to say despite the tightness of my throat. "I head to the palace after we are done here." The very thought of seeing Isabela again had my heart aching. If he treated her poorly...

"I will go with you for moral support."

Like the good brother he was. "Thank you. Are you ready?" I asked.

Nate ran a hand through his hair. The muscles in his jaw flexed as he stared at the plain building. "Is there such a thing as being ready when it comes to Father?"

"I suppose not." One of us had to take the first step, and the other would follow. Either way, I knew that the sooner I was done here, the sooner I could see Isabela.

Hopefully not for the last time.

No. I would not allow it unless she wanted to be apart. I touched the small box in my pocket, assuring myself it was still there.

First this, then Isabela.

Each step felt heavy.

The prison guards let us in almost immediately, the warden hurrying to escort us.

"Call me Isaiah," he insisted. "I am sorry for the predicament your family is in. Please, follow me."

Most prisoners kept to the back wall of their cells, not making eye contact. There were a few who watched us pass by, and one who dared hiss at Isaiah through broken, rotting teeth. I tried to keep as close behind the warden as possible, wanting to be out of reach in case one of the prisoners decided to try something. The ceilings were so low that I had to duck under the doorways as we moved into a hallway that brought us to heavily guarded rooms for visits. I noted that the guards were in groups of three with one rune-writer in each, black attire marking them when the others were wearing grey.

"He is in here," Isaiah said, gesturing toward the small room. "I will wait nearby in case you need me."

I gave him thanks and glanced over my shoulder to make sure Nate was still with me. He gave a solemn nod, and we walked in together.

The grey of the bare walls, floor, and ceiling added to the morose atmosphere. Father—in plain brown rags like the attackers had been— sat on a wooden chair, his hands and feet shackled to the floor. If he could get up, the chains gave him very little radius of movement.

The door was kept open in case the guards were needed. I took a little comfort in it: even with my conflicting emotions and hurts he caused, could I defend myself against my father if he attacked?

"My sons finally deigned to see me," he said, lifting his stubbly chin. "Guilt eating away at you?"

Nate looked down at the floor. I forced myself to meet our father's intense stare.

"Why did you do that to Isabela?"

He sighed in exasperation. "I was keeping you safe, Thomas. She had you under her spell, and you needed to be set free. We were so close to raising our social status. The Elite were considering making our family line part of them."

"She did nothing to me," I argued.

"Then how do you explain your quick infatuation with her?"

"The love rune *you* gave me. I would have fallen for her regardless, but that made it happen much faster."

His eyes gleamed with hatred that made me want to recoil. "How could you blame me when all I have ever done was for my family? For you two? For your mother? You are ungrateful—"

"Do not pretend with us," Nate snapped. I looked at him in surprise, seeing him lock eyes with Father in a way he'd never done prior. "We are a thinly veiled excuse for you to do whatever you please for your own selfish gain. If you genuinely care about us, you will leave us out of it and speak the truth."

Father stood and straightened as much as his shackles allowed. Nate did not so much as flinch.

"I will not be spoken to like that by anyone, least of all a boy playing at being a man." Lip curled in a snarl, he spat at me, "You'd best keep him under control. He is your problem now, *Lord* Grahm."

I almost smiled at the shock on his face as I said, "That is not my title."

Father's eyes flitted back and forth between us, trying to make sense of what I'd just said and not wanting to believe it.

"It is mine," Nate confirmed, not bothering to disguise his delight at Father's dismay.

"You—" Father scowled at me, and for a moment I thought he was going to lunge. "How could you? You gave it up for what? That spellcaster?"

"It was never something I wanted. I believe Nate will be a lord this country needs." *And if not, at least he will be memorable.*

Father's expression abruptly changed to one of desperation; he reached toward me, the manacles holding him back. "Thomas, let me remove the love rune. You are not thinking clearly. Please, let me do this."

"I no longer have it." I was grateful for the salve and bandage Henrietta had given me to keep the blistered skin from being intolerable. Hopefully, in a few weeks, it would be nothing but a light scar. "I made this decision of my own free will and clear mind."

The hatred returned in full force. "You came here to mock me. You might as well drive a dagger through my heart and be done with it."

As I looked at him, I found that no fear remained, only pity. In all sincerity, I said, "I had hoped this conversation would go better. If you wish to make amends and salvage your relationship with your family, have Warden Isaiah reach out to us. Goodbye, Father."

Chapter Fifty-Nine

Isabela

Freedom

Esteban barely gave me a few minutes' notice before Thomas was supposed to arrive. I quickly washed my face and fixed my hair in a half-up style so that my forehead was exposed, the rune on display. Then I stood and waited, trying not to fidget. Esteban watched in amusement. Lorenzo did not so much as look at me as he waited by the door.

Thomas's knock echoed the thudding of my heart. The moment he stepped into the room, I looked him up and down, seeing nothing new other than the tiredness in his face. He lit up when he locked eyes with me, and he moved like he was trying to keep himself from rushing to me. I wished he would.

Thomas looked away briefly and bowed his head. "Prince Esteban, thank you for arranging this. May I begin?"

"By all means."

I had to clench my hands into fists to keep from throwing my arms around Thomas as he stepped closer to me. I inhaled, welcoming his familiar scent, letting that be enough for the moment, which passed all too quickly.

Thomas retrieved his pocketknife and made a slash across the back of his wrist. Using the welling blood, he gently traced over the rune on my forehead. It tingled as the rune came undone, but I focused on his face, taking in the small details I had been dreaming about since our separation. How was it possible that he was even more handsome than in my dreams?

He finished by wiping my face with a handkerchief. "It is done," he said, his gaze dipping to my mouth before jerking away to look at my father. "Have you considered what we discussed?"

Neither of their expressions gave me any clue to what they were talking about, although I was certain it had to do with my freedom.

"I heard you refused the title of Lord Grahm," Esteban said. "Why would your brother agree to paying such a large amount for my daughter?"

"It is not for her," Thomas corrected. "It is to free her so that she can make her own decisions. My brother loves Isabela like family, as does my mother. We are all in agreement."

My breath caught in my throat, my heart full, knowing that they loved me as I loved them. They were my family just as Camila was.

Esteban stared at Thomas with an unreadable expression. "I refuse your offer."

I looked to Thomas: his shoulders slumped, his head shook.

"Is there anything you would take? Name your price."

"You said yourself that she is a person, not property, and therefore could not be bought or sold."

"Then what will it take for you to give her freedom?"

With a slight tilt of his head, Esteban said, "I heard you have a love rune on your chest. Perhaps you would no longer want her if it were removed."

His words pricked me, giving power to that secret fear I'd been trying to stifle.

"The rune is gone," Thomas stated. "I still love her. Even if you set her free and she wanted nothing to do with me—" He swallowed hard, taking a moment. "Even then, I would still fight for her freedom and take a small comfort that she was her own person, that she was happy."

The silence was overwhelming.

Esteban walked toward us; Thomas tensed as if he were ready to protect me. I kept my gaze locked on Esteban as he drew close.

"I would not fight you, *mija*. If you ever need me, you know where I will be." He planted a gentle kiss to my brow.

It took me a few moments to process what he said. "You are releasing me?" I asked, dumbfounded.

"Your priest friend came to visit me, as I'm sure Camila told you." My eyes widened; he continued, "I've thought about what he said. He told me that my actions need to show the change I want to see before anyone else will accept them and follow." Esteban smiled bittersweetly. "I hope you will accept the apologies of an old, overprotective, controlling fool… and that you will consider letting me be a part of your life in some small measure."

I stood there, shock keeping me from moving and speaking.

He then turned to Thomas. "Take care of her."

"I will," Thomas promised.

Esteban turned to leave the room, but I grabbed his shoulder.

"Thank you," I whispered as tears welled. He nodded, patted my hand, and took his leave, Lorenzo behind him. No sooner had the door clicked shut than I faced Thomas, my grin matching his.

"You are free," he said, his voice thick with emotion. "I meant what I said: I want you to be happy above all else."

"Then kiss me."

His long legs crossed the distance between us in no time. Every kiss, every touch, soothed over all the fear and pain and despair until there was nothing left but us.

"Isabela," Thomas murmured against my mouth as if my name meant everything to him. I arched into him as pleasant shivers went down my spine. My hand slipped down to his chest, hovering where the rune used to be.

"Why did you get rid of the rune?"

Thomas turned serious. "If you had decided you did not want me... I selfishly hoped it would lessen the pain."

He pulled away, and I frowned at him.

"I did not give you permission to stop," I teased, reaching for him.

"I want to make something right." Thomas pulled a small box from his pocket and lowered to one knee. He opened the box, showing off a gorgeous ring of diamond and sapphire. "Isabela, will you marry me again?"

The words had barely left his mouth before I replied, "Yes! I would have been furious with you if you hadn't asked."

Thomas chuckled, stood, and slipped the ring onto my finger. "I missed you."

Before I could start crying again, I kissed him, hoping that would express everything I wanted to say.

Chapter Sixty

Thomas

Happily Ever After

"Are you ready?" Priest Abel asked.

"Yes." I smiled at him. "Thank you for doing this again."

"I am happy to do it." He leaned toward me and whispered, "I am giving you a wedding gift: a kitten that seemed rather fond of Isabela. I'll be sure to have someone bring her to your house after you have returned from your honeymoon."

"I'm sure Isabela will like that. Thank you."

Instead of an intimate indoor wedding like the first one, we were outside just behind the palace, rows of attendees standing side-by-side with space in the middle for people to walk through. As per Camila's and my mother's insistence, the men wore their best suits, and women wore dresses in various shades of light to medium blue, which matched the flower petals scattered about on the rolled out white carpet that ended at my feet.

Esteban escorted Isabela down the aisle, but all I saw was her, how radiant she looked in the flowing white lace gown that had been tailor-made for her. She beamed, locking eyes with me, and I could not remember ever being happier.

When they reached us, Esteban released her with a quick kiss to the cheek and took his place near Lorenzo and his nieces. Well, most of his nieces: Camila stood next to Nate, their fingers interlocked. He winked at me. Near them was Mother with Queen Eleanora and her sons. August shot me a reassuring smile and nod.

The ceremony went smoothly, and everyone clapped and cheered as we kissed and Priest Abel once more proclaimed us married.

We went indoors to the ballroom for the party. Camila and Mother had worked together to decorate it. They bought more crystal chandeliers so that the candlelight would reflect in beautiful colours on the floor; tables were full of food and pastry dishes from both countries arranged in aesthetically pleasing ways; even the curtains had been replaced with blue silk.

"Congratulations," said the Queen as she hugged us in turn. "Isabela, I am proud to have you as the new ambassador between our countries."

"I am honoured you asked me," she replied sincerely.

"And Thomas, I am proud of you for taking the position of Elite. I need rune-writers I can trust."

"Of course, Your Majesty," I told her with a bow of my head.

The Queen left, and then Mother hurried over to us. "Welcome to the family," she said to Isabela, hugging her tightly. "I am so happy to finally have a daughter."

"Your sons love you too, Mother," Nate said from behind her, Camila on his arm. "Here I thought we were your pride and joy."

"Of course you are!" Mother swatted his elbow with her fan. "But there is something different about a mother-daughter relationship."

"Jealous, Nate?" Isabela challenged teasingly.

He shrugged. "I'll let you have this one. It is your wedding day after all. Just know that I'm still her favourite."

"You'll always be my baby boy," Mother crooned, reaching for his cheek.

Nate batted her hand aside and moved out of the way. "Well, Camila, that is our cue to leave. Care for a dance?"

"Yes." Camila looked at us. "There is lots more planned, so no disappearing. Understood?"

Isabela and I were obedient until after a few dances. Then we slipped away while everyone was distracted by the fireworks outside.

"This dress has such a long train," Isabela complained, trying to hold it bundled in one arm.

"You are so beautiful," I told her, stealing a kiss before I pulled her outside and swept her off her feet. She made a startled noise and wrapped her arms around my neck. "I thought this might be easier since your train is so long."

Out in the cool night air, I carried her to a spot outside that was hidden from the ballroom windows.

"Camila will hunt us down, and I'm sure Nathan will help her."

"I just want a few moments alone with you, Mrs Grahm. If it please you, that is."

Isabela laughed, and the sound filled me with more joy. "It pleases me."

I set her down slowly, my hands lingering on her and pulling her close to me. "Good." I kissed her neck, enjoying the sound that came from her throat. "It is hard to believe that just a short while ago we were strangers."

Her fingers wrapped themselves in my hair, playing with my curls. "Just a short while ago I was running away from the only life I'd ever known."

I looked at her. "I prefer to think that you were running to find me as fast as you could."

"You are a terrible flirt, Mr Grahm." Isabela stared up at me with so much love and adoration that it was intoxicating. "I love you, Thomas."

"I love you, Isabela. *Mi Sirena.*"

Hello!

Thank you for reading *A Different Kind of Magic*. Whether you loved it or not, I'd really appreciate it if you left a rating and review on Amazon and Goodreads so that I can see what I'm doing right and what I can work on. If you are interested in continuing reading, check out the rest of the series as well as my other works on Amazon.

You can also check out my website **www.chesneyinfalt.com** and any of my social medias under @chesneyinfalt. I'm also on Patreon and will be releasing exclusives.

Acknowledgments

This book was different for me because I'm not used to writing something that has this much focus on the romance—I'm glad I did it though! I had some wonderful help along the way:

Nicole Scarano: Thank you so much for the cover! It's beautiful. I'm obsessed! You did an amazing job.

Lydia Russell: I think it'd be a shorter list if I looked for things to not thank you for. From alpha reads to edits to feedback to encouragement, you've been there from the earliest parts of the story and influenced certain characters getting more spotlight than they were supposed to (*cough cough* Nate *cough cough*). I'm so thankful to have you as a writing buddy and look forward to what else we come up with!

Rebecca F Kenney & Sarah Sutton: Thank you for beta reading. You two are great authors, and I'm grateful you took the time to read through my work and give me advice.

My Infalt crew: Thanks for your support and honest feedback. I have the greatest in-laws anyone could ask for!

Corina Chance: I appreciate that you took time to sift through some chapters with me. Those early chapters were a mess!

Neil Infalt: You've given me the best real-life fairy-tale. I love you!

Charlie & Maximus: My adorable fur babies. You two are great company. I love that you rest at my feet while I write.

Lastly, I want to thank my Patreon supporters and my readers: because of you, I get to do what I love. You are awesome!

Much love,

Chesney Infalt

One More Thing...

Initially I wrote this book as a standalone. With how many books I plan on the *Warrior's Song* series having and the plethora of projects I expect to release, the last thing I wanted was something longer than one book. I had great intentions, I promise.

But then Nate happened. He was originally supposed to be a background character, no one of consequence... but he quickly became one of my favourites, and my alpha reader fell in love with him. She constantly reminded me when he was not getting enough page time and insisted he deserved more. And the more I wrote, the more I realised that Nate has a story to tell and growing to do. At first I thought to give you, my readers, a short story, but I've come to terms with the fact that he needs his own book to tell his tale *properly*.

His story is in the works, not at all ready for your eyes just yet, but I will leave you with the letter Nate couldn't bring himself to send to Camila.

Dear Camila,

~~I thought we had something.~~

~~What happened? What went wrong?~~

~~I was at the ball and I saw you accept his proposal~~

Why not me?

Chesney Infalt has been writing stories since she got her first notebook at the age of six. While those are under lock and key, her books *The Three, Worth Fighting For, Haeven Short Stories Collection,* and *Warrior's Heart* are available now on Amazon.

Made in the USA
Columbia, SC
09 January 2023

74988964R00207